Year
of
Jubilee

Books by

PEGGY TROTTER

Year of Jubilee
Reviving Jules

~Unchained Souls Series~
The Secret Things
The Secret Storm

~Society of Outcasts~
The Misfit Bride
The Lowborn Lady
The Spellbound Schoolmarm

~Up from the Miry Clay~
Tattered Blossoms Rise
Wild Daisies Bloom
Flawed Roses Flourish (Releasing-2024)

Spun

Year of Jubilee

PEGGY TROTTER

Year of Jubilee

First Edition/Updated 2023
ISBN: 979-8-9897864-0-4
Printed in Monee, IL, United States of America

All Scriptures used with this work are from the King James Version (KJV).

Cover Art by Zanne Davis
Edited by Susan M. Baganz

DEDICATION

Thank you, Lord, for using my hands to write your story. I pray it encourages others in their walk with You so that we can truly embody Psalm 34:3.

"Oh, magnify the Lord with me, and let us exalt His name together."

Psalm 34:3 KJV

I thank my husband, Barry, who has supported me throughout this process—my true better half. May my stories enlighten readers to the blessings of a union ordained by God.

And to Megan, Renee, Misty, Nancy, Diane and many others, thank you for your fingerprints upon this novel.

CHAPTER ONE

Gibson County, Indiana, December 31st, 1849

Jubilee Stallings' forehead collided with the wall. Stars flashed behind her closed lids. She lay completely still. Her face heated and her body ached, yet she dared not move.

"You're worthless," her husband's slurred voice continued.

She heard his footsteps stagger across the floorboards.

"You're nuttin' but a dog, and…and…a piece…of dung."

The floorboards thundered as his body hit the floor. Scraping sounds emitted from the other side of the room.

"I…oughta…"

6

He continued mumbling unintelligibly. Jubilee pressed her bruised brow against the icy wood of the wall and prayed. Fresh tears wet her face. *Please fall asleep.* Almost on command, Colvin gave a snore. Jubilee continued to lie immobile, although, now that the initial rush of adrenaline had worn off, the frigid air made her naked body want to shake. She clenched her teeth and fought against her body's urge. Snores filled the air.

She pushed to a sitting position and eyed the straw mattress where Colvin had sprawled. Moving as cautiously as a newborn colt, she crawled to her dress by the door. She pulled it on as a set of shivers ripped through her body. With her sweater in hand, she crept to the fireplace. Only dying embers remained, but Jubilee couldn't risk adding another log. Her teeth chattered as she tucked her feet beneath her skirt and pulled up the ragged cardigan to ward off the chill.

She grimaced as she rubbed the swelling on her neck where he'd choked her. The moonlight broke through the clouds, highlighting the marks scratched into the wall near the stone mantel. She'd carved the last one this morning— December 31, 1849. More than a full year had come and gone since she'd begun marking. Tomorrow would be her second birthday in this house. Once again, tears threatened. She'd be eighteen.

The day had dawned in a gray haze, but the day of her birth marked a new year, which always buoyed her with hope. The hours had passed pleasantly. She'd filled the wood box, baked fresh bread, and gone to bed looking forward to tomorrow. Until Colvin had exploded through the door, startling her from a deep sleep. She closed her eyes and her mind. It was always the same. More tears spilled from her swollen eyelids.

She tensed as Colvin sputtered a few times before going back to his ear-splitting snores. Noting where his pants had dropped, she decided to wait a little longer before she pilfered a couple coins. Any more and he'd notice and beat her senseless. Now, time to rest and recover her strength. She'd make sure she wasn't near the cabin when he woke. Hopefully he'd follow his usual pattern and be off and gone for the next several weeks. *Let it be months,* she prayed. *I don't care if he ever shows up again.* For now, she needed rest.

She woke a short time later, collected a few coins from Colvin's pockets, and opened the door, thankful for the quiet leather hinges. Because of the cold, she wouldn't head to the woods, her favorite hiding place. She'd settle for the barn, a huge hulking structure. Her breath formed a ghostly fog about her in the chill, crisp air. Fear licked at her, and she ran from the evil sleeping in the cabin.

Inside the barn, she moved quietly so as to not stir the cow, who loved to greet her in the early morn. She scrambled into the loft and buried herself in a cave of hay. The exertion left her body panting, but warm. With the protection of the sweet hay around her, she fell asleep.

* * *

Jubilee started. She blinked a few times before she realized where she was. Dust tickled her nose. Noises caught her attention. Colvin saddled his horse in the stall below. He spoke in gentle tones. The man had always been kinder to his beast than he had been to her. A door opened with a creak and a low thudding indicated man and horse made their way to the exit. *Good riddance,* she thought as the barn door closed.

With Colvin gone, Jubilee took up residence once more in the cabin. Her hands were like ice blocks as she started a fire from the few remaining embers. Once her fingers warmed, she brought the coins out of her pocket. They needed to be hidden. Jubilee climbed on the rough table and located the canvas bag she kept behind a loose board in the eaves. Not much left. The stash might last two months if she were careful. After climbing down, she pulled the bench as close to the hearth as possible. *Some birthday.* She sighed. At least a warm fire burned in the fireplace. Perhaps now she'd have a time of peace.

* * *

Spring arrived and by mid-April, Jubilee's desire for peace fought with her need for food. She'd dropped a good amount of weight since Colvin's visit. All the meager supplies she'd managed to purchase in January had long since been used. She'd run out of flour six weeks ago, and out of salt in early February.

She'd killed five of the chickens, one by one, save the last hen and one rooster. Now she only took an occasional egg for breakfast, hoping there'd soon be a new brood of babies. Otherwise, the chickens would be gone too.

Elsie, the old cow, had been nothing but a sack of bones wrapped in leather in early March, although now she found tender grass to revive herself. She'd gone dry, and without a bull, she wouldn't freshen soon.

Jubilee turned her attention to the task at hand and drove the cutting edge of the shovel into the packed sod once more with her bruised heel. She paused a moment to wipe the sweat from her brow and survey her accomplishment. The small eight-by-ten patch of newly-turned soil made it hard for Jubilee not to let discouragement grip her.

Her stomach clenched in hunger. A drink of water would help, but the bucket and dipper stood a good twenty feet away, which was too much work. She thought of the thin wild onions and dandelion greens she'd laid on the table for lunch. The meager meal duplicated what she'd eaten every day for weeks, but she could hardly wait to devour them. Yet she had to wait. This garden was vital and had to be big enough to allow her to store sufficient food until next year. She sighed. It needed to be four times this size.

Jubilee pushed herself away from the handle of the shovel and rambled to the water bucket. She settled in the new grass and grabbed the dipper. Her life depended on getting the ground dug, raked, and ready for planting by mid-May.

Her ears picked up another sound. Her brow wrinkled and her eyes flew open. A horrible dread washed over her. Hoof beats. Distant, but very real. Her head snapped up.

Colvin.

Of course him. Who else? Seldom did anyone come out this far. Her weary body, so tired before, tensed with fear. She glanced from the woods behind her to the barn. *Where could she hide?*

The creak of saddle leather was audible now. He'd soon be coming through the tree-lined pathway. The cabin blocked his line of sight if she headed for the trees now. But it had to be *now.* She turned and trotted past the outhouse, praying she'd reach the woods before he saw her.

Another sound stopped her dead in her tracks. *Whistling.* Colvin never whistled. She changed direction and crept to the side of the cabin.

* * *

Rafe sat easily in the saddle. He tilted his head toward the sky and shielded his eyes with his right hand. Had to be near past lunch. He looked ahead and saw a break in the thick branches. That had to be it. He urged his Appaloosa to a faster pace, anticipating laying eyes on his new property.

Sure enough, the trees broke and Rafe took the path. He located a clearing up ahead. As he emerged through the tangle of limbs, he pulled the animal up in surprise. The barn, the biggest he'd seen in the area, greeted him like a castle on a hilltop. He grinned. Colvin had said it was worth twice the land and he had, for once, told the truth.

He swung his gaze to the cabin. The front porch sagged, nearly detached from the main house since the foundation had given way at the steps. He'd have to walk uphill to reach the door. Stumps, waist high, littered the yard. The place would require some industry, but he hadn't come to sit on his thumbs.

His eyes caught a movement at the edge of the shack. What was it? A face?

"Hello?" he called.

Silence greeted him. His hands yanked the shotgun from the scabbard at his leg, and he urged Horse closer to the house. He dismounted quietly and motioned the animal to stay. Horse, well trained, stood steadfastly, watching him.

Rafe sidled up to the left corner of the cabin with his gun held across his chest. In one swift movement he stepped out, weapon raised, prepared for anything. But the yard stood empty. With quick movements, he pressed himself to the wall. He reached the back corner again and popped out in ready stance, shotgun cocked.

It was a girl. She stood with hands out next to the outhouse, about fifty feet away. Hunched over, she poised for flight. He took a deep breath and brought the gun down. As thin as she was, she presented no threat. *Must be a neighbor girl.*

"Hello?" he called again, and she back-pedaled a half a dozen steps. "Wait. This the Stallings' Place?"

She stepped behind the outhouse and peeked at him.

"Hey there. Can you tell me if this is Colvin Stallings' place?"

She never moved. Was she addled? He strode toward the outhouse. Time for some answers.

No sooner had he taken a step, when she took off running. He jogged to get a good glance at her, but by the time he reached the outhouse, she neared the edge of the trees beyond what had once been a cleared field. Now, scattered with young trees and weeds, it'd soon turn the open meadow into a woods. He gave a sigh. What did it matter? She was probably trespassing and wouldn't return.

He turned and took a step toward the shack. The hand pump caught his attention. Ah, that would come in handy after a long day of tending crops. His eyes fell on another sight. A shovel was stuck in the soil, the handle straight up in the air, mid-row in a small patch of freshly turned dirt. He stopped short, wheeled around, and studied the edge of the woods. Why would a woman be digging in Colvin's yard? This had to be the place. The barn matched the description.

He moved to the back door of the shack and pushed it open. What he saw made him want to choke his dead cousin. The floor appeared swept. In front of an ashless fireplace, a table stood, topped with a bowl of dandelion greens and wild onions. Herbs and strips of cloth hung from the ceiling. But, worst of all, was the worn quilt on a straw mattress on the floor, directly to the right of the door. The bed was carefully made.

He stuffed his hands into his pockets. Colvin had sworn no one lived on the place and now this. Rafe turned and looked toward the trees. Did that girl live here? Was she a squatter?

Well, he could hardly set up house until he found out. With an aggravated grunt, he left the shack and mounted Horse. He'd have to find her.

* * *

Jubilee climbed higher. This had always been her lucky pine. Never once had Colvin located her when she'd shimmied up this tree. The problem was, the farther she scrambled, the thinner the trunk. And, although she'd slimmed down quite a bit, the five-inch trunk tilted dangerously and creaked louder at each sway.

She closed her eyes and hugged the bark to her face. The pine smell always soothed her, the sap did not. The rough bark made a plumb uncomfortable seat. In her weakened condition, she knew she couldn't clutch this tree for the rest of the day and into the night. Already she shook from the effort of climbing and holding her position in the rocking tree.

Snap. She caught her breath and her eyes flew open. The stranger had found her. Twigs continued to crunch under the horse's hooves as they neared.

"Hello? Can you hear me? I must talk to you."

Jubilee shivered and her muscles trembled. Sensing him below the tree, she squeezed her eyes shut.

"I need to know who you are." His voice grew fainter. "Colvin Stallings is dead, and I own the property now."

Jubilee nearly lost her hold on the trunk. Had she heard right? Colvin was gone? Her breathing sped up. How? Surely she couldn't be free of him. Her face puckered in distaste, disgusted she'd be thrilled at the possibility of a man's death. She prayed the Lord understood.

But, if the first part were true, the last part must be true as well. A sob rose in her throat. She was free of Colvin, but now had no home. Nowhere to go. Stickiness clung to her hand and face as she wiped the moisture from her eyes and contemplated her situation.

She needed to think. Her throat constricted with tears. Her numb mind grappled for something practical to do. First, she'd stay hidden until he left the woods. She'd check her fishing lines. Then make her way back to the house. Maybe, by some miracle, this invader would've disappeared.

With a mind full of worries, she carried out her plan, begrudging the time she should have spent digging the garden, and landed a middling catfish at the creek. A blue cat was more appetizing than the yellow belly she held by the string, but she wouldn't complain. She'd carefully cut out the mud vein, fry it up, and feast. Now, if only her visitor had vanished.

Near dark she crept toward the outhouse and paused long and hard, searching for signs of the man she'd seen earlier. *Please let this all be a horrible dream.* Cautiously, she stepped past the garden and approached the house. Her hunger drove her to be careless. She grabbed a couple of pieces of wood from the meager pile against the cabin to start a fire and reached for the door. Suddenly, he loomed before her. She gasped and dropped her load to flee for the woods.

But his hand, like a steel trap, clamped down on her arm and she screamed. He had her. Jubilee kicked and flailed for all she was worth until he released her. She collapsed in a writhing fit and clawed her way through the tall grass until she reached the hand pump. Her arms hugged the metal as if it were a lifeline.

CHAPTER TWO

The thin girl's strength startled Rafe. She'd tussled in terror, fighting for her life, and he'd let her go. He could've easily held her, but he knew that would terrify her more. Her feeble attempts were laughable if it hadn't been so plain she lacked energy because of starvation.

"Whoa," he said quietly, as if calming a spooked horse. "Stay there, I won't touch you."

Rafe put up his empty hands as she heaved with effort. "I need to talk with you."

She panted and studied him with huge, brown, eyes.

"My name's Rafe Tanner. I'm Colvin Stallings' cousin."

This statement didn't seem to reassure her as she tucked her body behind the narrow pipe. He ran his gaze over her. Thick, dark hair shimmered with cinnamon highlights. She wore it pulled back and braided, doubled up and secured at the nape of her neck. Flyaway hairs surrounded the thin, frightened face like a halo.

Her skin was tanned already in mid-April, and the dress was an absolute rag. Now that he approached her, she didn't appear as young as he'd first thought. He stepped back and let her breathe and realize he meant no harm.

"Listen, I'm gonna take your fish and clean it. I'll fry it over at the campfire, and then we can eat and talk. I've got some bacon and a few rolls left over from my lunch in town. Just don't run off. I promise I won't hurt you."

The horror on her face eased, yet her eyes followed his every move. He maneuvered himself backward and gathered the catfish and the wood, leaving as much perimeter around the girl as possible. He settled beside the campfire. This wouldn't take long. Then this whole misunderstanding would be cleared up.

* * *

She assessed his distance, popped up, and scampered to the cabin, stumbling with exhaustion. After wrenching the door open, she slammed it shut. After two attempts, she managed to throw the heavy chunk of wood into the cast iron rests. She collapsed onto the floor and sucked air. Curled up in a fetal position, her body quivered. What was she going to do? Exhaustion trumped her fear. She blinked. *Stay alert.*

Nearly an hour passed as she lay there, mustering some strength. A soft knock sounded behind her. She flinched and lunged away.

"Ma'am, the fish is done. I'm gonna set the plate here on the back steps if you wanna get it. I'll be over by the fire." Jubilee strained to hear his soft voice. "You oughta get it soon or a critter might drag your fish off."

She struggled to a sitting position. Dare she open the door? Her stomach clenched in reply. *Is this a trick?* She glanced to the table. With the greens and onions, she could make do. But the thought of a raccoon getting her fish repelled her more than she could bear. Yet that *man. What if he...?* She refused to contemplate.

She chewed her lip. Finally, her stomach won. She knelt, hoping to snatch the plate—if it were really there. Certainly worth the chance. With the stealth of a Kickapoo, she removed the bar and the door yawned open.

A platter came into view, and the smell of food filtered to Jubilee's nostrils. An onslaught of saliva flooded her mouth. Throwing caution to the wind, she pushed the door wide to search for him. Her gaze caught him quick and, like his words, he sat next to the campfire, his eyes on her.

She swallowed. Why would he give her this food? *Enough pondering, grab the fish.* After seizing the plate and plopping the platter to the floor, she snatched the leather handle and yanked. Shouldering the wooden bar, she secured the door. She froze and panted. What was he doing? She pressed her ear against the wood, trying to calm her breathing.

Nary a sound. She looked at her plate. Some of the precious fish had scattered across the dirty floor. Scooping it up, she noticed several strips of bacon and two rolls also graced the tin platter.

She didn't take time to ruminate, but hurried to the table to rinse the dirty pieces of fish in the water bucket on the table and jammed them into her mouth. Grabbing an onion to season the fish, she hoped to finish it. *Oh, the bacon.* When had she last tasted its salty goodness? She ate in a frenzy for a few moments before slowing her pace. Her stomach could only take a few bites at a time. Her plate was still plenty full when she stopped. She was stuffed.

She dunked the dipper in the bucket and took a long drink of water. Her satisfied stomach caused her to pause and think. Why had this stranger shared his food with her? She glanced toward the door and shrugged one thin shoulder. Right now, she'd exhausted herself. She'd mull the thought later.

Jubilee picked up the plate and the bucket of water and plodded to the straw mattress in the corner. It only stood two feet from the back door, but Jubilee's energy was depleted. She set her load next to the bed and lay down. If she woke in the night, she'd try to eat more. She'd need her strength tomorrow. Snuggling under a threadbare quilt, she fell asleep in moments.

* * *

Rafe drank his coffee and listened to the coyotes howl in the distance. This farm appeared a lonely place for a man used to family at every step. His gaze shifted to the doorway of the cabin. Did this woman live here, day after day, by herself? How frequently had Colvin come back to actually occupy the house? Considering the state of the farm and the condition of his wife, if that's who she was, not often.

He thought over his position. Where he'd bunk was the easiest to plan. The barn, the best building in the area. Who this woman could be, and what to do with her, completely perplexed him. He threw the leftover coffee on the fire. This problem wouldn't be solved tonight. He'd just as well find a comfortable spot in the barn and hope daylight would answer some of his questions.

* * *

Jubilee's gritty eyes cracked open. Weak morning light washed across the floorboards from the lone window on the far side of the cabin. Her breath formed clouds in front of her face. With reluctance, she rubbed the sleep from her eyes and sat up. Last night's events cut through the fog of her brain. She leaned back against the wall and reached for the plate, which still contained a few bites of fish, bacon and roll.

For the first time in months, she'd awakened with a feeling of real strength. Shortly after downing the water from the dipper, she realized another need. The outhouse. She glanced around, wishing the chamber pot hadn't been left outside the back door. Her only option was to leave the sanctuary of the cabin.

The chill air raised goose bumps across her arms and she rubbed them, her teeth chattering. That man no doubt lingered, but he'd been kind enough to clean and cook the fish. He'd given her some of his food. But he'd grabbed her, just like Colvin. The fingers of her right hand worked a nervous circle in the thin fabric of her skirt. What choice did she have? An incredible need to know if Colvin was really dead rose in her. But, if this information were true, she had nowhere to go. The farm would belong to a stranger.

She glanced up to the old, rusted shotgun over the fireplace. The thing was useless. The weapon had greeted them when she and Colvin had arrived. It'd never been fired, and she had no bullets. However, this stranger didn't know that. She hoisted herself from the mattress, pulled one of the table's benches to the fireplace, and reached for the firearm. The rusted metal was cold to her touch. Even without ammunition, the gun made her appear a little more in control.

She unbarred and opened the door without a sound. With trepidation, she stuck her head out, glanced around, then crept down the steps one at a time. The frosty air nipped at her skin, and Jubilee shivered. She tried to hold the gun across herself, as if she could raise the barrel at any moment and blow off a varmint's head. Unfortunately, the heavy thing weighed down her arms. Nonetheless, she arrived at the outhouse without incident.

On her return journey, her eyes searched for movements. Then, she heard it. A whistle. She gasped and glanced toward the cabin. It was a good ways from safety when he popped around the corner of the house, carrying a rake and a rifle. He spotted her and froze. Jubilee swallowed and raised the gun a bit.

"Mornin'." He nodded and continued to saunter to the garden on her left. He began whistling again.

Jubilee's arms quivered under the weight of the gun, and a shudder, which had nothing to do with the temperature, snaked down her spine. He propped the rake and the rifle against a tall stump while she sucked in small breaths to calm her pounding heart. He took up the shovel from the very spot where she'd buried it yesterday and began to dig. She narrowed her eyes. His strong, thick arms finished the row without much effort.

"Help yourself to some bacon left in the pan." He motioned with the tip of his shovel towards last night's fire.

A cast iron skillet sat on another stump nearby. She licked her dry lips. The leftover fish proved more breakfast than she'd become used to, but fresh bacon beckoned. Unfortunately, that salted pork rested fifteen feet from where he stood. He shrugged and walked toward her. She lifted the shotgun. He stopped as he came to the end of the row and began digging. The muzzle drifted down.

"You live here?" he asked as he dug.

She juggled her thoughts. Time to find out. Enough of this sneaking around. She needed to know. "Yes."

He paused a moment to glance at her. "You know Colvin Stallings?"

Jubilee watched him dig. "He's my husband."

The digging stopped, and he stood. He was tall, much taller than Colvin. The shoulders on this man were next to frightening. She knew Colvin's power firsthand, and this man's larger build put her on edge.

They evaluated one another for a second or two, and the point of Jubilee's shotgun inched up. He took a deep breath, pulled the hat from his head, and raked a hand through his blond hair.

"Ma'am, I don't know how to tell you this, but Colvin Stallings is dead."

"Did you see his body?" The wavering point of the barrel went center on his chest.

"Ma'am?" His brow lowered and he pressed his hat to his thigh.

"Did you see him dead?" she persisted and, despite the cool temperature, sweat beaded across her brow.

His eyes narrowed before he plopped the hat back on his head. "Yes, Ma'am, I did. I stood outside the saloon where he was shot."

"Did you see him laid in his box?"

He shook his head. "No, ma'am, but I attended his funeral."

Likely story. She tightened her lips and pressed her cheek to the cold barrel of the gun, focusing him in her sights. "How'd he die?"

* * *

Rafe paused and wondered at the coolness of her questions. It was difficult enough to tell someone their husband had keeled over dead, but should he reveal the truth? He glanced down and kicked at a clod of dirt hanging on the shovel.

"Ma'am, I have no reason to hide facts. He cheated at cards and Mose Brown shot him clean through." He paused to gauge her reaction. When she gave none, he continued. "Mose is in jail now, waiting judgment."

She stood with that pitiful gun. More than likely the weapon was more hazardous to her than him. Her lack of reaction set him to digging, and he was on his way back to start a new row when she finally spoke.

"You own this land now?"

He stopped again and nodded. "Yes, Ma'am."

She let out a shuddering breath.

"I apologize about all this being sprung on you, but Colvin never mentioned a spouse. As a matter of fact, he assured me the place had been empty for six months."

Rafe dug the sharp edge of the shovel into the sod with new effort. A wife. Or worse yet, *a widow*. A very neglected one. Anger roiled inside him. He wished Colvin were alive so he could thump the side of his head with this shovel. Here he'd purchased this land in the middle of nowhere, intending to build a successful farm, recover from humiliation, and avoid female entanglements. Now, he'd inherited a widow.

With teeth gritted, he tore into the soil. After turning over another three rows, he paused. She still stood there. Fine. He'd tell her the way it had to be.

"Listen, I'll be glad to pay your fare anywhere. You just let me know, and I'll go to town and buy you a stage or a steamer ticket. Shoot, I'll even buy you a horse if that's how you wanna go. Colvin had no business doing this to you and, as his cousin, distant though we were, the least I can do is get you home."

Rafe had never seen hope slide off of a person's face quite like it did from hers. Her skin paled and her mouth parted. The small woman's intense eyes, dark as night, pleaded. For what? For kindness? For understanding? For help? Rafe wasn't sure. Despite the mixed messages, he recognized the despair in the sag of her body. Uneasiness teemed in his gut.

She shook her head, her voice a mere whisper. "There's nowhere."

"Surely you've got somewhere you can go. Your folks' house maybe? An aunt or uncle or even a cousin?"

She glanced away and the shotgun lowered until the barrel stabbed the ground. "I'm an orphan."

CHAPTER THREE

*A*gh, *of course.* The way his luck ran, what else would she be? Rafe took his frustration out on the ground once more, deftly covering three extra rows before he stopped. An orphan. *An orphan.* He straightened and stared at her. What must it be like to have no one?

Rafe shook his head. He had no clue. He'd grown up in a large family with many brothers and sisters, surrounded by aunts, uncles and cousins. For a moment, he put himself in her shoes. Being an orphan would be horrible. He glanced back up. No, not horrible, because she wouldn't know the difference. How sad. He sighed. What a mess.

She spun, threw the shotgun to the ground, and took off like a deer toward the woods. He stepped away from the garden and watched her run, barefooted no less, across the field. *Good gravy. What now?* He tossed the shovel down and strode to the pan of bacon. Another one of her disappearing acts. He was getting nowhere fast. Well, at least food would be waiting when she returned.

He marched to the back door of the shack and entered. Again, the absence of material things struck him. To his left was a trunk, to his right, the mattress. An old trestle table with two bench seats sat in front of a cold fireplace. Other than the herbs hanging from the ceiling that totaled out the entire cabin's furniture. No shelves, dry sink, chairs, rockers, cabinets—nothing.

He bent to retrieve the bucket and tin plate. Outside, he washed them and refilled the container with cool water. He returned to the table where he loaded the platter with bacon.

For the rest of the day, he threw himself into work. He finished digging the garden and raked the soil out. Next, he repaired the fence, noting the supplies he'd need. Horse, tethered inside the would-be corral, nipped at the fresh grass, eyeing his owner's busyness. Rafe bent his back in the task of cleaning a stall for the animal before dumping the vile water from the trough and filling it with clean from the hand pump. Every once in a while, he paused and perused the woods.

The stumps came next, and he turned most of them into firewood, stacked almost past his head, several layers deep against the cabin. After a quick lunch, he assessed the damage of the cabin's roof and front porch. He added more lumber to his growing list of needed items. On toward dark, back aching, Rafe cleaned the barn. Was the woman gone for good? He grunted as he tossed straw into a pile.

Well, if she never showed herself again, that would solve his problem. *Or would it?* He stuck the pitchfork into the ground with a little too much force, strode to the door, and looked out. He sighed and crossed his arms. No. Now, worry for her needled him.

* * *

Jubilee arrived at the creek in record time. Her breathing slowed as she stood, hands resting on her hips. She had to think…why couldn't she think? At last she bent and gathered the fishing line she'd hidden under a log. She tried not to concentrate on being homeless, but moisture rushed to her eyes and her heart ached.

Finding a bare spot in the soil, she raked with a sharp stick. Soon, she was rewarded with several plump worms. Tears fell to the ground as she snatched them up and wound them around the hooks. She sniffed as she collected the rock with the hook tied at the end of the long piece of an old sweater's yarn. With all her might, she slung it into the water and repeated the process with the other two.

Finally, she settled on her favorite log and stared across the creek. Now what? Where to go? To return to the Orphan Society in Philadelphia was out of the question. Her eighteenth birthday had come and gone. And Mrs. Galston had no further affection for her than any other bound-out stray. Besides, the rich widow would be furious at her unexpected departure. She swallowed. No reason to re-live that horrible night.

Maybe she could return to Philadelphia and throw herself at the mercy of the Society's board and beg for help. Yet she knew it wouldn't, in all probability, put her in a better situation. Pastor Sheffield talked about God taking care of folks. Perhaps his preaching had been some big lie. Was it really true? Had she been carried away by his gentle smile and green eyes?

Yes, she confessed. She'd had a horrible crush on the man, even while his dear wife sat with their three kids on the front pew. She'd adored him and hung on his every word. With a shiver, she took a deep breath. But she'd learned about the Lord, too, and she'd given her heart to Him.

She sighed. No sense sitting all day and gathering wool. None of these ideas would solve her trouble. Her stomach reminded her lunch approached. She rose and searched for greens and onions, stopping to check her pitiful rabbit trap as she walked. As if any animal were stupid enough to run inside and kick out the stick. Tears moistened her eyes and she rubbed them away. *Face it. I can't even take care of myself.*

Jubilee passed the time with her meager lunch and paced the property, delaying the obvious outcome. Her hopes for a home of her own were shattered. This stranger owned this land, and she had to go.

* * *

The dimness in the barn made Rafe call it quits for the night. He wiped his brow with his sleeve, walked to the door, and surveyed the farm. Already the yard looked better. And by the end of the summer, it'd be a different place.

His eyes darted towards the woods, wondering about Colvin's widow. His thoughts stopped short. Why, he didn't even know the woman's name. His gaze raked the tree line once more. Where was she? She needed to eat. Had she found something? He shook his head in frustration. Here he was taking her on to raise. *What a dolt.*

There had to be a solution to fix this situation. It would be cruel to send her away, a woman with no means to support herself. She'd already been abandoned and practically starved to death. He could hire her for sundry household duties, but…

A hoot owl's haunting echoes reverberated outside and he paused, clenching the pitchfork handle in his hand. Somehow he had to formulate an agreeable arrangement.

He exhaled a rush of air and laid aside the pitchfork. A large portion of the barn was finished, so he picked up his rifle. The bacon in his saddlebag would make one more meal. He glanced at the sky. Just enough light left to hunt. And, as much as he hated feeling responsible for the woman, he knew they both had to eat. He saddled Horse and set out to find some game.

* * *

Jubilee glanced at the sky as the light turned orange. Hiding wasn't the answer. Besides, she trembled with hunger. After she checked the fishing lines, she knew there'd be no fish tonight. The air she inhaled chilled her lungs, and she closed her eyes in acceptance. She had no choice but to return to the cabin. Shivers ran down her spine, either from the thought of returning or from the chilly wind that had picked up, or both. Rubbing her hands up and down her arms, she set off back across the field.

As she approached the outhouse, she slowed and became wary. No fire burned near the garden like yesterday. Her eyes scanned the area and spotted a new campfire about thirty paces from the barn. Her skin was numbed by now from the cool air, and her feet raw and frozen. Maybe getting close to the fire wouldn't be such a bad idea. Could she outrun this big man? Doubtful. Outrunning an inebriated Colvin had been a different matter.

Reluctantly, she approached the ring of flames. She squinted at his kneeling form lit by the campfire, and he grabbed the rifle and cocked it, aiming in her general direction.

"Who's there?" he demanded.

His tone made her want to flee back to the woods. But she stood her ground and called out, "It's me."

The rifle instantly lowered, and she stepped into the circle of light. He had a tripod set up and a pot, full of something bubbling, caught her eye and her nose. Her stomach growled.

"Have a seat." He indicated a bench across from him.

Jubilee wondered where such a bench had come from, but pushed the thought away as she tentatively sat down. Her eyes shot around the dark landscape, reminding herself that she knew the lay of the land better than he. Surely a dozen hiding spots existed just around the barn.

"I've cooked up some rabbit stew." His voice rumbled low. "Don't suppose you've got bowls? It'd make eating a lot easier."

She jumped up like a bee had stung her.

"I'll get bowls." She took off through the darkness, trying not to run lest it indicate her fear. At the cabin, she quickly gathered the bowls and spoons and made her way back to the fire. Handing them to him would prove a tricky thing.

* * *

Rafe eyed her. By his estimation, she was plumb out of her mind with fright. He spooned the thick stew into the dishes, wondering how he'd hand it back to her given her reluctance to approach him. He chose to stretch out as far as he could without actually standing and setting it on the ground. She all but snatched it, yet didn't devour the contents as Rafe would've suspected.

"Thank you."

"You're welcome." He stuck the spoon in the hot stew.

They ate quietly for a few moments. Then Rafe spoke. "No fish today?"

She shook her head, her eyes drifting back and forth from him to her meal.

"I guess we oughta talk," he murmured. "It'd be easier if I knew your name."

She gave a one-shouldered shrug. "Jubilee."

"Have you thought of a place to go?"

Again, a shake of her head.

"I see." He went back to eating. "You need some more?"

"No."

She could probably barely eat what he'd given her. He helped himself to a second portion and didn't speak again until they had both finished.

"Okay, I've been thinking about this all day." He paused and fixed his gaze on hers. "I gotta lot of work in store for me on this property."

She clenched her hands in her lap and stared at him with those huge, dark eyes. The fire's light revealed dirt smudges across her forehead. He returned to focus on the campfire.

"It might work to have a little help around here. Like a 'business arrangement,' of sorts." His eyes flicked back to her.

The woman's eyebrows drew together. Rafe cleared his throat and kept talking.

"You'd stay in the cabin and cook dinner and clean up. I'll occupy the barn. You could also tend the garden, put up the harvest, and take care of the barn animals." He paused as if he'd just thought of something, "You do cook, don't you?"

Hesitantly, she nodded.

Satisfied with her answer he continued, "I'll clear the land and plant the crops according to my plan. I'll make sure we have food, clothing. The basics. The whole thing will sort of be a cooperative effort."

The woman's hand set to kneading the fabric of her skirt. His eyes narrowed. What was going through her brain? Didn't she understand the arrangement?

"Course, folks roundabout will soon get wind we're both living out here, and to keep any damage to our reputations, we probably ought to marry."

She gasped and her hands flew to her mouth.

Rafe shook his head. That hadn't gone well. "We'd still stick to our arrangement of you in the cabin and me in the barn, but to everyone else we'd be just...a married couple."

It was finally out. Rafe took a deep breath. Jubilee blinked at him.

"Now, you'll probably need a night to think it over. Either way you decide, we'll be heading into town tomorrow morning." He cleared his throat and stood. The woman nearly broke her neck trying to jump up and stutter-step behind the bench.

"Well, I've got a few chores to tend to." He strode to the barn.

* * *

Jubilee stared after him, then covered her face with her hands. He had to be kidding. She shook her head to clear her thoughts. A *forced* marriage? *Again?* Tears gathered at the back of her throat. Well, at least this time she'd have a choice. Colvin had kindly set a revolver to her temple.

She shivered, having left the relative warmth of the fire. Waiting until he disappeared into the barn, Jubilee took off at a run to the cabin, tears streaming. Not bothering to gather wood, she barred the door and pounced into bed to cover up with the quilt. She blinked in the darkness, and her brain grew numb. How had all this happened? Too much had changed in the space of twenty-four hours.

Yet, what other option did she have? It was this or…it was just *this*. Pulling the ragged blanket tighter, she sobbed into the pillow. If she wanted to stay, she'd have to marry a stranger. Another stranger. Colvin's cousin. *Oh, glory. What am I going to do?*

* * *

Back at the barn, Rafe picked up a brush and began to groom Horse. He disgusted himself. Horse sidestepped to avoid the rough strokes, and Rafe gentled his hand. *Why had he suggested marriage?* Because he felt responsible for her, that's why. Horse nickered, turned his piebald face to him, and butted his arm.

"Sorry, boy." He scratched the swirl of hair between Horse's blue eye and his brown one. With a tender hand, he detangled the streaked mane.

But what did it matter, really? The one he desired was lost to him. God's plan, his father claimed. Rafe gritted his teeth, annoyed that this piece of advice had crossed his mind.

Bad things happened to people all the time. Wrong things, awful things. *God's plan.* Was there such a notion? He pulled a burr from Horse's mane. What was the difference if he married a strange girl? The woman he wanted was out of his hands.

CHAPTER FOUR

Rafe rubbed his smooth chin and patted the old wagon he'd worked on till late in the night. A fresh paint job and it'd be good as new. He flicked his glance toward the cabin. No use trying to waste any more time. Horse stomped his indignation at being harnessed, bringing a grin to Rafe's stiff face.

"Sorry, old buddy." He thumped his flank. "This is your job till I get my hands on a good harness horse. Trust me, we're all making adjustments."

She appeared and rounded the corner of the house to the front porch. He shut the barn door, then leaped to the buckboard seat and slapped the reins. Horse took off with a jolt. Humph. They'd have to work on that. He pulled Horse to a halt as he neared.

"Mornin'." He greeted and touched his hat.

She bobbed her head.

"Am I loading your stuff, or are we driving in to meet the preacher?"

"I don't have anything."

So, she was leaving. Rafe took a deep breath and rubbed his neck. Hard to understand why that didn't set well.

The woman's face appeared white and strained. "I have a question."

He nodded, climbed down from the wagon, and approached the rickety porch. "All right."

She cleared her throat. "If I stay…would you…?"

His gaze dropped to her hand working circles in the soft ragged material of her dress. She kept her gaze on the wagon but didn't finish.

Finally he spoke. "Mrs. Stallings, I…"

"Don't call me that. Please," she begged, her soft, brown eyes round as she pressed a hand to her breast.

He leaned against the porch support. "Fine, how should I address you?"

She shrugged one thin shoulder.

He sighed and shook his head to clear it. "You had a question?"

"Yes. If we married and had a…'business arrangement,' would you agree not to…" she swallowed and stepped back, "…beat me?"

Her dark eyes fastened on him again. Their neediness mesmerized him. Anger at Colvin seared the pit of his stomach.

With exaggerated slowness, he removed his hat and ran the brim around in his hand. He kept his eyes on the dirt to keep the anger toward his cousin from showing in his face. Finally, he looked up and waited until her gaze latched to his.

"Ma'am, as a gentleman. I would never strike a woman." He spoke with deep conviction. "Never."

She studied him for a long moment. "Then, I will agree to the…'business arrangement,' as you explained last night."

* * *

Refusing to let fear choke her, she stepped from the porch, leaving a wide berth around the huge man who'd soon be her husband. A sob rose, and she forced it down. Scurrying to the other side of the wagon before she changed her mind, she set her foot on the base of the bed to swing herself aboard.

"Here, let me…"

She screamed and leaped away from the wagon. The man moved so silently, and he loomed terribly close. She pinned him with her eyes. He shoved his hands into his pockets, his face puckered. Surely he wouldn't break his promise already.

"Ma'am, a man usually helps a woman up to her seat in the wagon."

She shook her head swiftly. "I can ride here in the back, and I'll board myself."

He placed his hat back on, and Jubilee glanced at his golden-blond hair lit by the rays of the sun.

"Ma'am, it's polite manners for me to help you up, and I'd much rather you ride up front where it's more comfortable. I've already promised I won't hurt you. You've got to trust me if this is going to work."

She raised her chilly fingers to her face. To be that close to him. To let him touch her. Jubilee inhaled a trembling breath and stepped forward. It took all her courage to allow his big hands to encircle her waist and lift her. Her throat went dry, fearing he wouldn't let go. But he did, and he circled the wagon to the driver's side.

As he boarded, his big body juggled the seat and she, panicking, grabbed hold of the seat.

"Sorry, didn't mean to jostle you."

He settled in and grasped the reins. Jubilee struggled to keep her leg from touching his, but he required a lot of room.

"I've got a coat if you're cold," he mentioned, pulling the long garment from the back.

Jubilee gratefully slid her bare arms into the huge sleeves. The outerwear was nearly big enough to wrap around her twice. She kept her head turned as she pondered the man. His physical stature intimidated her. He was a hulk of a man, a great deal larger than Colvin. As a matter of fact, they seemed opposites in many ways. Colvin had been small and wiry, with dark hair and close-set eyes, much like a mouse with his narrow face.

Rafe stood well over six foot, with broad shoulders, blond hair, and striking hazel eyes. Brown one minute, green the next. His nose stood out a bit strong and he wasn't overly handsome, yet, he was appealing. Nothing Jubilee could remember had been appealing about Colvin. She took a deep breath and tried to calm the trembling in her middle. Perhaps they'd be opposites in personality, too. Jubilee certainly hoped so.

* * *

Rafe's stomach clenched in pity for the woman next to him. Why, she'd trembled when he'd lifted her to the wagon. She weighed less than a newborn calf. And he couldn't deny he admired her pluck to have survived the struggles she'd seen in her young life. He pulled himself up short. Hmmm, how old was she?

"May I ask you a question?" He rephrased her words, emphasizing, 'you.'

She nodded and gave a one-shoulder shrug.

"How old are you?" He glanced at her. She shrank from him.

"Eighteen."

They rode in silence for a while.

"What about you?"

"Twenty."

The creaks of the old wagon and the soft plodding sound of Horse's feet were the only sounds for a long spell. Finally Rafe spoke.

"I'll drop you at the mercantile while I go make arrangements with the pastor." He gripped the reins as the faces of his family flitted through his brain. They'd miss the wedding. "Then I'll stop back and pick you up. Make sure you purchase several yards of fabric. You'll need a couple of dresses, and I'm sure you'll want curtains for the cabin. A new quilt for winter will come in handy, and I figure you'll need one too. So get plenty, and any other necessities. We'll load up the wagon with food and head home."

She gaped at him. "I can get fabric?"

"Yes, for all the items I mentioned. Get plenty. We're set pretty far from town."

She stared for such a long time that he finally turned. "Problem?"

With a quick shake of her head, she turned her gaze from his.

All right now. This was going to work. Rafe whistled a made-up tune as the wagon plodded to town. It was better than he could've planned. She'd cook for him, so he could concentrate on farming. She'd take care of the laundry needs, so he had no worry with that. The garden would be tended to, the cow milked.

Yep. Almost like hiring a servant. Better even, because she had a vested interest. He leaned back in the seat and relaxed. The woman next to him recoiled. He cleared his throat. Except for that. Uneasiness needled him and he shifted again. He had to remember that, without him, she'd be homeless. Yep. This was for her own good.

* * *

New dresses? Curtains? Quilts? He could afford all this? A shot of dread rippled through her. What would he want in return? Selecting fabrics, yard after yard, then multiple threads, was like a dizzy dream. Jubilee could barely believe the volume after so much want. That, with the rest of the supplies Rafe had ordered, came to a very large amount.

On a bench outside of the mercantile, she shivered and laid her hand upon the brown package containing the precious material. Could it be true? Was she really going to take all of this fabric home? She glanced up and searched the street. Fear raced through her. Perhaps this was the way it'd be. He wouldn't show up and she'd be abandoned here in town. Just as the treacherous thought leaped to her mind, she saw the wagon appear from the direction of the sawmill.

He waved, vaulted from the high seat, and loaded the stuff in the back of the wagon. When he reached for the brown package in her hand, she hugged it to herself and shook her head. He gave a half-grin and encircled her waist to heft her to the seat. She sat for a moment, trying to still her frightened heart. Would she ever get used to that?

He strode into the building to pay for their purchases and reappeared. "We're supposed to be at the church at one." He climbed aboard. "So I figure we ought to eat before we head over."

Eat? Were they going home? She didn't question him as the wagon set in motion. But he didn't turn around to head back to the cabin. He went a block up the street and drew to a stop. Jubilee studied her surroundings.

"Pastor told me this place had good food."

Jubilee waited for him to reappear at the side of the wagon. After he set her on the ground, she stepped back with a puzzled look on her face.

"We're eating here?" She motioned to Millie's restaurant, with the red-checked curtains at the windows. Her hand grabbed the side of her skirt.

"Yep."

He started for the door, but she froze. When he shuffled back to her, he rubbed the back of his neck and raised his brows. "This not a good place?"

"I don't know, I..." They were eating in a restaurant? She licked her lips and stepped hesitantly toward the door.

He hurried to open it, and she halted, eying him. A gentlemanly gesture. Perhaps he'd been telling the truth, though it did seem strange for someone to hold the door for her. He motioned with his hand to precede him. Once inside, Rafe selected a table and waited for her to sit, then helped her to slide her chair forward. Jubilee gave a gasp and grabbed the table edge. He sat opposite her, his eyes probing hers.

"Do all men open doors and push in chairs?" She scrutinized him.

"Yes. Gentlemen do."

This would explain Colvin's lack of manners. He'd been no gentleman. She continued to analyze Rafe a moment as she fingered the flatware. "Oh. They have a lot of silverware. Why are there so many forks?"

Rafe removed his hat and set it in an extra chair.

"Well, the small fork is the salad fork. The large fork is for the main course."

Her brows drew together. Realizing her mouth hung open, she snapped it shut. The place setting resembled the table at Mrs. Galston's house. "Can't you eat your salad with the same fork?"

He chuckled softly. "I suppose you could."

The waitress appeared, rattled off the specials of the day, then took Rafe's order. Jubilee paused and dread filled her chest.

She leaned forward and whispered,

"I don't have any money."

He smiled. "I do. Get what you want."

She swallowed and glanced at the waitress again.

"I…" Oh my. She turned pleading eyes to Rafe.

"You like roast beef?" At her nod he told the waitress to bring another plate of roast beef.

Jubilee scanned the interior uneasily, feeling totally out of her element.

"Have you ever eaten in a restaurant before?" He gentled his voice.

She shook her head and saw the pity in his eyes. She glanced away.

"Pastor Barnett said they have good food."

Her tense muscles wouldn't relax. She was to be married in a little less than an hour. Again. Her nerves quaked, and she took short breaths. Her hands knotted in her lap.

"I don't remember thanking you for the fabric. I've never had so much." Her voice came out as a whisper. Oh dear, that made her seem even more stupid, if that were possible. Any moment now he'd stand and announce she was too much of a dunce to marry. But he just nodded and leaned back in his chair. He smiled good-naturedly.

"Reckon it just means work for you."

He probably thought her a simpleton. She glanced away. Her voice was hoarse when she spoke. "Oh, no, I'll be glad to get started. I haven't done sewing in a while."

It grew quiet at their table, and Jubilee scanned the room. The people seated seemed like regular folk. It must not be uncommon for most people to eat at these establishments. A fancy-dressed couple sat at the corner table, he with his long black coat and vest, complete with his top hat resting in the chair beside him, and she with an enormous amount of ruffles and a large, strange-looking gathering of fabric at the backside of her dress.

The lady wore a crazy-tall feathered hat covered with ribbons, and tied beneath her chin, that looked plain uncomfortable. Surrounding another table, a group of older men in casual clothes told yarns to each other and slapped their legs with glee. Three ladies dressed for tea, pinkies up, sat nearby, deep in conversation.

Rafe shifted in his seat and she flinched. She'd almost forgotten him. It could've been enjoyable to sit and study the people as they came in and out, if it weren't for the fact she accompanied a virtual stranger whom she'd agreed to marry. She lifted her eyes. He stared out the window, watching a horse and buggy. She patted the brown paper package of fabric in her lap. He'd been very kind to purchase the fabric. Was it a ruse to get her to marry him? Her stomach clenched. Jubilee wasn't sure if it was from hunger or from wedding anxiety.

The waitress arrived and plopped the plates onto the table and scurried away. Jubilee eyed the huge portions covering her plate. This was enough food for two days.

"Do you mind if I pray?" Rafe asked quietly.

Her eyes flew to his. Was he a preacher?

CHAPTER FIVE

W hat a silly question. The man farmed. She muddled this thought in her head, thankful she hadn't blurted her thoughts aloud, and barely acknowledged his simple prayer. He tore into his food and she did likewise, wondering how she managed to eat. But experience had taught her to take meals when they became available.

She was struggling to eat a mere half of the roast beef, potatoes and gravy, when he pushed his plate back clean. She stared at the rest of the food on her plate.

"You know you don't have to finish every bite." A trace of humor lit his voice.

She swallowed. "What will happen to the scraps?"

He shrugged. "Probably get added to a big slop bucket and hauled out to the pigs."

She gasped and looked down. They threw good food out to the hogs? Positively unthinkable. Even cold Mrs. Galston had sent the leftovers home with Mrs. Perkins.

She'd endured weeks with relatively nothing to eat. Her eyes went to him in astonishment. "Really?"

He laughed. "Yes. Don't worry about the leftovers. We've got bigger fish to fry."

Suddenly, her belly sank, as if filled with a thousand lead marbles. The wedding. Oh, dear heavens. She pushed her plate back. It didn't appear so appetizing anymore.

* * *

As he held the door for Jubilee, his mind lit on his family. It was true, Rafe supposed, that their marriage wasn't a real wedding of sorts. Still, they ought to be standing with him. Especially Sarah. They were going to be crushed when he wrote and told them. He sighed. Nothing to do now. It was a deal he'd see through.

At the wagon, Rafe came around to gently lift his bride-to-be. As he set her in her seat, his eyes caught that dress. Real marriage or not, he hated for folks to view his fiancée in such a get-up. She looked positively…well, like a starving orphan. Something twisted in his gut. That was exactly what she was.

Inside the church, four people puttered around, putting out fresh flowers, sweeping, and arranging books. They all stopped in their duties when they came in. An aging gentleman with white hair, and a small woman with equally white hair, stepped towards them.

"Pastor Barnett." Rafe greeted him as they shook hands.

"Ah, Rafe. All ready?" The older man smiled, his face wreathed in wrinkles. "My wife, Esther."

The tiny woman approached with a big smile.

Rafe nodded before turning to Jubilee. "This is Jubilee."

Esther stepped forward and put both hands on Jubilee's cheeks. "Why, you are practically the spitting image of my daughter, Fanny Nell."

Jubilee's eyes opened wide.

"Oh, I'm sorry, dear. I certainly didn't mean to startle you." The woman took her by her hand and patted it. "Why don't you and I step next door and let these men tend to the details?"

* * *

Jubilee turned, eyes on Rafe, fully engaged in conversation with Pastor Barnett, then mutely followed the strange woman.

"We don't have too many weddings here, so this is a real treat. That's why I had my sister and her husband come in and get the church ready. I thought some nice fresh flowers would dress the church up on your special day."

Jubilee said nothing, aware she was being pulled into the residence next to the church. It must be the Barnett's home. Esther guided her through the house, not stopping until they reached a back bedroom. Jubilee's eyes swept the immaculate room, coming to rest on the silver-backed hairbrush set lying on the dressing table.

"Now, you sit here," the woman urged, patting a quilt-covered bed, and Jubilee seated herself on the edge.

The woman swept over to a large armoire and swung the doors open. To Jubilee's surprise, the closet overflowed with dresses. After pulling a stool over to climb up, Esther searched a moment before bringing down a frilly peach one.

"Now I realize this is a bit out of fashion, but I believe this outfit is a near-perfect fit."

What? Did this woman intended to give her a dress? She swallowed as she studied the gorgeous fabric. Never had she even been close to such a creation, let alone worn one. She started to speak, but Esther was quicker.

"Fanny Nell's Aunt Ruby, who lived in New York, delighted in sending her the newest dresses. Why, Fanny never even wore this one." The woman stroked the fabric and removed an imaginary speck of lint before snapping her attention back to Jubilee. "Here, let me help you."

Jubilee stood with her hands up. "Oh, ma'am, I can't wear your daughter's clothing."

The woman's face grew puzzled. "Whyever not?"

Jubilee could only shake her head and stare at the peach creation.

Esther fluffed the ruffles. "You don't like this one? Why, there's several more. You can have your choice."

"Oh, no, nothing like that. That's the prettiest dress I've ever seen."

The woman smiled. "Well, I do believe it complements your coloring. Your dark eyes and golden skin will look absolutely glowing in peach."

Jubilee dared to touch the fabric. Oh, the material was heavenly. She stepped away. "I just couldn't."

Esther laid the garment across the bed and approached Jubilee. She placed one hand on Jubilee's cheek and her weathered blue eyes searched hers.

"Now, why deny this old woman's desire? Look at all these dresses." She swept her arm to the armoire. "I can't wear a one of them. Wouldn't want to if I could. They were Fanny

Nell's, and she's been gone near thirty years now. You'd do me and Fanny an honor by taking one."

Jubilee stared at the woman. Never had anyone been so kind. Finally, she gave a small nod, and Esther squealed in glee, unfastening the tiny buttons on the beautiful dress as she chattered like a magpie.

"Now, this one has a matching bonnet and bag, which is handy for going about town. It can easily be worn to church, if you so desire. We'd love to have you both in morning service. Can't tell you what a blessing it is to meet a new couple. Does this old heart good, and I know Raymond prays for it all the time. Young folks are the growth of the church."

Before Jubilee could think, the gorgeous garment settled on her shoulders. The coolness of the silk gave her a shiver. Esther directed her to the oval, full-length mirror in the corner. Jubilee stared at her reflection. It hung around her waist a bit, but the garment had transformed her from a ragamuffin to a lady. Esther buzzed about her, pinning the skirt before directing her to remove the garment again.

"It'll take a few moments to tuck these in, dear." Esther pulled a needle and thread from a basket near the bed.

Jubilee stood in her threadbare chemise while Esther sewed.

"Now if you get in that trunk at the end of the bed, you'll find a fresh crinoline to hold this dress out. I believe one will fit you." She licked the thread and attempted to insert it into the eye of the needle.

Instead of going to the trunk, Jubilee walked to her, pulled the needle and thread from her hand, and in one deft motion threaded the needle.

"Why, thank you. You're a wonder. My old eyes can hardly thread it through anymore."

Esther's hand drew out a long stitch. "Don't forget the trunk."

Jubilee sighed, tired of fighting the inevitable. A plethora of white, lacy underclothes popped out when the lid lifted. How did one come to own so many fine things?

"See, you're really doing me a favor." The woman laughed softly. "My oldest son has harped on me for years to get rid of all this." She sighed, and her gaze grew sad. "I just can't."

Jubilee ran a hand over the soft material. "When you said Fanny Nell was, gone, did you mean she's passed?"

Esther's eyes deepened with sorrow when she glanced up. Her busy hands rested in her lap. She nodded.

"Yes," she said. "She got the pox at seventeen. Never had been strong, and it took her quick. Plumb broke my heart."

For a minute she sat, looking far back over the years, before sighing and getting back to work.

"She's with the Lord now and there ain't a better place." A sad smile crossed her face. "I know she'd be as happy as I am to share a few things with you. Go ahead. Pick any one you want."

Jubilee watched her stitch, her mind on a young girl dying before she'd even lived. Then she dipped her head and began digging through the beautiful things. How would she choose? In the end, Esther whisked one of the stiff crinolines from the chest and helped Jubilee dress. With Esther's skilled hands, the garment fit her like a glove, the puckers adding volume to her thin waist. Jubilee fingered the silky ruffles of the skirt and stared at herself in the mirror.

"Well, now, let's work a little magic with your hair." Esther guided Jubilee to a chair. Meekly, she obeyed.

Esther continued to chat as she combed, braided, and tucked. A surreal feeling captured Jubilee, like a lovely dream. When she'd finished, Esther led her to the mirror and Jubilee squinted at herself. Her hair had been brushed to a shine and wrapped to the back of her head, where the locks hung in vibrant waves. She caught her breath and touched her coifed hair. *I'm a stranger.*

After grabbing a brown ribbon from her sewing basket, Esther whisked her to the back door once again. Pausing outside, the older woman picked white tulips from her flower bed. The older woman's stories never paused as she wrapped a brown ribbon around the fragrant flowers' stems.

"Every bride should have a bouquet. Yes, oh yes. Pretty as a spring day." She presented them to Jubilee's trembling hands and looked her over. "Now, I suspect your groom awaits, so we must hurry. We've kept them long enough."

Jubilee swayed as the church door swung open, trying to adjust to the dim interior. A large, firm hand caught her arm. Rafe. Gracious, the man was tall. Her eyes searched his for a moment, and his gaze swept over her hair and dress. A frown settled between his brows, and he released her. She took a shaky breath and stepped away. He hadn't approved. Well, it wasn't as if they married for love. Rubbing her arm where he had touched her, she wasn't sure why his disapproval shook her.

Biting her lip and dabbing at the moisture in her eyes, she stepped toward Pastor Barnett. The contents of her stomach rocked, and she had a horrible feeling the roast beef might make a reappearance. A hot wave washed over her and she swallowed. She was only vaguely aware Rafe had stepped next to her. Pastor Barnett held his Bible aloft. Jubilee closed her eyes as her stomach rolled again. Rafe mumbled something, and she opened her eyes. Pastor Barnett looked at her expectantly, leaning slightly forward with a small smile pinned to his face. Bile gathered in her throat.

"I do." She fought the nausea for a few moments more before hearing, '...the power vested in me.'

Her stomach lurched, and she took flight toward the side door, her hand firmly clamped over her mouth. Around the back of the church she sailed, before throwing herself, and the contents of her stomach, all over the grass. When the heaving stopped, she rolled over and lay on her side, covering her face with her hands. *Please don't let them find me.* The thought had barely run through her mind when a large hand touched her arm. "Please, leave me."

She could hear Esther's melodic voice approaching and wished she were at home where she'd spring up and run for the woods. Instead, strong arms gathered her, and suddenly she floated.

"Please, no."

"Oh, dear, oh dear, the poor thing. Let's get her into the house." Esther's voice appeared much closer.

Someone pressed a handkerchief into her hand. Jubilee buried her face in the strong column of Rafe's neck. Before she protested, her new husband answered.

"I think it's best if I took her home."

The floating continued and Jubilee clenched her eyelids closed.

"You're more than welcome to spend a few nights with us until she's up and ready." Esther spoke again.

Jubilee grabbed tightly onto Rafe's collar. He cleared his throat and stretched his neck. She let go of his shirt.

"No, she'll be much more comfortable at home."

He placed her in the back of the wagon, and Esther brought a quilt to cover her. She buried her head under the blanket and let the tears squeeze through her lashes. In the background, she heard Rafe thanking the couple, then the wagon began to move. She was married again. Married to another stranger. She stuffed the edge of the quilt in her mouth to stifle the sobs.

* * *

Rafe mentally wrestled with himself all the way home. He hated that she was sick and knew the stress of marrying him had brought the illness on. Yet, if he hadn't married her, she'd be homeless. But she'd be free. If only she hadn't appeared all dolled up. He didn't like her being so…attractive. It was much easier dealing with a homeless young orphan.

How did a dress and a few hairpins make such a difference? He squelched the emotion down. Didn't matter.

Didn't matter a hill of beans. He was here to make this farm become successful and, by dog, he would. No brown-eyed doe-child-turned-woman would waylay him in the process. And what was his problem anyway? So she was pretty. So what? His heart still bore open sores from the agony Rosemary had inflicted.

No, this arrangement was for the best. In the long run, Jubilee would have a home, and she'd be a good housekeeper, laundress, and gardener. Yes, this was for the best. She was just his…employee, that was all. He had to keep that in mind. She'd recover, and would realize all of this was for the best. He'd just about convinced himself of this when she snuffled. She was crying under that quilt. He frowned and grunted.

He was definitely a mean, low-down sack of bones, that's what he was. He gave a heavy sigh and shook his head. It'd take a miracle to right this situation, and Rafe wasn't sure he believed in them anymore.

CHAPTER SIX

Despite Rafe's misgivings, life fell into a pattern on the farm with Jubilee. He saw little of her during the first few weeks, as if she were hiding out. He had no doubt she was, but he found plenty to keep himself busy. He'd stored the food items for Jubilee in the cabin, noting her distance with some amusement as he carried in the huge bags.

His first project was repairing the hole in the roof. Then he finished reconstructing the entire front porch. Happy with the outcome, he decided the time had been well spent. Still, he knew he had to get at the fields. The new pair of oxen he'd invested in would be a great improvement over Jubilee's one-man shoveling team.

Rafe rounded the house with his axe, intending to cut more firewood before harnessing the oxen to the plow. When his eyes fell to the woodpile, he stopped short. The height remained nearly the same as last week. Did the woman use any fuel? The back door swung open and Jubilee gave a start, her eyes huge.

"Mornin'." He dipped his head in greeting, wondering at the same time if she would ever meet him without fear.

She bit her lip as she eyed the axe. "Morning."

He motioned to the stack. "I thought you'd near be out at this point. How come you have so much wood left?"

He set his hand high against the cabin and leaned against the wall. She closed the door a little more, and Rafe realized he'd been a bit abrupt. He'd have to tone it down to gain her trust. His eyes shifted down, but she hid behind the door. He knew her well enough now to imagine one of her fingers spinning a nervous circle in her skirt fabric. He shifted his gaze to her face, knowing she watched every move he made. She gave that thin, one-shouldered shrug.

"I don't know. Preparing a meal doesn't require much of a fire." Again the shrug.

She only used fuel to cook? He cocked his head. "You ain't been keeping a fire?"

He took a step towards her. Her eyes widened, and she shook her head like a child in trouble. Rafe grunted and pulled the axe from his shoulder to let it swing to his side, his hand wrapped around the wooden handle. Jubilee closed the door a bit more.

Rafe scratched his neck. "Listen, Jubilee. I want you to burn wood anytime you're cold. Don't suffer through this chilly weather when you've got plenty of fuel out here. I don't mind keeping you supplied, you understand?"

Her head bobbed up and down.

He took a deep breath. This trust thing would develop, or at least he hoped so. Just blamed frustrating for her to fear him so much. He stuck his free hand into his pocket.

"All right. After breakfast, I'm off to plow the west field. On Saturday, I'd like to set out the seed in the garden, and I'd appreciate you being there to see where everything is planted. The weeding and harvesting will be part of your chores."

"It's not a problem."

He nodded and started on his way to the barn when she called to him. He stopped and watched her disappear into the cabin, then return carrying a colorful quilt. She approached and handed it to him. "What's this?"

She stepped back before she replied. "For you. The barn must get cold, too."

He looked down at the quilt. The simple design in rust, dark green, and mustard squares appeared well-made and heavy. The thickness would definitely stave off the chilly temperatures. He smiled and nodded.

"Thank ya much," he said, not sure what else to say.

She turned and withdrew into the cabin.

* * *

Jubilee barred the door, rested her back against the rough wood, and chewed her lip while working her skirt fabric in a circle. Her brow puckered in thought. Use the wood? Just for a little heat? She rubbed her free hand across her face. The weather hadn't even been below freezing the last week and a half. Colvin would've slapped her silly for wasting fuel in such a way. At the Orphan Society, they often slept five to six in a bed to ward off the cold.

Besides, she had the new cape Rafe had bought her, the wool blanket he insisted on getting, and the dress Esther had given her. This was the warmest she'd been in years, yet keeping a fire banked throughout the day would be rather nice. A luxury even.

Jubilee collected her thoughts and headed straight for the food stores. There was breakfast to fix, and a fire to build as well as tend. Never one to stall, she set to work. As difficult as the decision to marry Rafe had been, things had smoothed out. He'd patched the hole in the roof, the porch was redone, the garden tilled, and the pantry contained plenty of food.

Her thin frame had a pinch of health back, with energy to boot. Now, apparently, there was also plenty of wood to burn. She had a couple of dresses, a cape, a blanket, and plenty of cloth to make several more quilts and shirts for Rafe. Really, she felt almost rich. So why did she harbor such a fear of the man?

Jubilee arranged the bacon on Rafe's plate beside the scrambled eggs and fresh bread smeared generously with creamy butter. She put on her cape and took the cheesecloth-covered platter to the barn. He'd be harnessing the oxen in readiness for plowing. Stopping at the newly constructed cold box on the porch, she retrieved the milk bucket and headed across the new grass.

It seemed silly the man had to take his meals in the barn. He owned the place after all. A man should be able to eat at his table, same as she did. Her steps slowed. He really ought to dine in the cabin. If Jubilee's hand had been free, it would've clutched at her skirt seam. Instead, she came to a halt. Rafe *should* eat in the house. At his table. That meant she'd have to share or take her meals elsewhere.

Her face scrunched in thought. Sharing the cabin would be the decent thing. She let out a loud sigh. Time to get past this fear. She'd tell him he was welcome to take his meals at the cabin.

She set the pail of milk down and opened the heavy door. The barn's size resembled a mansion. Since the hour was early, the inside appeared still and shadowy. The rustling above made her wonder if he gathered hay in the loft. Like an answer from on high, a large wad of straw fell to the middle of the floor.

"Hello?" she called and heard a muffled response.

She went to the rough-cut bench, the same one she'd sat upon the first night Jubilee had met him, and set the platter and pail down. He suddenly appeared at the top of the ladder with a lantern, which gave a soft glow that brightened as he climbed down. He nodded his head at her and made for the bench. She stepped back but did not leave as customary. After hanging the lantern, he pulled a bucket from a peg and washed his hands, drying them on the towel from atop the plate. He paused and looked at her.

"You needin' something?" Like the barn, his voice was quiet.

Jubilee swallowed around the knot in her throat.

"Yes," she began, her fingers fixed in the seam of her skirt. "I think it'd be more proper for you to eat at the table. In the cabin."

He rubbed his hand down his chin, and Jubilee could hear the rasp of whiskers.

"What's brought this on?"

She shrugged one shoulder.

"More proper, huh? You know, there's not too many folks watchin' us eat our meals that I'm aware of. I'm all right here."

Jubilee stared at the plate to avoid his eyes. Heat spread up her neck.

"Well, I suppose I didn't really mean proper. Maybe I meant more comfortable." Checking his reaction, she caught his crooked grin.

"More comfortable for me, or for you?"

She cleared her throat, hoping the shadows of the barn hid her hot cheeks. *How do I answer that?* Her hands clasped behind her. She refused to shrug again. "Well, I wouldn't have to carry all this out here and back inside. If you wanted seconds, I'd be right there, and you could sit down at a table and..."

He grinned again. "Fine. As long as this arrangement suits you, it suits me. But I won't be in tonight. I'll be plowing 'til dark-thirty."

Jubilee swung around and all but flew to the cabin. Glory be, she hoped she didn't regret doing that.

* * *

That night, Rafe settled in on the small cot and arranged the new quilt over his body to suit him. He couldn't help but smile as the smell of fresh hay surrounded him. The blanket warmed him, and he admired the muted colors, which satisfied a masculine taste. No, what made him grin was her nervousness at asking him to take his meals inside the cabin. That oughta be a hoot. She'd probably sit across the room, right next to the back door, with her breakfast balanced on her lap. If he even spoke, her plate might tumble to the floor. He grunted, yet the smile slid from his face. The image was humorous, but the reasons behind her fear were definitely not. Perhaps sharing a meal would take the fear from her eyes.

He couldn't complain. The food was good and filling. And, even though she was hardly bigger than a bird, she didn't shy away from hard work. This quilt was proof of that. He stretched his arms out and laid his hands behind his head, elbows out.

Yep, things were coming around. Most of the fields he'd planned on planting this year were plowed. He'd fixed the fences, hacked down weeds surrounding the cabin, fixed the roof and replaced the porch. The garden was ready to plant, the new cow would soon drop her calf, and the old one was healthy enough for breeding again. After planting the garden and the fields, he'd start digging up the rest of the stumps from the front yard.

Thoughts of his family crept in to dampen his spirits. He'd sent off a letter to let them know of his marriage. He'd kept the note short and sweet. There really wasn't much to say. His younger sister, Sarah, would be heartbroken to learn of his unexpected wedding. He sighed. This certainly wasn't what he would've chosen.

Rosemary's face crossed his mind. He shook his head to deny a stab of pain. His pride still stung to think of her sneaking off and marrying Dale. If it'd have been anyone but his best friend, it wouldn't be quite so hard to take. He groaned and pushed away the disturbing thoughts.

What did it matter anyway? He'd married Jubilee, and as far as folks knew, this was a normal marriage. His family would support him, and soon everyone in his hometown would receive the news. The distance might aid in appearing as a regular married couple. He and Jubilee, just an average man and wife.

Suddenly he grinned in the darkness. He at the table, and Jubilee sitting primly at the back door with her plate in her lap.

CHAPTER SEVEN

Jubilee scurried around, flour flying into the air. What was wrong with her? Her usual morning routine seemed shot to pot. Now the biscuits were burnt. She huffed. Too late to fix another batch since Rafe's heavy boots sounded on the new porch floor. She scooped the eggs and bacon to the plate, almost throwing the biscuit basket on the table when she heard a small knock on the door.

"Come in." She had to utter it twice to be heard, then caught her breath as his huge form filled the doorway.

"Mornin'," He removed his hat and hung it on the peg near the window.

The table was a simple trestle with two bench seats on either side. Rafe chose the one against the wall in front of the only glass pane. Jubilee fidgeted nervously by the stove.

"Okay if I sit here?" He gestured.

She nodded and shrugged one shoulder. The man owned the place yet asked her where to sit. She snatched up a fork, a knife, and a clean cloth napkin to lay them on the table close to the lone plate.

He sat and stared at her. "Is this my plate or yours?"

She cleared her throat. "Yours."

He glanced around the table before spreading his search to the kitchen area. "Where's yours?"

"I...thought I'd eat later. This way I can get you anything you need and such..." She gnawed her lip and looked away from him, but not before she caught the half-smile that crossed Rafe's face.

"So you're just gonna stand and fetch while I eat?"

Jubilee made the mistake of letting her gaze wander back to his. There he sat with that quirky grin, eyebrows lifted, humor lighting his eyes.

"I..."

And she could think of nothing, absolutely nothing to say. All she could concentrate on was the way the early morning sunlight lit the blond highlights in his hair. *Holy moley.*

* * *

Rafe shook his head. If the woman thought she'd pretend to be his servant, she had another thing coming. He stood, retrieved a plate from the shelf, and laid it directly opposite of his. He collected a fork, knife, and napkin, and arranged them next to the empty dish. He went to the stove and picked up another egg.

"What are you doing?" Her question came in a rush.

He turned to face her, still gripping the oval shell.

"Jubilee, I'm not gonna eat alone while you wait on me hand and foot like some lowly servant. Let's both sit down and have breakfast. It'll be a great time for us to discuss business. We're partners on this farm and we've got to work together to make a go."

With that he stepped up to the stove and cracked the egg into the pan, and it immediately began to sizzle.

* * *

He could fry an egg? She stared, opening her mouth in disbelief as he scooped it out and plopped the finished product onto her plate. She'd never seen a man cook. He held out his hand toward the bench, indicating she should sit. She did so, eyeing him the whole time. He immediately bowed and said a simple prayer of thanks so quick Jubilee hadn't even collected her wits enough to bow her head. Then he peered at her, eye to eye. He seemed very close.

"I'll switch ya eggs if you don't like my cooking." A rumble echoed from his chest as he laughed at his own joke.

Jubilee's hands sweated. She wiped them on her skirt. "No, this is fine."

"Could you pass the biscuits?" he asked.

Jubilee reached for the basket and remembered some were overdone. Perhaps by chance he'd reach in and get a good one. As luck would have it, a black-bottom one filled his hand. She held her breath. He picked up the knife and sliced the biscuit in half. The utensil clattered to the table and banged on the bench beside him before clanging across the floor.

* * *

Jubilee's reaction to his accidental dropping of the knife reminded Rafe of a small, crisp leaf whipped by a rush of wind. She leaped up, literally jumped over the bench, and knocked it to the floor. In a flurry of skirts, she darted across the room. He barely had time to stand before she hovered at the back door, shaking like a frightened rabbit.

"Jubilee? What's going on?"

She shook her head vigorously. "I didn't mean to burn them. It was…an accident. I'll be more…careful next time, I promise. I think I had the stove too hot or…"

Rafe slowly stepped towards her, and she flinched. Her eyes were huge, muddied pools.

"Jubilee, listen to me. I accidentally dropped the knife. I'm not mad about the biscuits. They're fine. I'll just cut off the bottom. My sister Sarah used to do this every time she made bread. Trust me. No big deal."

She continued to hover at the back door, her fingers worrying her skirt in a circle.

"Please come and sit down." When she hesitated, he returned to his bench and eased his body down. He couldn't feel less like eating now, but he'd stuff this food in his mouth nonetheless, to show her everything was fine.

He retrieved the knife, wiped it clean, and quickly severed off the charred section of the biscuit, then buttered the cut side. After a bite, he tried to chew, ignoring the awful tumble in his stomach at her violent reaction. Somewhere along the way she'd learned physical punishment accompanied burnt food. Stoically, he forked a wad of egg into his mouth and waited for her to return to the table. She did, and even sat down.

Jubilee picked up the fork and poked at the meal without actually eating. Her head stayed down.

Rafe tempered his next words with an extra soft tone. "Remember what I promised you before we got married?"

"Yes."

He took a deep breath. "I'm not going to break that promise."

Rafe stared at the top of her head, waiting.

"Jubilee. Look at me."

She raised her head and met his eyes.

"Whether you burn the biscuits, or drop a dozen plates, or destroy the garden, I'm not gonna hurt you. Understand?"

Her head bobbed.

"Do you believe me?"

He took in her perplexed face, her eyes glistening with tears. Finally she gave that one-shouldered shrug.

Rafe placed his hands on either side of his plate and leaned forward. "Jubilee, you can take my oath to the bank because whether you trust me or not, I'm gonna keep it like I said."

And with that he rose, excused himself, and left the cabin.

* * *

Anger drove Rafe to work harder than ever, and planting the last field didn't take long to finish. Oh, what he wouldn't do to Colvin if that dag-burned idiot hadn't gone and got himself killed. She was no bigger than a child. The scene at the table repeated through his mind, ending with her at the back door, arm up to fend off blows. And her eyes, her huge, pleading eyes. The incident made him sick.

Finally, he threw himself on the new grass that ran along the fencerow. Shielding his face from the sun, he prayed. *Oh, God, let Jubilee heal. Help her forget the meanness and be able to forgive.*

He groaned, but a peace entered him, and he realized it was the first time he'd really prayed since he'd lost Rosemary. He sat up. Praying hadn't felt awkward. He hadn't double-thought the process or anything. The prayer had just come as natural as his prayers had before he'd been jilted. He sighed. *I'm sorry God. I shouldn't have quit praying.*

He recalled Pastor Barnett and how he'd promised they'd try to attend the morning service. Here, some four weeks later, they'd never once darkened the church door. Rafe bowed his head and rubbed his hot neck. Maybe now was time to keep his promise, not only to Pastor Barnett, but to God.

* * *

Jubilee was in a jumble. She was an idiot. An idiot. Why did she leap across the room for such a simple thing as a knife dropping to the floor? She swallowed around the lump in her throat as the tears filled her eyes. Why, if she burned the biscuits when Colvin had been home, she'd left his meal and disappeared into the woods until he was gone. But this wasn't Colvin. This huge man who now occupied a place at the table was hard to read.

Rafe was quiet. He was calm. Or at least he appeared to be. Jubilee knew only time would prove whether he really possessed these qualities. He seemed honest, he even appeared...godly. If only he weren't so large. If he decided to, he could tear her apart. And that was, plain and simple, why she had such a difficult time letting go of her fear.

She took a shaky breath and scrubbed the frying pan harder. *Trust.* The words entered her mind like a wisp. Her movements ceased. Had this been her own thought? She shook her head. It didn't matter. Trusting Rafe might have dangerous results. *Help me trust, Lord, if he is worthy. If he is not, Lord, keep me safe.*

* * *

"Church?" The word came out of her mouth as a squeak and brought Rafe to a stop in the middle of his sentence. They sat across from each other, having a delicious, stilted dinner. Then he'd dropped his idea of going to the morning service.

"Do you not want to?" he asked.

She blinked. Of course she wanted to go. She'd yearned to attend since coming to this lonely cabin with Colvin two years before, but he wouldn't even discuss the possibility.

"I..."

Dared she tell the absolute truth? Surviving the Orphan Society, being bound out to Mrs. Galston, as well as life with

Colvin, had taught her to filter her answers to reflect what the hearer wanted. Examining his friendly, warm expression, she decided to take a chance. Warmth spread up her neck.

"I'd love to go."

A grin broke across his face and Jubilee caught her breath. She flicked her gaze to her plate.

"Excellent. I'd hoped you'd want to. I promised Pastor Barnett, after all, and I remembered the other day we hadn't been yet."

She contemplated the new shirt she'd finished for him. The garment was burgundy and would look fine for church if he had no other. She'd make sure she gave it to him before he took his leave tonight. Her thoughts came to a halt as he continued to speak.

"Uh, I've also got some more news."

She gazed at him. His face had lost its carefree grin and had now been replaced by a puckered brow.

"I received a letter from my family," He took a drink of water before his eyes came back to hers. "They're inviting us to come so they can meet you."

Jubilee's stomach practically hit the floor. She clutched the table edge and looked down. Had this plate contained tasty food? Because, right now, the meal looked awful. Her hand worried her skirt and, when she didn't reply, he continued.

"I thought the best time to go would be in the next couple of months while the crops are growing. I can get one of the neighbors to take care of the animals. Perhaps one of the boys could weed the garden. We'll go by steamboat up the Ohio. It's a long haul in a wagon."

His voice was so calm and quiet. Yet a buzzing began in her head. Visiting family? People who'd believe they were just any ordinary couple? An actual family? What did one do with kin? How in the world would she cope in a house full of strangers?

"Should I go ahead and get the tickets?"

She tried to wrap her brain around the matter. Had he asked a question?

"Jubilee?"

She jerked her head up.

"I'd really like for us to go and visit my family. Is it okay?"

She could do nothing but echo his last words. "Is it okay? I…you're asking me?" A little bit of her fear turned to surprise.

He nodded. "I know we're business partners in this farm, but we need to work and make decisions together. Please feel free to tell me what you want. In a lot of ways, we really are a married couple like other people see us. We oughta get along and have happy lives. This is a big decision, and I aim for you to have your say."

* * *

Rafe watched her face go from fear to confusion to surprise. The poor girl had no idea how transparent her emotions were most of the time. Teasingly, he gave a small smile to take away the seriousness of the moment and watched as a pink blush covered her cheeks before she lowered her head.

Maybe she needed a spell to think on it. "You can decide over the next couple of days and let me know on the drive to church. That sound okay?"

She nodded but didn't lift her chin again. Rafe's smile grew as he excused himself and went whistling out the door.

CHAPTER EIGHT

Next day, after breakfast, Rafe whistled again as he headed for the garden shed to collect implements. He stopped dead when his eyes caught Jubilee, bent over, sticking seeds in a long furrow. The shovel, rake and hoe lay next to two bushel baskets full of seed.

"Well, I guess this is one way to know where everything is." He ran his eye over the patch. "Is this the corn?" He indicated the mounds running east to west on the north side.

At her nod he smiled. "Good thinking. Don't want to shade the rest of the garden. What's here?"

"Cucumbers."

"That's a good use of the space around the corn. Now what?" He walked down the row toward her as she started the green beans. "Give me a handful and we'll work two rows together."

The beans went in quick, and they started a row of squash. Rafe grabbed the seed potatoes from the bushel basket and cut them into fours with his knife, leaving an eye in each piece.

"Shoulda got these potatoes in earlier." He grunted and shook his head as he placed several potato chunks in each dirt hole. "Guess we'll have to remember for next year."

Next year. Shoveling the dirt to fill the hole, he wondered. *Will I be planting with Jubilee again next spring?* "Seems you're experienced in garden layout. You've done a fine job."

Jubilee stood up, and Rafe could sense her assessing him.

"I guess you've done this before?" He was determined to get an answer from her.

"Yes."

That one word contained loads of information. "Colvin teach you?"

"No."

Rafe smiled to himself as her blunt answer spoke volumes. "You must've been educated at the orphan's home, then."

"Some."

He dug a few more holes for the potatoes before taking another stab at conversation. "What orphan home were you in?"

"Philadelphia."

Rafe stopped and cast a glance at her. "As in, Pennsylvania?" At her nod, he let out a whistle. "Now that's a piece away. How did you get all the way to Gibson County, Indiana?"

"Hog tied to the back of a horse."

Rafe's hands froze, and he snapped his head up. "What?"

She ceased planting to look at him. "What's not to understand?"

Rafe's brows furrowed. "You mean to tell me Colvin tied you up and hauled you here?"

"After kidnapping me."

He watched her bend and poke the seeds into the ground, as if they were talking of the weather. Kidnapping? Not sure what to say to that, he tore into the rest of the row, shoveling like a madman. Finally, he stopped.

"He *kidnapped* you?" He rested his hand on the top of the shovel handle.

"Yes." She never paused.

He shifted his feet and thrust a hand in his pocket. "From the orphan home?"

"On my way there."

"Listen, I…" He wiped his brow. "I'm sorry. I had no idea."

She shrugged and continued to plant. A thousand questions leaped to Rafe's mind. He ran a hand through his hair and glanced off to the fields. "How old were you?"

Her hands never paused. "Sixteen."

A heaviness settled in Rafe's heart. His glance flicked to her, but his hands stayed busy. His thoughts turned to prayers and soon the row was completed. They finished the onions, radishes, and peppers in silence. Rafe's back ached, but his heart even more.

"You're gonna need some help with hoeing and such," Rafe commented, avoiding the subject he wanted to discuss, as he gathered the implements. "This garden will be more work than a whole field." He cast his eyes over the finished result. It was huge and had to be to get enough food stored away for the both of them for a whole winter.

"I can do it."

He took her in. There was no way he would open that can of worms by denying her claim. Best to stay silent. Besides, she probably *could* hoe the garden alone. He dipped his head to hide a smile. Dirt clung to her face, hands, and skirt. Sweat beaded across her brow. At just under five foot, the girl had pluck. He had to give her that.

"I'll take care of these." He leaned forward to take the empty bushel baskets from her, and she withdrew from him. "Guess I better check that last field."

He turned, then paused at her quiet words.

"Thanks for the help."

He nodded his head and flashed a smile. "Anytime."

* * *

Jubilee's brow knitted as he sauntered away. She supposed she'd been rude with her short-change answers. But he couldn't know the thoughts darting through her brain. This whole trip thing had her tied in knots. Plus all his questions. Was it safe for him to know all the details of where she'd come from? Or how she came to be here? He could easily decide to take her back and she was beyond the age to return. The Orphan Society of Philadelphia only let girls stay until they turned eighteen. Jubilee shuddered as she thought of the night of her eighteenth birthday.

She moved to the corner of the cabin and stood watching him as he went to the barn. He moved so easily for a big guy. *Why did he take time to help me?* The garden was to be her chore. The man was a mystery. She snorted. *All* men were mysteries.

She shrugged to herself. What did it matter? There was a bigger problem here. What would await her at his home? And why in the world did he want her to go? Perhaps this was a trick to remove her from the farm. She expelled an aggravated breath. *Why didn't I ask some questions of my own?* She caught herself circling a nervous finger in the seam of her dress and clenched her hands in frustration. *Because I'm a little 'ole fraidy cat. That's why.*

And, scarier still, she wasn't sure what to do about it.

* * *

With the wagon seat jostling her into her large companion, Jubilee berated herself for forgetting to give Rafe that new burgundy shirt to wear for church. Not that it mattered. He had on a well-made white one, tucked into black pants, which set off not only his wide shoulders, but also his tight waist and hips. Her face heated even as the thought entered her head.

She patted the peach creation Miss Esther had bequeathed to her on her wedding day. Perhaps she'd be a bit overdressed. It certainly felt that way. Yet she couldn't help but appreciate the wide smile Rafe had given her when she opened the cabin door.

She'd done her best to lower her gaze to keep him from seeing her hot face while he lifted her to the wagon seat. What a goose she was. Scared to death of him, yet uplifted at his attention. He spoke and startled her from her thoughts.

"You give any thought to taking that trip to see my family?"

She gazed at the wildflowers along the path as they drove. "Yes." She cleared her throat. "I think we should go."

"Good. I hoped you'd agree."

She turned her face to look at him. "What would you've done if I'd said no?" She felt his shrug before he spoke.

"I'm not sure. Maybe I'd have gone alone eventually. I'd like to see everyone. Sarah will be thrilled."

Her curiosity piqued, she glanced his way. "Who's Sarah?"

"She's my sister, my little sister. We're pretty close."

She studied him from beneath her lashes. "How many people do you have in your family?"

His fingers rubbed the leather of the reins, and it caught Jubilee's eye. He had large, capable hands.

"Well, there's Mom and Pop, my oldest brother, Everett, and Forrest. I've got two older sisters, Anna and Phoebe, and there's Loyal, who has a house in Ohio. Last, there's Benjamin, me and Sarah. Everyone else lives close to Mom and Pop, plus one set of grandparents, my grandmother, three aunts and two uncles."

Jubilee fought the anxiety rising within her. That was an awful lot of names to remember. "It must be nice to have so many people in your family. Are any of your brothers and sisters married?"

He laughed. "Yeah, everyone now except Sarah, and she's only sixteen. But she's a beauty. She won't be single long."

Jubilee turned her head to stare at the landscape and digest all of this. What must it be like to have such a large family? She'd nothing to compare it with except the children she'd grown up with in the home, and they'd scattered here and there. The rest of the wagon ride was made in silence, Jubilee's emotions going in circles about this family trip.

The church looked beautiful among the maple trees, now fully leafed out. Irises bloomed around the foundation in a multitude of colors. The simple building sported a tall steeple above the two white entry doors. Pastor Barnett and his small wife stood at the top of the stairs, greeting people.

After Rafe lifted her down in silence, Esther bustled to meet her with a smile and a hug. Jubilee wasn't sure what to do. It was a new sensation for someone to receive her in such a welcoming manner. The pastor's wife chattered away, escorting them to the sanctuary. Her husband descended the stairs to greet them with a handshake and a grin. Jubilee's face grew warm at the parishioners' stares as the Barnetts made a fuss over them. Finally, they entered and took a back seat behind a young, blond-haired couple with a baby.

The congregation stood to sing after the pastor gave a short introduction. The song was unfamiliar to Jubilee, so she moved her lips to hide the fact that she didn't know it. Next to her, Rafe's low voice joined in. He knew the words and his tone was pleasant and deep. They sat and Jubilee looked around discreetly, having the advantage of sitting in the back.

Her mind returned to her companion who shifted, bumping his leg against hers. She tried to focus on the pastor, who stepped to the front to start the sermon. He wasn't a yeller, he was quiet. She had to strain to hear some of his words. He appeared to have a real burden for lost people and a deep conviction of reaching out to everyone in the area.

Somewhere in the middle of the sermon, the baby in front of her began playing peek-eye. Jubilee tried not to pay attention to the little imp, but it was difficult. With blond hair and a flash of bright blue eyes, she was adorable. When at last they stood for the benediction, the baby, whose face now peered over her father's tall shoulder, grinned openly. Jubilee did her best to keep her gaze toward the song leader. After the closing hymn, the couple in front of them turned to introduce themselves and apologized for their child's antics.

"Ve are most sorry. She not good on church." The father grinned and the baby dove for her mother's arms. "I am Ivan Larsson. Dis Elsa. And dis, dis Britta."

"Ve are neighbors." Elsa smiled, her green eyes warm as she wrestled the bouncing child. "Ve move in few months back."

Rafe reached out and gave Ivan a firm handshake. Jubilee couldn't help but smile at Elsa's friendly face. Elsa was taller than her by a good six inches and slightly plump. Her dress was a plain blue, yet well-made and new.

"You plant fields? My done. Is gud wetter for da planting." Ivan, with his strong Swedish accent, started a conversation with Rafe while young Britta reached out, babbling for Jubilee.

Startled, Jubilee looked at Elsa. But she offered the child to her with a laugh. "You hold? She like you."

Uncertain, Jubilee held her arms out for the chubby little girl who grabbed for her bonnet ties, knotted loosely to allow the hat to hang on her back. Britta clapped and threw her arms up in delight, grinning and showing her four white teeth. Jubilee was captivated and caught her breath at her antics. Britta squealed and held out her pint-sized hands, opening them and closing them towards the beams of light through the shutters.

"Yah, likes the light, she does." Elsa beckoned Jubilee to bring the sprite closer to the windows. The baby reached out to the window and let out a happy squeal. Jubilee's smile widened.

"She's adorable." Jubilee laughed. "How old is she?"

"Britta be one next month." Elsa nodded.

"Oh." Jubilee giggled as the tot lunged again to the shutters. She patted the baby's back and crooned to her. The child turned to her and gave a big baby grin before becoming fascinated with Jubilee's dress. She reached out to squeeze the ruffled sleeve caps.

"Oh, no. No, no, Britta, pretty dress. No wrinkle." Elsa fussed. "You want me take her?"

"No, she's fine."

"That dress—so beautiful." Elsa's eyes widened.

Jubilee smiled. "The pastor's wife gave it to me on my wedding day."

"Oh," Elsa's face brightened. "Miss Esther nice woman. You come visit? We have tea."

Jubilee glanced to Rafe. "Perhaps."

* * *

Rafe scanned the trio at the window as he muddled through Ivan's poor English. He caught his breath. Jubilee positively glowed as she held Ivan's babe. She bounced the child on her hip and pressed the little girl's hand against the slants of light, earning a happy squeal. He pulled his eyes away and blinked, remembering to nod to Ivan as he paused to search for the right word, but his gut tightened. She seemed so at ease and happy to be cradling that child. Her laughter floated to him.

Rafe pulled at his collar. He made his getaway from Ivan and walked toward Jubilee, and saw her eyes go from joy to guarded watchfulness. She handed the baby back to her mother and waved at her new friend as she moved to Rafe's side. After assisting her up onto the wagon seat, it was complete and utter silence all the way home.

CHAPTER NINE

Rafe and Jubilee attended church faithfully each Sunday. The pastor and his wife always welcomed them with a firm handshake and a hug. He enjoyed getting to know Ivan. As he talked to the big Swede, Rafe's gaze usually drifted to Jubilee chatting with Elsa and reveling in Britta's escapades. He tried to harden his heart to Jubilee's joy when she held Britta. Children were a gift from God, Rafe knew, but there were no babies in Jubilee's future. Their marriage was a business arrangement. Rafe clenched his jaw. This plan had been his idea hadn't it? *At least she isn't homeless.*

Rafe wrote a letter to his folks to let them know the exact date of their visit. They'd stay two weeks with his parents while Ivan took care of the farm. Sure would be good to get back home and visit the family. But the thought of meeting up with Rosemary again set his teeth on edge.

* * *

The night before the trip, Jubilee lamented and fretted over every item she put in her newly purchased satchel. Rafe had packed the wagon the day before so they could pull out early in the morning.

Nerves had Jubilee staring at the rafters when she should have been sleeping. Relief washed over her when the clock hands moved to four a.m. She threw the covers from her and began to get ready. Rafe had told her at dinner the night before that the stagecoach left out of Princeton at five a.m. They'd board Horse at Griffen's Livery and Blacksmith Shop nearby.

She dressed quickly in the darkness, her anxiety growing when she stepped onto the porch to wait for Rafe. Streaks of pink appeared in the eastern sky, lighting the darkness through the heavy woods. The air was moist, and God's creation seemed to hush at the wonder of daylight. She tried to concentrate on the beautiful morning, but her hand worked a circle in her skirt. *Please let everything be all right, Lord.*

There wasn't much conversation on the trip into town. Rafe made short business of boarding Horse, transferring the carpetbags and purchasing their tickets. Jubilee's tummy tumbled as she viewed the aging Concord stagecoach. But it had new wheels and the leather looked sturdy. A boy with a ragged jacket ran to and fro to bring buckets of water to the four horses harnessed to the front.

The men threw the luggage to the top and strapped it to the back as well. The driver was a grizzled tough nut, and his partner of the same sort, with wiry beards and sweat-marked hats.

"Looks like we had plenty of time." Rafe grinned.

Jubilee nodded, then watched as the driver and his cohort disappeared into the stagecoach office.

After another twenty minutes, they began to board. Jubilee, the only woman on the stage, boarded first with the help of her husband's hand. She chose the third row of seats and sat against the far wall, facing forward. The interior was terribly tight once the others were in, and Rafe threw his arm around Jubilee to afford a little room for his large shoulders.

She clenched her sweaty hands, wondering how she could sit so stiffly for five hours. The coach shuffled as the rest of the passengers climbed in. She turned her head toward the window to get a small puff of air. Jubilee leaned forward and saw the driver climb up the side to the top of the vehicle. Another jostle shook the coach as the shotgun partner mounted on the other. She heard the driver yell out a 'Hi-O,' and they were off.

She caught her breath as everything swayed, but she soon settled, enjoying the ride. Leaning back, she relaxed against the seat and Rafe's arm. The movement of the coach was pleasant but the seating arrangement was not. The passengers, like one being, lurched with each jolt of the coach.

There was no concern of losing one's seat as the passengers melded as one flesh sandwich with the conveyance walls as bread. A breeze picked up as they left Princeton. As they increased in speed, dust came in with the air and Jubilee turned her eyes inward. The window would be a mixed blessing.

"Well, this is certainly a perfect opportunity to get to know one another," the man on the other side of Rafe commented.

Jubilee leaned forward to catch sight of his red face and ample girth. The man was at least fifty, with a hat sitting jauntily on his wispy head. He had a gold chain that ran from his buttonhole to a pocket on his satin vest. His blue eyes were merry and friendly.

"I'm Clyde Lane from Vincennes. I own Lane's and Sons Mercantile."

A rumble sounded from Rafe's chest. "Well, Mr. Lane, I'd shake your hand, but at the moment, I can't move. I'm Rafe Tanner from Princeton."

The man chuckled back. "And the lovely lady?"

Her husband cleared his throat. *Yes, explain that one.* However, he answered without a hitch.

"This is my wife, Jubilee."

The man leaned forward and gave a smile showing a gold tooth. "Mighty fine to meet you folks. What business you in?"

"Farming," Rafe answered smoothly.

"Ah." The man let out a breath. "The salt of the earth kind of people. I always say, that's the best type. Me, I'm on my way to Evansville to scout out new merchandise. Got some competition across the road now, and I figure to expand my wares."

Rafe nodded.

"Yep. You make this trip often?" Mr. Lane asked.

"Ah, no. Actually, I'm somewhat new to the area," Rafe replied. "My folks live over toward Louisville."

The older man let out a chuckle. "Ya don't say? I have a sister that lives in that neck of the woods. They own some fine horseflesh down Kentucky way. You ever been to Three Pines Horse Farm?"

Rafe adjusted his arm along the back of the seat, and Jubilee fidgeted. "No, can't say I have. Heard of the place, though. My folks are on the Indiana side. They own a farm northeast of New Albany."

"Can't beat the Hoosier State. Bet you were born and raised there, huh? I hail from Virginia originally."

"Yes, I was. My grandparents came out of Maryland and settled in Indiana. My wife came from Pennsylvania,"

Jubilee could feel the vibrations of Rafe's voice against her shoulder and a warmth spread through her that he thought to mention her roots.

"I see." Mr. Lane caught Jubilee's gaze. "From Penn's wooded land, eh? My guess is you're headed to Pennsylvania or New Albany. Am I right?"

Rafe's answer came out as a jerk as the coach lurched. "New Albany, this trip."

This trip? "Oh." Jubilee's hip ground against the wall.

The merchant leaned forward again. "You all right, little lady?"

"Yes."

Mr. Lane chuckled. "There's a few bad spots in this road. Might be best if you climbed in your husband's lap."

Jubilee's face burned, and her gaze caught Rafe's dimple. She quickly averted her eyes.

"Don't worry, though. We'll soon be at the Log Inn Stop, and they'll give us a fresh set of horses. We can get out and stretch our legs. 'Tis a mighty fine eatery, too."

Jubilee's glance went to the seat in front of her, which only had a leather strap to support the passengers' backs, and grimaced. The men in the first two seats faced one another with their knees intertwined. She glanced at Rafe's legs and realized his knees were jammed against the wood of the middle seat.

"Won't be long they'll lay that railroad track. They're saying now the construction should be started by next year." Mr. Lane slapped his leg. "I'm banking on those steam engines to haul up my merchandise to Vincennes, lickity split. I suspect traveling to Evansville will get much easier than this old Concord."

Rafe grunted his agreement.

"You know anything about Vincennes?"

"Can't say I do," Rafe answered.

"Well, I can certainly pass the time telling you of our rich French settlement. We have a college, also. It's a right fine city."

Thus began the lesson of the founding of Vincennes by Mr. Clyde Lane, well-to-do merchant. He remained interesting enough to help pass the time, but Jubilee was thankful when she caught sight of a double-gabled building. The coach stopped and the first and second row of passengers emptied out, groaning and stretching their legs.

Mr. Lane hobbled to the exit, his head bent to avoid the roof. Rafe went next. Jubilee, her legs unsteady, stood and moved to the door. Rafe's eyes swept her face and, instead of handing her down, reached both hands up, caught her around the waist, and lifted her to the ground. She hated to admit it, but she was grateful for his assistance since her legs seemed to have locked up. Most of the passengers made their way into the Log Inn and Rafe held his elbow out to assist Jubilee.

"May I escort you, my lady?"

With a swallow, she slid a trembling hand into the curve of his arm, thankful for once for his strength. Mr. Lane continued walking on Rafe's other side.

"Why, Mr. Henry Clay's presidential campaign came through here in '44, headed up by a…let me think, oh, what is his name? Levinson, Linton…Lincoln! Yep, that's it. I believe his first name is Abraham. 'Course Polk won, so I guess he's not that noteworthy. Lincoln gave a fine speech, though."

Jubilee took in the log interior as they wandered to a table. Seats quickly filled and Rafe invited Mr. Lane to join them, along with a couple other male passengers as well. Jubilee watched two woman scurry around to feed everyone as the men made small talk, Mr. Lane taking the lead. The special was fried chicken, and it wasn't long before a huge basketful was plunked on their table. Mashed potatoes, beans, and cornbread finished out the meal. About an hour later, the driver and his partner rose.

"Stagecoach leaves in fifteen minutes, folks." They plopped their worn hats on their heads and walked to the door.

The talk quieted as everyone rushed to finish their food. Outside, they were soon forming a line at the stagecoach. The generous meal made the inside of the Concord even tighter, if that were possible, and Mr. Lane's incessant chatter lengthened the second leg of the journey. Jubilee's body waxed sore and her ears weary by the time Evansville came into view.

They ate dinner in a hotel dining salon near the Ohio River. Rafe guided Jubilee to her room. Thanks to her previous sleepless night, she practically dozed on her feet.

"I'm right across the hall." Rafe indicated the door directly opposite of hers. "Knock if you need something."

She nodded, too tired to respond. Clicking her door shut, she barely registered the small white room with only a bed, a nightstand, and a lamp. The last bit of sunlight crept through the thin curtains on the window. Not bothering with a light, she undressed and slipped beneath the cool sheets.

* * *

An earsplitting horn filled the air. Jubilee edged behind her large husband. She'd seen her fill of paddleboat packets on the Delaware River as she ran errands for Mrs. Galston in the Old City of Pittsburgh. But never had she contemplated boarding one. The thing was huge, and smoke poured from the two chimneys. The name, 'Lil' Bluebell,' was painted in blue across the pilot's house and in larger letters on the wall of the main deck. Rafe, tickets in hand, didn't seem to have any qualms as he turned around with a crooked grin, eyes dancing in laughter.

"It's quite an invention, isn't it?" Rafe's dimple appeared and he gestured toward the ship.

She nodded, in awe of her exciting, yet curious surroundings.

"Are you ready to board the wild dragon?" His left eyebrow rose in challenge.

He seems to be enjoying this. Does he just like paddleboats, or is he laughing at me? She looked toward the steamboat, eyeing its huge, dripping wheel and gave a shrug. He grinned, making heat fly up Jubilee's neck. He stuck his elbow out toward her.

"It's quite the experience. You'll love it."

Clutching his arm, she stepped toward the beast. Once on board, however, she agreed as she marveled at the sparkling water as it meandered around the bend. The front of the steamer was crowded with both humans and animals, but Rafe led her to an empty bench on the side of the boat.

"We'll sit here awhile and enjoy the view."

Everything fascinated her. The people. The river. The huge waterwheel.

Rafe settled his big frame in the seat beside her. As more passengers loaded, folks nudged and stepped in front of her, blocking her line of sight. A scruffy man sat to her right, and Rafe put an arm around her shoulders. She inhaled a shuddering breath.

"Perhaps we should find an empty spot along the rail." He spoke softly in her ear.

At her nod they stood, and he guided her to the starboard rail among the crush of people, breaking through to the side. He placed his hand on her waist and shifted her in front of him as he leaned against the wood. She caught her breath as the breeze brushed her face. The horn blew again, and Jubilee gasped and plugged her ears.

"We'll launch here in a minute. I think you'll actually enjoy it." Amusement lit his face, steadying her as the boat moved.

Jubilee gave a start. He must consider her a dolt. She set her gaze determinedly toward the river, hiding her eyes from him.

"I wasn't making fun of you." Rafe dipped his head to catch her eyes.

When she didn't turn, he spoke again. "I enjoy your curiosity."

"It's not that I've never seen a boat. It's…" She stopped and gave a small cry.

The steamer pitched forward and, without thinking, she grabbed whatever was available—Rafe's lapels. Much to her surprise, she couldn't seem to let go as the ship inched forward. Jubilee's lips parted, and her eyes swung to the moving landscape. The sound of falling water thundered behind them as the engine began to pick up a little speed.

She attempted to speak, but the floating motion and the breeze across her cheek made it hard to breathe. The wonder of the ship's departure caused her to flick her gaze to Rafe, who had a gentle grin on his face. One of his brows lifted as he surveyed her expression. Jubilee stared at him a moment before realizing her mouth was open. She snapped it shut and detached her hands from the fabric of his jacket.

CHAPTER TEN

"Sorry," Jubilee murmured.

Rafe couldn't take his eyes from her as she stroked the material until satisfied it was straightened. Looking up, she caught his gaze and blushed. She turned to the white rail. A bird flew close to their heads and drew Rafe's attention. Birds of every kind were all around. Plovers ran swiftly across the sand bars. Flocks of ducks and geese paddled near shore as well.

"Interesting, huh?" Rafe asked.

She nodded.

"The boat is loaded with supplies and going upstream. I doubt this sternwheeler will reach New Albany until morning."

She leaned over to watch the animals below on the main deck. Bales of hay and cotton lay alongside stacks of barrels. Grubby men milled about, smoking and chatting.

"This is a beautiful packet, isn't it?" He gestured toward the large Dining Salon behind them.

"Yes, but..." She stopped.

"What?" Rafe prodded.

She turned her eyes to his. "They're very dangerous, aren't they?"

A scuffle behind Rafe caused him to bump into Jubilee. A red-faced gentleman mumbled an apology.

"Excuse me, Jubilee," Rafe said. "Yes, I suppose they are. Boiler explosions are the main concern. But I've met the pilot, and he's well known as a man with great expertise below the Falls of the Ohio."

"What's the Falls of Ohio?"

Rafe grinned. "It's where the Ohio River drops near Louisville. Impossible to go up them in a steamer and only a few can navigate one down. We'll be getting off before then."

She examined the large cabin to the right through the crowd. "Is the boiler on this deck?"

Rafe shook his head. "Well, this is the promenade deck, or the boiler deck, but it's actually below us."

Jubilee's eyes widened. "So, if it does explode..."

Rafe took a deep breath and looked to the river where a small boat passed. "I don't reckon we'll really know."

"Guess we'll just trust the Lord."

Rafe's head snapped down to look at her, but she'd turned back to the landscape. The woman never ceased to amaze him. He'd searched to formulate some comforting words to ease her mind, and out she came with such faith. Her statement shamed him that he hadn't mentioned it first. *God's plan.*

The red-faced man nudged Jubilee, and Rafe gripped the rail as a barrier. "Yep, the Lord's got it well in hand."

People soon lost interest in the river plodding by, and Rafe and Jubilee found an empty bench. A few hours later, in the huge gingerbread Salon, they dined on boiled fish in gold-rimmed plates set on white tablecloths. Dark gentlemen served, and Rafe noted Jubilee taking it all in with great interest. They explored the hurricane deck later in the afternoon, but the sun was so strong they returned to their bench below.

Dinner came and went and soon dusk approached. Rafe kept an eye on the crowd, realizing riff-raff made their rounds on folks' money pouches. They sat on the front side of the promenade deck, and he glanced at his partner. She was like a kid in a candy shop with wide eyes, taking in the activity. She never seemed to tire of the surroundings.

"So," Rafe stretched out his legs. "Are you enjoying the ride?

It was a safe question.

She turned shining eyes on him. "Oh, yes. Thank you."

He smiled, and she dropped hers gaze. "I don't suppose you've done much traveling?"

"No."

"Me either." He crossed his arms. "But I did ride a packet up to Wheeling, Ohio back in '48. My brother, Loyal, was married there, and now that's where he and Elizabeth live."

"Is that your oldest brother?"

Rafe laughed. "Definitely not. I have four brothers and three sisters."

She remained silent for a time. "What are their names again?"

Rafe chuckled. "You sure you're ready for that?"

Her large, dark eyes blinked at him. "I suppose."

He cocked his head. "All right. But remember, you asked for it. The oldest is my brother Everett. He's married to Addie, and they have six kids, Rachel, Rebecca, Joshua, Calvin, Orie, and Liza. Forrest and his wife, Mollie, have Elijah, Cora, Hiram, and baby Zekiel. My oldest sister, Anna, is married to Amos, and their children are Hugh, James, Samuel and Levi. All boys. Phoebe is married to Isaac, and they have two girls,

Lucy and Emma. I already told you about Loyal and Elizabeth. He's a doctor, and they have two kids, Lizzie and Garvin."

He gave her a crooked grin. "I'm almost finished. Benjamin is married to Caroline, and they have Evangeline and new baby Nellie. That just leaves Sarah and me. 'Course, there's Ma and Pa, my grandpa and grandma, Henry and Blanche Tanner, and ma's ma, Grandma Louisa Priddle, as well."

"That's a large family."

"Yep, and all but Loyal live within a few acres of each other." He straightened and gentled his tone. "What about you? How did you end up at the orphan's home?"

* * *

Anxiety welled in Jubilee's chest. Could it be safe to tell him such things? For all she knew, he was fishing for information. She pulled her gaze from him, wishing she understood his intentions. He seemed kind, and she was having a grand time on this steamer, but...

A distant horn sounded ahead of them. People moved to the front of the boat and the hubbub distracted Jubilee and Rafe from their conversation. A few men broke away, yelling, and jogged back to the stairway.

Jubilee stood. "What did he say?"

Rafe shook his head as he craned his neck to see over the crowd. "Something about a boat that's hit a snag. Come on, let's find out."

He gripped her arm and escorted her to the starboard rail, near the front. Sure enough, as they rounded the bend on the right, a small side-wheeler leaned precariously, some thirty feet from the south bank. On the stranded boat's main deck, a group of people waved and shouted toward the *Lil Bluebell*. The steam engines growled as the big paddle stopped and reversed.

"Looks like we're going to pick them up." Rafe glanced back at the stern.

"How will they do that?"

"Not sure. But they're in for a swim if we don't."

The captain was as skilled as Rafe claimed, and they butted against the smaller craft, a day excursion steamer with twin side wheels fully covered from view. The name, 'Rosemary Marie,' was emblazoned across the small pilot's house. Next to her, Rafe groaned.

Jubilee searched his pale face. "Are you sick?"

His Adam's apple bobbed. "No."

Jubilee pulled her eyes from him and watched the group cross over the makeshift gangplank to the main deck of the *Lil Bluebell*. Seven people in all boarded. An older pair, dressed in sleek, impeccable clothing, a captain with a crew of two, and a younger couple. The woman caught Jubilee's eye.

The flounces on the woman's sky blue dress glittered in the sunlight. The circumference of the bottom of the skirt made it difficult for the elegant young man to escort her across the beam to safety. The woman's erect carriage had the boisterous group on the main deck parting in awe. As she stepped over the chasm, Jubilee was struck by her beauty. The dirty brutes down below stumbled toward her to assist her aboard.

She swept the boat with a haughty gaze, settling on Rafe with a slight lift of her chin. The smile she gave the grungy mule skinner close by was dazzling, and she leaned forward to speak to the man. He pointed off to the stairway that led to the promenade deck where Jubilee and Rafe stood.

The crowd gasped and Jubilee's eyes followed the crowds to the handsome, white-sided wheeler as the entire boat slipped below the surface. Only part of the pilothouse remained above water. Her glance returned to the newest passengers below but found they'd all disappeared.

* * *

"Rafe? Rafe Tanner? Rafe Uriah Tanner, I knew you'd be back."

Her husband stiffened beside her as he turned toward the woman's silky voice. Jubilee shifted as well. The beautiful woman from the sinking day steamer strode straight toward them. Behind her, a man skipped along to catch up, calling her name softly. The man's face became bland and his walk slowed when he caught sight of Rafe.

The stranger cut quite a figure in his black suit and topper. There was no denying he was handsome. He was dark-haired and olive-skinned with a dimple in his chin, but he lacked Rafe's height and had to tip his head back to look him eye to eye.

"Yes," the woman stepped up to Rafe, her gaze coy, and ran her fingers under his lapels, "people said you were gone for good, Rafe Tanner. But *I* knew better. You can't stay away for long."

Rafe cleared his throat before removing her hands from his suit coat. "Hello, Rosemary."

A giggle tinkled through the air. "Now, Rafe, dear. Are you pretending you don't know an old friend? Here I've just been rescued from the cold waters of the Ohio, and you've no comfort for me?"

The handsome stranger next to Rosemary stepped up and held out his hand. Rafe hesitated only a moment before clasping it in his own. "Dale."

The man nodded, but the skin around his lips whitened.

"Oh, Rafe. Who knew our day excursion would join us up with you? What luck." She linked her arm with his and tugged at him. "Let's sit and chat, shall we? We'll catch up on old times."

Rafe pulled from her grasp.

"Actually, I'm here with my spouse." Rafe sidestepped her and reached back for Jubilee. "This is Jubilee, my wife."

The woman's beautiful porcelain face became ice. Her head turned stiffly on her starched neck, and Jubilee worked hard not to cringe.

"Married?" The ice princess's answer spun to a higher pitch.

Rafe nodded and firmly affixed Jubilee's fingers around his forearm. "That's right."

At the hard note in his voice, Jubilee glanced toward him. His jaw was clenched and his face seemed a bit flushed.

Rosemary sniffed. "I see."

The stranger next to Rosemary smiled and slapped Rafe on the shoulder. "You old fox, you."

Rafe's body swelled as he took a deep breath. "Yep, there's an old fox here, that's for sure."

Jubilee's eyes went from one man's face to the other. The stranger dropped his gaze to the river, and Rafe's nose flared.

"Forgive me, Jubilee," Rafe said. "This is Dale Harper. He and I went through the schoolhouse together." He gave a broad exaggerated sweep of his hand. "And this is Rosemary Harper. His wife."

The man locked glances with Jubilee. "Nice to meet you."

"Mr. Harper." She nodded. She glanced at Rosemary, who perused her with a frosty gaze. "Mrs. Harper."

"We had a lot of good times." Rafe's tones indicated otherwise.

Dale lifted his head with a dash of regret in his eyes. "Yes, we did."

Rosemary snapped her face toward Rafe's, her gaze melting to pleasure. "We simply must dine together. Father will be here shortly. Getting rid of a ship's captain is such nasty business."

"I'm not sure I follow you." Rafe's voice was cool.

She gestured back in the direction of the small craft, now beyond the wake of the huge steamer. "Father won't continue to employ such an incompetent man as Captain Gains. We just christened the new 'Rosemary Marie' two weeks ago. And I'm sure his crew is finished as well." She clapped her hands gracefully and gave a sly smile. "Perhaps he'll listen to me now and commission a full-size steamer. After all, he does own the company."

Jubilee's gaze flicked to Rafe's. His face grew stiffer and his eyes narrowed.

"I'm afraid we've already eaten and it's rather late. Terribly nice to meet you both again, but we're ready to retire to our cabins." And, with that, Rafe bid them farewell over Rosemary's complaints and escorted Jubilee toward the women's section.

* * *

Jubilee said goodnight to Rafe as he made a hasty exit to the gentlemen's quarters. She should be exhausted from all the excitement, yet restlessness filled her. Her cabin was small, almost claustrophobic. The bed lay against the wall, which provided more walking room. Once she pulled it down, there'd be little space. A tiny built-in dresser with a small mirror hung near the door. Her satchel rested on the floor next to the wall under a petite round window. No other chair or other amenities graced the area.

But she wasn't ready for bed. Instead, she paced. Her stomach churned from the awkward meeting with the Harpers. The encounter reminded her of when the Orphan board reprimanded one of the children. Everyone would be called to the large downstairs foyer where the offense was plainly outlined for all viewers, and the offender caned severely. Jubilee hugged herself and shuddered.

More puzzling still was the transformation of Rafe. On the farm he appeared so informal and at ease. Even his speech had a tint of a lazy southern drawl. Tonight his words had been clipped and formal, nothing like the man she'd come to know in the last few weeks.

Rafe. She stopped pacing and looked around the small wooden space. A few short weeks back she'd possessed only a complete and utter fear of the man. Now, bereft of his presence, she missed the man's bulk and comfort.

Sighing loudly to herself, she realized the idiocy of her thoughts. *Do I trust him or not?* Maybe it was just pity. Yes, that was surely what she was feeling. And perhaps a dash of resentment toward the Harpers for ruining the evening.

She pulled the bed down with a bit more force than necessary. At least the linens appeared clean. The cabin was now completely ensconced in darkness, and she saw no sense in searching for a lantern. She undressed quickly and lay on the hard, narrow bunk. It'd take a long time to fall asleep, she was sure, with Rafe's granite face swimming before her eyes.

Tomorrow will be better. The steamer would creep along all night, and they'd arrive at New Albany sometime in the morning. The Harpers would be nothing but a memory after they stepped upon the dock. Then she and Rafe would only have to deal with his family. She yawned. *She and Rafe?* Drifting off to sleep, she pondered the slip in her thoughts.

CHAPTER ELEVEN

Rafe opened his eyes and brought his hands up to rub his face. He groaned. *Rosemary*. On this steamer. He threw off the covers and swung his legs to the floor but made no effort to get up. Avoiding the Harpers became the main goal today. They'd be pulling into the dock at New Albany soon, so it was possible.

He lifted his head to stare at the wall. Rosemary's beauty hadn't waned a bit. No way around it, she appeared as gorgeous as he remembered. Blonde hair, blue eyes, flawless porcelain skin, the slight pout to her full mouth, and an eyebrow that had a tendency to lift as she twirled her lacy parasol. She wasn't a short person, maybe medium build, with a tiny waist and that haughty way of carrying herself with her chin elevated.

Clad in the height of fashion, usually pastels, she displayed the manners of a high society lady. Rafe's stomach tightened, as did his jaw. He still craved the sight of her, still cared for her, and at the same time detested her. He gritted his teeth. She was now married to Dale. *Someone else's wife.*

Jubilee. What in the world had she thought about the Harpers? Particularly Rosemary, with her hands on his lapels. He ran a hand through his mussed hair. He and Jubilee had agreed to appear as a normal couple. Rosemary's presence, however, would make that a difficult task.

He rose and dressed. No sense in making Jubilee wait. He steeled his innards against the inevitable meeting with the Harpers. Jubilee's innocent eyes came to his mind. He knew Rosemary could eat Jubilee in one gulp. He had to protect her and himself. His best defense was his marriage.

Jubilee seemed subdued as they made their way to the Salon for breakfast. The rumor circulated that they'd be docking around ten o'clock. Rafe took a deep breath. The sooner the better.

They were seated without encountering hide nor hair of the Harpers, and Rafe relaxed a bit. He smiled at Jubilee, taking note of the fullness in her cheeks now. His gaze flicked to her dark hair, which shone like crystal. Never had he seen anyone with such shiny locks.

Many people frowned at her sun-darkened skin and sun-splashed hair, but he thought it gave her a healthy look. Her best feature, though, were those dark eyes, now looking quite puzzled as they gazed back at him. She differed so much from…his heart skipped a beat when he realized he was thinking of Rosemary.

"Is everything all right?" Jubilee's brows drew together, and her lips pursed.

"Right as rain."

Breakfast arrived with greasy gravy slung over hard biscuits, but they managed to polish off most of the meal and left the Salon in record pace. Rafe led Jubilee to the hurricane deck, hoping she wouldn't mind the sun, given the early hour. They were the only ones on the top. He escorted her to a bench that would afford a wonderful panorama of New Albany once they came abreast of the curve.

"You'll love the view from here," Rafe said, almost convincing himself they weren't simply hiding. It went down his gullet easier.

* * *

Jubilee opened her eyes and rubbed them with her fingers, taking a slow breath of air to awaken herself. She raised her head and realized they were still on the hurricane deck on the same bench. The sun's rays shone bright, and her face grew warm. As she stretched her neck, something dawned on her. She'd been lying against his shoulder—asleep. Her eyes grew wide, and she covered her mouth with her hands. Glancing at him, she found him smiling and the sunlight caught the green in his hazel eyes.

"I'm so sorry," she whispered.

Rafe grinned. "Didn't inconvenience me none. Look."

He motioned ahead of them, and she noticed the steamer had slowed. Shielding her eyes with her hand, she saw the docks and scanned the houses and businesses along the banks.

"We'd better collect our satchels and get below." He rose and assisted her. "The horn will soon go off and we don't wanna be here when it does."

They took the stairway and collected their baggage from their quarters. Rafe carried both of them in his right hand while she gripped his left, maneuvering through the crowd. The whistle blasted and Jubilee cringed, thankful not to be on the hurricane deck.

The captain skillfully slowed the huge ship to ease into the slope at the bank of the river, where several other steamers were beached. Excited chatter twittered all around and the throng pressed in from every side. By now, the heat had become oppressive. It took time to disembark on the dirt bank and climb to the wooden walk. Rafe hailed someone Jubilee couldn't see and a shiver of apprehension shot through her.

A few moments later, the crowd parted and they were surrounded by a puddle of family, all talking, smiling, and hugging. Jubilee blinked and caught her breath, still not entirely awake. There were so many. Rafe pulled her toward two older people, the lady wiping her eyes and grinning at her already.

"This is my mother and father, Jennie and William Tanner." Rafe introduced them. "And this is my wife, Jubilee."

She smiled and was pulled into a hug by Rafe's mother. "Oh, what a beautiful girl you are."

Jubilee blinked. *Beautiful?* Then Rafe's father embraced her, his height an obvious clue as to where Rafe had inherited his stature. Then the names began to fly, Everett, his wife Addie, with way too many kids, Forrest and Mollie, more kid names, then Anna and Amos, Phoebe, Isaac, Benjamin, Evanga-something and so many children running, jumping, and being held that Jubilee grew dizzy.

Then grandparents, Henry and Blanche Tanner, and Grandma Louisa, Jennie's mother, leaning heavily on a cane. Jubilee moved to the edge of the crowd, her hand gripped in her skirt. Rafe pulled himself free from his father's embrace and stepped to her, wrapping his arm around her back while he continued to talk. She hated to admit it, but his presence added a measure of security.

"We've brought our luggage, so maybe it's best if we head to the house. I'm sure meeting everyone is a bit overwhelming for Jubilee." Rafe chuckled.

"Oh, of course, dear. We are a bit much, I suppose. We're so sorry." Rafe's mother wrapped her in another hug.

Jubilee breathed a sigh of relief as they moved off the busy platform. Horse-drawn buggies crisscrossed everywhere, but the Tanners wove confidently through the crowd, laughing and jostling the children.

She clung to Rafe, marveling at the easy atmosphere of the family. Grandpa Will swung one of the many smaller girls up in his big arms, thundering a laugh at her pouty expression.

"Never gonna get cherry pie with a face like that!" he teased before tickling the little girl. She burst into giggles and wiggles. Rafe seemed engrossed in full conversation on the state of his new farm with the eldest brother...Everett? Jubilee wasn't totally sure. Sarah skipped to Jubilee's left, eyes alight at every word Rafe spoke, punching in questions about his new place when she could. Jubilee swung her gaze around and noticed how tall the men were, and that most of the women were taller than she. Even Sarah towered half a head above her, and Jubilee remembered she was only sixteen.

Reaching the wagons, Jubilee learned they'd brought four. She and Rafe ended up in the driver's seat of his mom and dad's wagon, while they occupied the backseat. Sarah and a couple of the older children got in the back on a colorful quilt and made themselves comfortable, chatting and singing.

Rafe took a hold of the reins and gave a gentle slap on the backs of two fine black horses and they began rolling north. The road was busy with the docking of the steamer, and she surveyed the businesses that lined the main street while the Tanners talked.

Jubilee glanced at her husband, and he flashed an encouraging smile. Rafe's father, Will, seemed abuzz about his son's new farm, and Rafe's eyes sparkled as he told him of the improvements he'd made since his arrival.

"The barn is one amazing building. You should see it, Dad. It's one of the biggest I've seen. And it's well built, all pegged together. I'll have no problems getting the hay and feed stored for the winter. I'll be able to house the cows and the young livestock on the coldest of days."

Rafe continued talking about crops with his father for several minutes until his mother interrupted. "Now all this farm talk can wait, Rafe. I want to hear all about your sweet wife.

Why, she's hardly spoken a word, poor dear. Don't you ever give her a chance to speak?" Jennie chuckled.

Jubilee turned wide eyes on him and he, taking pity on her, smiled and answered. "Well, Mom, she was just thrown in with about thirty strangers all loaded with questions and such, so I'm thinking she needs some time to warm up."

"You must've had a whirlwind courtship, being as you were only gone from home a few months, Rafe. You left here so besotted with Rosemary, and the next thing we know you're married."

Rafe's body stiffened. Ah, Rosemary. That explained a lot.

"Now, Jennie," Will began, "no need stirring the pot before we even get them home. They'll tell us when they're ready."

"Oh, Jubilee, don't think I'm not thankful you're here. I'm pleased as punch. Why that ole' Rosemary…"

"Jennie," Will's voice rumbled.

This, however, did not put the woman off one bit. She leaned forward and patted Jubilee on the back.

"Oh, I'm sure it's this way when you go home, Jubilee. We're just all full of curiosity. I bet your folks are as curious about Rafe as we are about you."

Rafe cleared his throat to speak, but in cut Jubilee's quiet voice.

"Actually, I grew up in an orphanage in Pennsylvania. I don't really know who my parents were."

The silence thickened. Then Jennie answered softly. "Oh, I wasn't aware. I'm truly sorry for butting in. Please forgive me." She paused before continuing, "Well, I want you to know you've got a family now. If you ever need anything, you just ask."

Jubilee's hand buried itself in her skirt and began a nervous circle. This was going to be harder than she'd thought. Her mind rolled around as the rest of them conversed. They left the busy city behind as farmland surrounded them on both sides of the wagon. When they finally pulled into a long driveway, Jubilee noted a modest white house with a large porch, shutters at the windows and a nice-sized barn to the left, painted red.

They unloaded and everyone went their separate ways while Jennie chatted. She led them upstairs to a doorway on the right side of the hall.

"Now this was Rafe's old room...well, the boys' old room," she amended. "You two can freshen up. We've got a big meal planned under the maples in the side yard. I guess I better get down there and help. We'll give you both a couple of minutes." She started for the door and suddenly stopped. "Oh. And a few people from the church may be stopping by toward evening. They all know you're coming, so I thought I'd let you know." She turned to them, gave a big smile, and dabbed her eyes. "I'm so pleased you're here."

She stepped from the room and snapped the door shut. Jubilee turned startled eyes on her business partner. Rafe seemed much larger in the confines of a small room. His face puckered in thoughtfulness.

"Well," he brushed a big hand down his slightly bristled jaw. "I guess I didn't think all this through."

She glanced around the room. The bed to the left was large, with a trunk at the foot. Straight in front of them stood a dresser under the open window. A bedside table and a new chaise lounge to the right completed the furniture in the room. Jubilee froze. *Good gracious, what now?*

* * *

Rafe was all too aware Jubilee had become like a statue. His face grew warm. What must Jubilee be thinking? She couldn't possibly think he'd planned this.

"I'm sorry, Jubilee. I honestly never gave much thought on the accommodations. I'd really rather not reveal the true state of our marriage if possible. That leaves us with sharing this room. I…" He picked up the satchels and set them on the settee and slid his hands into his pockets.

Glory, what to do now? What to say? "I'll a…let you get ready and I'll…" he cleared his throat, "do something else. Uh, I'm sorry."

He strode to the door, stepped into the hallway and closed it with a click. Oh, lands, what a mess. Here he'd been congratulating himself for escaping Rosemary this morning. He'd gone from the pan to plop into the fire. Well, he supposed the chaise would be his bed for the duration. Short of telling his family about the arrangement, there was no other option.

He rubbed the back of his neck and took the stairs two at a time to join everyone, hoping Jubilee didn't decide to rat him out. Not only would that stir up major complications and a flurry of pointed questions, but it'd get back to Rosemary and his former best friend, Dale. He'd already been made a fool once. He'd like to escape another round of that.

* * *

Jubilee inhaled a shaky breath and lowered herself to the chaise. The odd piece of furniture had only a back on one end and a long armrest along the backside. But Jubilee's mind wasn't on that so much as it was the sleeping situation. How was this going to work? Would she survive two weeks sharing this room with Rafe?

Telling his parents wouldn't be an option. She had no desire to divulge the details of their marriage and its actual state. She gave a shuddering sigh and placed her hand on her throat. They'd have to share the room. Perhaps he could…. She glanced at the chaise. It was very small. Rafe was very large. She swallowed. *Oh, dear.*

CHAPTER TWELVE

Jubilee rose, pulled her brush from her satchel, and walked to the dresser where an oval looking-glass hung on the wall. Pulling her thick hair out of the braid, she brushed it through and studied herself in the glass.

A mirror was a luxury Jubilee wasn't used to. She stared long and hard at her face. Jennie had said she was beautiful. *Beautiful?* She sighed. No, definitely not. What had Esther said on her wedding day? Oh, yes, pretty as a spring day. *Had she spoken of the flowers I held or me?* She leaned forward toward the reflection. It seemed important all of a sudden that she was, at least, attractive. Her eyes appeared too big. Her skin tanned too dark. Her hair too thick. Her body too thin. She quickly re-braided her hair and turned from the mirror. *I am who I am.*

She brushed the lint from her blue dress. Such a plain garment, but well made with her own hands. It would have to do. *She* would have to do. Her chin tilted up. No use putting off the inevitable. She opened the door and ambled downstairs.

A head popped around the corner.

"Oh, there you are," Sarah exclaimed. "I wondered if I'd missed you coming down. Everything's ready."

She grabbed Jubilee's hand and pulled her through the kitchen, to the left, and out the back door to the right side of the house. Everyone congregated near makeshift tables under two red maples. More food covered the surface than Jubilee had ever seen. And a whole lot of people stood about, smiling.

"Here she is," Sarah announced gleefully.

Everyone hushed and gathered at the tables while joining hands. Jubilee found Rafe on one side with a gentle smile, and Sarah, grinning, on the other. Everything grew still, even the children, and Jubilee peeked around in the midst of Will's prayer of thanks for the food, and then quickly bowed her head.

When the prayer ended, Rafe guided her to a spot on a backless bench, and to Jubilee's relief, she noticed Sarah next to her. The two women across from her smiled. They resembled each other with long, blonde hair and green eyes.

"I'm Phoebe and this is Anna. This is my husband, Isaac." She motioned to a huge bear of a man with a wild, reddish beard. "Over there is Anna's better-half, Amos."

She winked at Jubilee, and put a hand up to guard a conspiratorial whisper from her sister, but spoke plenty loud. "I'd watch out for Amos. He's the practical joker."

Anna grimaced and giggled. "Sadly, yes. The night he proposed to me, he put a slimy slug in a jewelry box and left it on the table, knowing I wouldn't be able to resist it."

A look of revulsion swept over her face and she shook her head. "Of course I didn't. I flung the box and the nasty thing landed on my arm. It was disgusting." She leaned forward. "I despise slugs, and he knew it."

Those who'd caught the story laughed, Jubilee included.

A brown-haired, delicate woman on the other side of Sarah groaned. "Must we have such talk around the dinner table every time? Ugh. How disgusting."

Phoebe giggled. "And that would be Mollie, who gags at about anything, which makes the dinner table stories even funnier."

Rafe added, "She's Forrest's wife and has three boys and one tomboy, if you get the meaning." He leaned over toward Mollie. "How many snakes are you up to?"

Jubilee turned her head to observe Mollie's face pale. "Seven, thank you very much." Then she pointed at the child's table, teeming with giggles. "And my children know if they hide one more snake on me, they're in for some serious whippings."

The children's snickers broke out louder, with a lot of pointing, while others covered their mouths, eyes huge.

Phoebe grabbed a roll as the basket went by to add to her plate of ham and potatoes. "So, we've got to know what side of the fence you're on, Jubilee. Gagging or non-gagging?"

The two women giggled and looked at Jubilee.

Jubilee glanced at Rafe before answering softly, "Non-gagging."

Phoebe stood and clapped her hands while Anna shouted, "Alas."

Jennie shook her head disapprovingly. "Oh, girls, really. Show some manners."

Jubilee added corn to her plate.

Amos spoke up for the first time. "And now you know who the quiet ones are and who the loud ones are."

Anna gave him a mock shocked face, and an elbow thump to his ribs. "He's just trying to steal you from our camp. Tell us, Rafe, is she quiet or loud?"

Jubilee blinked and glanced at her husband, who had an open smile.

"Well, she's quiet. But she's curious."

Amos made his dark eyebrows dance up and down. "Curious, huh? Well, that could be dangerous. This one can't resist a jewelry box, that one," he said, pointing towards Mollie, "can't resist a covered pail in the middle of the yard."

Mollie's mouth flew open. "*You* put that snake in there."

Amos held up both hands, one big paw clamped around a piece of fried chicken.

"It wasn't me. Just my idea." He pointed to his temple with a wink.

"Amos Breckenridge," Mollie said, flustered. "You are in big trouble."

Forrest, Mollie's husband cut in. "Children, children, stop all this fussing and fighting. And I'm talking to the ones at the adult table."

Everyone laughed and dug into their dinners.

"So, Jubilee, Mom told us you were raised in an orphanage. What was that like?" Sarah inserted.

Jubilee finished chewing and shrugged one shoulder.

"It was okay. We worked hard and sorta leaned on one another. Life wasn't awful or anything. I learned a lot of things.

Sewing, gardening, cooking, stuff like that. When I got older I was bound out to an elderly widow."

"How in the world did you ever meet Rafe?"

Jubilee swallowed around a lump. She glanced at Rafe. What should she say?

Rafe jumped in. "She married Colvin."

A collective gasp sounded from the occupants of the table. Heat flew up Jubilee's neck to her face. The food she'd consumed converted into a large weight in her stomach.

"It wasn't a very good marriage, so we really don't want to talk about it." He glanced at Jubilee. "As you know, Colvin wasn't much of a fine human being. And you already know he's passed, and I bought his farm."

Jennie snorted. "My older brother was never known for his compassion. I'm afraid his son inherited his bad nature, God rest his soul."

Anna tilted her head with her hands together at her mouth. "Did you fall in love with her, Rafe, when you went to the farm? How romantic."

Jubilee clenched her hands and looked at her plate. Maybe it was best for them to think that.

Phoebe cooed, "How sweet. Look, she's so shy. Oh, Jubilee." She reached across the table and touched her hand.

"We're so glad you're with us. What a difficult time you've had."

Anna nodded. "And even though he's my little brother, and it pains me a bit to say this, Rafe's a great guy."

"Hey," Rafe protested.

Jubilee giggled. Despite the rocky conversation, she enjoyed the meal and Rafe's family. They told stories about one another and the laughter continued until her stomach ached. After the dishes were put aside, a large box was brought out and put in front of Rafe and Jubilee.

Addie, Everett's wife handed her an envelope.

"This is a gift to the both of you from all of us for your wedding. We hope you enjoy it."

Jubilee could barely shut her mouth long enough to open the card. It was lacy and painstakingly homemade. Someone had sketched a bouquet of roses on the inside and included a poem by Addie, wishing them the best. Encouraged by Rafe, she opened the large package. To her surprise, a gorgeous set of china dishes, edged with beautiful pink roses, rested in the box, complete with a matching teakettle and perfect, delicate teacups.

A lump formed in her throat. "Oh, my."

"That's great," Rafe filled in while Jubilee collected herself. "We haven't gotten any yet. Thank you."

"Oh, yes. I've never seen anything so lovely," Jubilee breathed. "Thank you so much."

Everyone saw how taken she was with the fine set, and they smiled and laughingly congratulated themselves on their idea. Jubilee found moisture forming in her eyes. These people, who were almost strangers, had been so very kind. She pressed her lips together to keep from bursting into tears. As soon as possible, she excused herself and made her way to the bedroom. Once inside, she sat on the bed and fanned her hot face with her hands. A knock sounded at the door.

"It's Sarah. May I come in?"

Wishing for a few more moments alone, she stood and called, "Of course."

The door opened and Sarah peeked in.

"I wanted to make sure you were all right."

Jubilee nodded, wiping the moisture from her eyes.

"Oh, what's wrong?" Sarah approached and put her arm around her shoulders.

Jubilee shook her head. "I'm just so surprised by the beautiful gift. You all really shouldn't have."

"Oh, of course we should have. We always get a special gift when someone gets married in the family. It's like a tradition. I've already got my dishes picked out, and I don't even have a suitor."

Both girls giggled. Sarah led her to the bed and they sat down.

"You remind me of my best friend, Cara. She's kinda quiet, and she's small, and she's so funny. You'll get to meet her tomorrow at church. I was so sad when Rafe left, but now he has you, and he seems so happy. I feel like I already know you."

Jubilee smiled. Even though Sarah was only sixteen she seemed more mature, and Jubilee felt a connection with her.

"Thank you for being so kind. I was very nervous to come. There's so many of you." She smiled and gave a one-shouldered shrug.

Sarah threw up her hands. "Oh, getting back to that, I'd better get back downstairs. The men wanta play that baseball game, and I want to get on a team. They always act like only they know all the rules, which gets tiresome, but it's still fun. You better come and play with us."

Sarah pulled Jubilee from the bed, escorted her down the stairs, and out into the yard. The men and the bigger kids organized into teams. Rafe laid out pieces of wood in a diamond shape while a couple of the children cried and begged to play. But Addie and Mollie corralled the smaller ones and began a wild game of duck, duck, goose under the maples, carrying the infants in their arms as they ran. Jubilee begged off playing, citing she'd rather watch and learn the game.

"We're the Knickerbockers," one of the older boys yelled and raised his hands.

"We'll be the Brown Shoes," a smaller child chorused.

"There's no such thing," the older argued.

It wasn't long before the bat and ball came out. The men hit the ball lightly, with the field spotted with much younger players, and made a great show while sliding into the bases, overplaying their triumphs. Finally the kids ran off to the creek to cool off, and the men smacked the ball to their fullest ability. Jubilee marveled when Rafe stepped up and hit it farther than any of his brothers.

"I always said Rafe could play," his father inserted as they clapped and whooped.

A wagon drew into the driveway, and an older man alighted from the seat. He assisted a lady down. Will and Jenny rose with a cry of delight, and escorted the couple closer. They appeared to be about the same age as Rafe's parents.

"You've just got to meet Rafe's wife," Jennie exclaimed as they approached.

Jubilee jumped up.

"This is Jubilee Tanner," she presented her when they all were facing one another.

"Oh, my, aren't you a young beauty," the woman exclaimed. "I'm Dottie, this here's my husband, Herbert Weaver. We're from Rafe's church where Herbert pastors. I can't tell you how fine it is that Rafe has found such a nice young lady."

"Thank you," Jubilee murmured.

"My goodness, that boy was all broke up when he left here," Herbert exclaimed.

"Now, Herbert, none of that." Dottie patted her husband on the chest.

"Well, we're right glad he's back to his old self. Oh." He gasped as Rafe hit a ball further than the last. "My, Rafe sure is a strong one."

The men, one by one, gathered beside the maple trees with the pastor and his wife to shake hands and greet one another.

"Well, I guess you should know, Will and Jennie. We spread the word, and instead of you all getting a bunch of company tonight, we're having a church dinner tomorrow after the service. A bit of a celebration for the newly married couple." He rapped Rafe on the back. "Glad to see this feller so happy."

Rafe gave a tight smile, and his eyes met Jubilee's. They all sat around the table and brought out the desserts, including cherry pie, and reminisced and laughed until past dark. The

Weavers said their goodbyes at last, and the mothers collected their children while the fathers fetched the wagons. Most of the younger ones were already asleep inside the house.

Soon, everyone except Rafe's parents, Sarah, Grandma Lou, who lived with the Tanners, and Rafe and Jubilee, were pulling away in their wagons. They waved to the departing families.

"Where do they all live? Do they have far to go?" Jubilee whispered to Rafe.

"Naw, their houses are just right down the road. We all farm the same patch of land together...well, they do," Rafe amended.

Everyone made their way into the house, proclaiming exhaustion, and Jubilee had to admit she was tired, too. Rafe's family went their separate ways, calling out goodnights. Jennie hugged Sarah and Jubilee again, and helped her mother to her room. She had no option but to climb the stairs with Rafe to 'their' room.

CHAPTER THIRTEEN

As soon as the door closed, Rafe turned to her with a soft apology. "I'm really sorry about this arrangement. I just couldn't say anything, I mean...you know."

Jubilee gave a small nod, her hand working nervous circles in her skirt.

"I plan to sleep on this thing," he motioned to the chaise, "if that's agreeable to you."

"Maybe I should sleep there. The chaise is...small."

Rafe shook his head.

"No, this is my fault. I should've figured something out...somehow."

Rafe stood thinking, with Jubilee equally still, but neither had another option. Rafe moved toward the trunk at the end of the bed.

"The trunk should have some blankets, pillows and such." He searched the wooden container.

He pulled out a blanket.

"Will you need a blanket?" Her voice sounded small.

Rafe cocked his head. She was right. It'd be a bit chilly as morning broke, but right now this room was stifling. She wandered to the window at the end of the room and pushed the window sash up a few more inches. Rafe headed for the chaise with a blanket, a sheet, and an extra pillow, sensing her eyes on his every movement.

"Look, I'll step out for a bit and you can..." he cleared his throat, "...prepare for bed. I'll be back in about twenty minutes."

With that he threw the blanket and sheet on the chaise and exited.

* * *

Jubilee hung her head. This was going to be so difficult. But, knowing she only had a few minutes, she closed the curtains and doused the light before quickly unbuttoning her dress and sweeping the garment off. She hung it on a peg next to the door, then grabbed the nightgown and popped it on. The bed screeched in protest as she lunged onto the mattress and yanked the covers up to her chin.

Time seemed to stop. Her rapid breathing slowed. She grew drowsy. Quiet footfalls sounded on the stairs, the doorknob turned, and the door opened a fraction. Rafe spoke just outside the room.

"Are you ready?" His voice rose barely above a whisper.

Wanting to yell 'no,' she instead whispered back, "Yes."

A huge shadow entered the room. Only the moonlight lit the room, but Jubilee's eyes, accustomed to the darkness, followed his form across the room. Obviously his eyes hadn't adjusted, as he ran his leg into the trunk and gave a sharp intake of breath. He moved slower, feeling his way to the chaise. A bubble of laughter formed, and Jubilee pulled the quilt over her mouth as if he could somehow see her smiling at him.

But the smile swept from her face when he reached down and removed his shirt. *O...oh.* She yanked the covers higher over her head. Underneath, she could hear the swish of clothing as he removed his britches. More rustling, and Jubilee hoped he'd settled into his comfy bed for the night. When all was quiet, she pulled the blanket down and, indeed, his large frame was stretched out across the chaise, covered with a sheet, his head propped up on the tall back. His feet stuck over the end at least a foot-and-a-half. He looked terribly uncomfortable.

She barely dared to breathe, let alone speak. He adjusted himself by pulling up and putting his head on the back. She watched as he squirmed for several minutes.

Finally she spoke. "Do you need another pillow?"

"No."

"I have an extra."

Silence. Jubilee pulled the extra pillow from her bed and tossed it across the room, landing it right on his chest. He stuffed the fluffy wad in the crevice between the high back and the seat cushion, which seem to help a bit. His fidgeting ceased.

"Have I told you how sorry I am?" His voice came as a mere whisper.

"Yes."

A long quiet moment stretched between them, and Jubilee thought perhaps he'd fallen asleep. But then he spoke. "Did you like the dishes?"

"Yes. Very much."

Again more stillness. Jubilee knew she had very little chance of getting a whole lot of sleep. Although she felt relatively safe with him now, this proved to be a nerve-wracking situation.

"May I ask you a question?" she ventured.

"Sure. I figure I owe you one."

"Who's Rosemary?"

The silence went on so long she concluded he must be angry with her, but when he answered his voice appeared low and sad.

"She was my fiancée."

Jubilee lay there, her eyes searching the room, and pondered if she ought to ask more. But he continued on his own.

"You should know the whole story. It's probable they'll be at church tomorrow. No sense in you being the only one who doesn't understand what's going on."

A few moments lapsed before he spoke, and Jubilee wondered if he were collecting his thoughts.

"We planned on a Christmas wedding. Well, on the twenty-seventh, while all the family was still here. That very day, a note arrived at our front door. It was from Rosemary. Nothing but a brief note. She didn't want to marry me and had left town"—he paused just a moment and his voice sounded strained—"with my best friend, Dale Harper. She and her parents had gone to St. Louis to arrange a marriage for them."

The story ended so abruptly that she threw a question to him without even thinking. "Did she not give you a reason?"

He breathed audibly before he spoke.

"Oh, yeah. Dale's an accountant and would be better suited for her family and more able to keep her in the type of lifestyle she enjoyed, or some gibberish like that. Her father's a steamship builder, as Rosemary was so kind to inform you, and he'd never been overly excited about having me as his son-in-law. Dale, however, had been working for him for a couple of years and is from a very wealthy family. I am, after all, just a lowly farmer."

She closed her eyes for a moment and prayed. Rafe, no doubt, still harbored some pain. "That's why you bought the farm."

"Yes."

And why you married me. A ball of tears rolled up Jubilee's throat. He couldn't have Rosemary, so anyone would do. No more words were spoken and, after a few minutes, Jubilee could hear his soft even breathing, indicating he'd fallen asleep. But it was a long time before Jubilee, her face wet with silent tears, could drift into an uncomfortable slumber.

* * *

When she awoke the next morning, Rafe had already disappeared from the chaise, his blanket and sheet folded neatly at the end with the pillow on the top of the pile. Jubilee jumped out of bed, shucked her nightgown and pulled her blue dress from the peg. Dressed, she stepped to the dry sink, poured a bowlful of water, and quickly washed. With her hair braided and up, she was bound for the outhouse in two shakes.

She heard several people in the kitchen, so she let herself out the front door without a sound, and swung back around to the backyard to the necessary. Outside, a fresh, dewy new morning greeted her, and by the chill and the slant of the light breaking through the branches of the oaks and maples to the east, it was still very early. She filled her lungs with crisp air.

After taking care of business, she strolled back toward the house, pausing to admire the soft petals of the yellow, purple, and white morning glories sparkled with dew. She looked up as she wandered, enjoying the flickering shafts of sunlight as they splashed across her face. At the front steps, she hesitated and decided to sit a spell and listen to the sparrows and robins in the trees and yard. Even a noisy jay joined in. Finally, reluctant to break the beauty of the morning, yet knowing church time quickly approached, she quietly entered the house the same way she'd left.

She padded up the stairs with nary a sound and opened the door to her room. There stood Rafe in his dress trousers, without a stitch of clothing to cover his torso. Jubilee gave an audible gasp. He'd leaned over to grab a shirt and continued that motion while Jubilee stared, mouth open.

His slight grin grew into a wide smile when she couldn't seem to tear her eyes from the expanse of his wide shoulders that nipped in nicely at his hips. Dark blond hair was sprinkled across his upper chest and continued down in a V-shape to his navel. His biceps flexed full as he pulled the shirt from the chaise.

"Sorry, I thought I could finish before you came back in."

Her eyes left his chest and crept to his face, where his smile and raised eyebrows met her gaze. Her cheeks blazed.

"I...I..." But no words came.

In a panic she turned into the hallway and, in a noisy flutter, stumbled down the stairs and back out the front door, not bothered that it slammed behind her. She ran past the house and the morning glories, then stopped. She put her hands to her thudding heart.

How long had she just stood and...stared? She groaned. Too long, way too long. The sight of his bare, naked chest seemed seared into her brain. Rafe's sardonic expression, questioning her intense interest in his state of undress, haunted her.

She groaned again and clutched her hair. Oh, she had to get away. She couldn't face him right now. Where to go? Her head swiveled, her eyes lighting on the large barn. Quickly, she ran barefooted to the door and whipped it open. Inside it was dim, and dust motes drifted through the air. The smell of clover and dried corn comforted her. She spotted the loft ladder and was up in no time, settling into a pile of hay.

Oh, dear heavens. She lay back and pressed her right hand against her forehead while her left twirled her skirt. She had made a fool of herself. An absolute idiot. Why hadn't she spoken? Why hadn't she closed the door? It was as if she'd lost the ability to move.

She swallowed and shoved the heels of her hands into her eye sockets before pulling her knees up to stick her feet in the hay. Oh, my, but he'd been fine. Tanned and well-muscled from the work in the fields, and he didn't seem to be in a great hurry to cover himself. She couldn't get the scene out of her head. Never before had she noticed such a thing about a man. What was wrong with her?

She continued to berate herself for several minutes until realizing she *had* to return to the house. They'd wonder what had become of her. They might even think she'd been in the necessary the whole time. Good gravy. Which was worse— everyone knowing she'd stared at Rafe's chest or everyone knowing she'd been in the necessary for a half-hour? She hurried to the ladder, rumbled down the rungs and hastened out into the sunlight. Her feet slowed as she approached the house.

What to do, what to do? She opened the back door to the kitchen—empty, to her surprise and delight. But as she neared the stairs, muffled voices from the back bedroom reached her ears. Sarah came out with a distraught look on her face. Completely forgetting the last half an hour, she went straight to Sarah.

"What's wrong?" Jubilee asked in a hushed voice.

"Grandma Lou fell in her room about fifteen minutes ago. Rafe rode into town to get Dr. Dodd, but he isn't back yet."

"Oh, no." Jubilee covered her mouth with her hand. "Is she all right?

"We think so. Her ankle is swollen and she's shaken, though. I think Mom's going to stay with her. Grandma Lou wants the rest of us to attend church." Sarah started to walk away. "If we do end up at the church, you better get ready. We'll have to leave soon. I've gotta find another pillow for Grams."

* * *

Jubilee wasted no time preparing for church after Sarah went on her errand. She chose Esther's peach creation and quickly slipped it on, even though she knew Rafe had left. Later, at church, she twirled her skirt hem with her finger as

Rafe sat on her right and Pastor Herbert stood up front, closing the sermon. Ashamedly, she'd hardly paid attention to one word, her mind so filled with her silliness this morning and with Grandma Lou's fall.

The congregation stood for the benediction. Pastor Herbert asked the Lord's blessing on the food, and only then did she remember the potluck dinner following the service. And they were the guests of honor. *Please, God, don't let the day get worse.*

The congregation moved into the aisles after the prayer and many made their way toward them. Will and Sarah joined them, but obviously everyone was interested in seeing Rafe once again and meeting his new wife. Jubilee couldn't even count the times she was introduced to a new person.

Rosemary approached, oozing with confidence, with Dale trailing, a reluctant look on his face. They'd arrived late and Jubilee had failed to get a bead on her.

"Rafe, I notice you arrived safely off that filthy steamer. So sorry about not meeting up with you the next morning, but I was exhausted from that chilling incident. A pure miracle we hadn't drowned." Her voice cooed. She shivered with a flash of drama.

Jubilee tensed. She'd grown up in a dormitory full of girls. Cattiness was not unknown or lost on her, and she detested it.

But she'd never seen it displayed at the level she now encountered before her. Rafe turned to face her, and Jubilee felt his body grow taut.

"Hello, Rosemary," he said. Looking beyond her, he greeted the man behind her with a nod. "Dale."

CHAPTER FOURTEEN

Jubilee's gaze flicked to the handsome man behind Rosemary. At least he had the grace to appear sheepish as he stayed a step behind her.

"Hello, Jubilee." Rosemary's eyes ran up and down her in a dismissive fashion. Suddenly the dress Jubilee wore felt like a rag. Rosemary's red satin frock drew everyone's eyes with its low cleavage, lace and beads. The garment was some creation, and no doubt the newest style.

"Gracious, Rafe, you must've put her to work next to you in the field as dark as she is. With those expectations, you should've picked a sturdier wife." A lilting laugh, high and delicate, trickled across the ceiling.

Rafe lifted his head, his jaw clenching. But before he replied, Jubilee cut in. "I've never worked in the field. I tend the garden among other things."

Rosemary blinked and really looked at her, her eyes narrowing. "Yes." She drew the word out. "Perhaps that explains skin dark as an Indian savage."

Dale attempted to interrupt at this point, but was smoothly pushed away by his domineering wife.

"No," Jubilee returned in a voice like silk. "I'm tanned because I'm outside under a hot sun. And I choose to do so without a bonnet. Rafe's too kind and considerate to use me as a field hand."

Rosemary sniffed.

The two ladies stared each other down.

"Yes, well, we need to be off. Nice to visit with both of you." Dale cleared his throat and towed Rosemary with him.

Rafe turned to her and dipped his head, his eyebrows drawn. A ghost of a smile danced around his lips. Her face flooded with heat.

"What a little bobcat you're turning out to be," he said softly, with a grin.

Jubilee dropped her eyes. Why had she defended Rafe with such ferocity? Sarah approached, and Jubilee pulled her mind from the whole scene.

"Was that Rosemary? Wow, she's nervy. Oops, sorry." Sarah grimaced. "She's such…well, never mind."

Pastor's voice rose above the hubbub. "Could we have Mr. and Mrs. Rafe Tanner outside, please?"

As they made their way to the front door, Jubilee's brain churned with myriad emotions. And it certainly didn't help calm her when Rafe's arm came up behind her back. She took a deep breath. This show was for appearances only, after all. Unfortunately, Rafe's torso appearance still remained very much uppermost in her brain.

Several tables had been set up outside and filled with baskets and small boxes. Jubilee caught her breath when she realized they were all for her and Rafe. Pastor drew everyone around, commenting on the large turnout to welcome the new couple, but mentioned his regret that Grandma Lou and Jennie were not able to attend. He prayed over the two of them, wishing them great happiness and many children, and asked God's blessing on the food.

Rafe and Jubilee, whose face now flamed, were invited to go through the food line first as the guests of honor. They were escorted, with their plates of food, to a new navy and yellow double-ring wedding quilt the ladies of the church had pieced together. Jubilee swallowed as she sat down on her patchwork pedestal. All this for a business arrangement. If they only knew.

She had settled her nerves by the time everyone else exited the food line. The whole congregation seated themselves on blankets and quilts around the churchyard. Between her and Rafe, dead silence filled the air. Finally, she ventured a quiet question.

"Don't you think we're misleading them?"

Rafe looked at her then scanned the crowd. "Not at all. We're married. We're not telling everyone we are and we aren't."

His eyes flicked to her face, and she glanced away. He moved closer to her, facing one way while she the opposite. She found breathing a little more difficult with him so near. He continued with his voice low.

"These are really good people. Most of them have known me since I was a baby. They just want to help us out. Someday, we'll return the favor."

He's so close. His breath brushed her ear, and she trembled.

"I can understand how this gathering seems odd to you, but this is what our church has always done. They arranged one for all my brothers and sisters as well."

Her throat grew dry when he laid his big, rough hand on her arm. She looked into those beautiful hazel eyes that couldn't decide which color to be, contrasting sharply against his tanned skin. "They're very kind."

"Enjoy it and be thankful." His gaze moved slowly down her face to her mouth then back up to her eyes.

Jubilee's breath caught in her throat and she jumped up. Her breathing came like she'd run a mile. "I need more...lemonade." She didn't wait for an answer but sped off to the refreshment table.

Thorns and briars. I'm behaving like an idiot. Finding excuse after excuse, she avoided going back to the blanket. The rest of the afternoon, Jubilee watched Rafe through her lashes. She glanced away any time his gaze swiveled towards her. Several conversations floated about her during the day, but she remembered very little. What she did recall was the way Rafe moved so fluidly, guiding his big, lithe body through the crowd, shaking hands with the men, dwarfing all of them, even his brothers, and throwing his head back to laugh during his conversations.

* * *

Rafe chuckled at a story Pete Miller told. He'd been an old fishing buddy of his from grade school. He missed spending time at the river, and Pete relayed a story of how his nephew had slapped him in the back of the head with a wet worm while they'd fished together a few weeks back. Rosemary walked by then, her brows drawn and her face an irritated mask, with Dale a half step behind, evidently the receiver of her tirade. They were too far away to catch their conversation, but from their body language it didn't look like an enjoyable discussion.

"You heard Dale's building the finest house round these parts." Pete motioned to the couple with his hand gripped around his lemonade cup.

"No, I hadn't."

Pete smiled. "Yeah, I guess everything is coming in special order. I don't know how Dale will be able to pay for it." Pete grimaced. "Sorry, I probably shouldn't be telling you this 'cause, well, you know, your relationship with her and all."

"Naw, no big deal." Rafe smiled. "Marrying her wasn't meant to be."

Rafe realized what he'd said rang true. He focused on Rosemary a moment, but looked away in case anyone should misinterpret his glance.

She was beautiful, yes, no one could doubt that. Yet, looking back on his pursuit of her, he realized that perhaps he'd pursued her for the wrong reasons. She'd been a much sought-after prize. He'd ignored obvious signs indicating her difficult personality, so nearly impossible to please.

Pete cut into his thoughts. "Well, good. Everyone knows she's making Dale miserable with this house. Maybe that's what he gets for sneaking around behind your back with her, huh?"

Rafe's jaw went tight. Yes, he'd grown weary of all the gossip. Remembering the deception still put him on edge. He glanced at Jubilee. She was opening the boxes and baskets at the table, her face wreathed in delight as she wiped moisture from her eyes. Everything delighted her. His lips quirked. Even his naked chest had caught her attention.

Jubilee appeared delicate among the women flitting about the table, so graceful. But he recognized her strength. He'd learned what she'd endured, and he'd personally experienced the fight in her. Her body appeared much healthier now, and curvier. Her cheeks had a healthy glow that tinged pink when he teased her. He stood there and let his eyes take her in.

Pete slapped Rafe on the back.

"Well, all I gotta say is congratulations. I had my doubts after the rumor mill claimed you'd married so quickly after Rosemary. But even an idiot can see you're gone over your wife. You're one lucky man."

Pete walked off to the dessert table, and Rafe froze. Gone over Jubilee? Well, here he constantly stared at her. Surely he wasn't...he couldn't...no. It was just being home, and feeling responsible for her and such. He cleared his throat and caught her glance toward him. Her eyes darted away. He pulled his thoughts from Jubilee and strode to grab a piece of pie.

* * *

Grandma Lou had shown improvement by the time the Tanners arrived home in the early evening, but was abed and asleep. Sarah took great delight in helping Jubilee show Jennie the beautiful gifts from the folks of the congregation. Jubilee's eyes still misted over as they brought out the lovely navy and yellow quilt to show everyone. Rafe's mother vowed she hadn't a clue they'd planned the beautiful gift, and remarked over the tiny stitches holding the pieces together.

After they all chatted a bit, Jubilee yawned. She finally excused herself and went to her room to dress for bed before Rafe entered. It'd taken what seemed like an eon to fall asleep last night, with her nerves on edge. Tonight would surely be a repeat. Her eyes flicked to the small chaise lounge. Poor Rafe. He hadn't even complained over what had surely been an uncomfortable night.

Footsteps padded up the stairs, and she all but leaped into her bed to pull up the quilt. A gentle knock sounded at the door, and Jubilee gave a hushed 'okay' for him to enter. He entered without a sound, and Jubilee covered her head when his shadow moved toward the chaise.

The sounds of clothing being removed indicated his state of undress. Her face heated as she remembered the scene of his naked torso with startling clarity. Had that only been this morning? Finally, the chaise groaned, taking on Rafe's weight, and he moved around to get comfortable. She'd laid the extra pillow on the chaise for him earlier and heard him punch it a couple of times to adjust it against his back. Finally he seemed settled.

"Busy day, huh?" his voice soothed in a low murmur.

"Yes." Her answer came like a breath, thrilled he'd spoken.

"I guess you liked the quilt."

She nodded into the night, and then realized he couldn't discern her silent answer in the dark.

"Oh, yes. The most beautiful one I've ever seen." She let a silence settle between them. So many questions about Rosemary swarmed in her head. Well, any subject would do, except her interruption this morning. "I supposed you enjoyed being back at your home church?"

"Uh-huh."

"Do you wish you could come back?"

He took a long breath as if he might be thinking. Several minutes ticked by before he spoke. Jubilee grew tense, fearful of what he'd say.

"No," he said. "I miss my family, and yes, my church. But I enjoy the quietness of our place. The ruggedness."

Jubilee gave a small smile. *Our place.*

He continued. "It's more like Rafe Tanner's place, not just Will Tanner's place. A farm where I make the decisions and take the consequences of those choices."

"Was it...difficult to see Rosemary?" There, it was out. She closed her eyes to harden herself as he answered.

"Actually, not really. It was much easier than I ever would've thought. I guess I have you to thank for that."

She caught her breath. "What do you mean?'

He stirred a bit. "Well, if I'd have come back alone, people would still be thinking I hadn't gotten over her. But I brought you, so everyone assumed I'd moved on and that helped a lot."

A trifle disappointed with his answer, she swallowed. "She is very beautiful." *Now why did I go and say that?*

"Uh huh. Yeah, but I realize maybe that was what it was all about."

Jubilee blinked and her eyebrows drew together. "Huh?'

"Well, when she moved to this area, I'd turned fourteen. All of us boys fawned over her. She'd come from the east and had high-faulting manners and ways, and she sure led a boy on. We yammered around about having a girl like her. Dale and I spent many a day fishing and discussing our interest in

Rosemary. I think anyone of us could've had her because it became a matter of who was willing to work the hardest for her affections."

Something akin to hope flared inside of her. She smiled again at the ceiling.

"I'd just turned a blind eye to her faults. I know it makes me sound a bit shallow that I could be so gone on a woman and six months later be counting my lucky stars I didn't marry her, but that's exactly what I'm doing."

It was quiet for a spell and Jubilee listened to his breathing even out into sleep. She'd never talked with a man the way she'd spoken with Rafe the last two nights. It seemed like they were almost a…real couple. A man and wife who shared their thoughts, feelings, hopes, dreams.

CHAPTER FIFTEEN

Jubilee woke up in the middle of the night bathed in sweat. Her hair had escaped its braid and was crammed around her neck. *Oh, I'm burning up.* The quilt was wrapped about her and, with the twisted gown, she felt like she'd fallen into a pot of hot water.

She threw the blanket off, pulled the damp hair from her neck, and waited to cool down. Her sleep-deprived brain realized she'd forgotten to open the window before getting into bed, and realized Rafe hadn't either.

She sat up and slid her feet to the floor. Tiptoeing to the glass, she hoped to slide the sash up and let a puff of cool air waft across her face. She glanced at Rafe. He hadn't moved.

The moonlight danced through the curtains as she swiped them away to grip the wooden frame and give a gentle tug. The pane didn't budge. Setting her tongue in the corner of her mouth, she squeezed the wooden frame and shoved with more force. Nothing.

Now how could this be happening? She'd easily flung this silly window open the night before. Shaking her head, she heaved again. Suddenly two strong arms reached on either side of her and slid the sash up without a bit of struggle. She took a shaky breath as she turned around, his arms still resting on the sill behind her. She looked up, up, even farther up, in her bare feet, and in the silvery moonlight, there stood a sleepy-faced Rafe with a gentle smile.

"Sorry, I was having trouble," she whispered.

"I can see that." His lazy grin grew.

He reached and drew out a lock of shiny, dark hair, spiraled from the braid, reaching to her waist.

"Your hair is long." His voice sounded husky. "I've never seen it down."

She could hardly breathe.

"I haven't ever cut it," she murmured.

"It's beautiful," he said.

He brought his hand out to the lock's full length and let it slip between his fingers.

They stood for a long moment, blinking at one another before he spoke again. "I guess we oughta get back to the business of sleeping."

"Uh, huh." She could barely speak.

He motioned with his left hand, indicating she should go first. Jubilee was very conscious of the thin nightgown which, before Rafe's help, had seemed so heavy. She climbed into the bed, thankful for the cooling breeze blowing into the room. Rafe settled on the chaise and all became quiet.

"Goodnight, Jubilee."

"Goodnight."

As the crickets chirruped outside, Jubilee listened as Rafe's breathing slowed and evened, indicating he'd drifted off to sleep. Her head turned to take in his long form stretched across the chaise. Her brain lulled over the term, 'business.' She was beginning to not like that word.

The next day, Jubilee saw Rafe occasionally as he helped his father and brothers harvest the wheat. She enjoyed getting better acquainted with all of Rafe's nieces and nephews, but enjoyed cradling the babies in her arms most of all. Jubilee helped cook, garden, clean and feed children, then laughed with the rest of the ladies as they sewed and drank cold tea on the porch. What an enjoyable time experiencing a real family.

* * *

That night Rafe stretched out on the chaise. The odd piece of furniture wasn't impossible to sleep on, but he did wish it extended a couple of feet longer. His knees ached from curling his legs.

Jubilee stirred in her bed and thoughts of her opening the window last night flitted across his mind. The moonlight had spun her dark locks to crystal. Hard on his self-control not to bury his hands in the heaviness of her hair. He could've easily drowned in her dark beauty and the deepness of her eyes. But he wouldn't. He had to remember how fragile she was. Not to mention they were just 'partners.'

He inhaled and changed the path of his thoughts. However, images of Jubilee and Colvin honed in.

"Jubilee?"

"Hmmm?"

"Are you sleeping?" He rolled his eyes at the ceiling. *What a stupid question.*

"No." She gave a soft laugh.

He smiled in the darkness, and sobered. "Can I ask you something personal?"

Silence.

"I suppose."

"Was it…bad with Colvin?"

She didn't answer, but he heard her take a sharp breath.

"Listen, forget I asked."

"No. It's okay."

"I shouldn't have asked." He adjusted the sheet over his body and stretched his neck. *Did you think she'd blurt out her most intimate thoughts?*

"I want to tell you."

He stilled.

"Maybe I should start at the beginning."

Rafe didn't dare move.

"In Pittsburg, the orphanage bound me out at age 12, to an elderly widow woman. Her name was Gertrude Galston. She's known as Granite Galston. She's a hard lady, but she treated me all right. Her house is in the Old City, a huge mansion, and she had a full-time cook and butler. I helped whenever and wherever they needed me. I ran errands a lot and worked in the garden most of the summer."

Jubilee paused here, whether to organize her thoughts or control her emotions, Rafe wasn't sure.

"Your Uncle Hilmer, Mr. Stallings, frequented the neighborhood. Mrs. Perkins, the cook, always said he had his eye out for a rich widow." She gave a small laugh. "He even tried to melt Mrs. Galston's heart as well, so he'd show up and do different handyman jobs. We had a bad storm in April of '48, which tore off some of the shakes on the roof, and Mrs.

Galston hired Mr. Stallings to patch it. When he arrived, he had Colvin with him, and they began to repair the roof."

Jubilee stopped and the pause grew longer. The breeze stirred the curtains.

"He...always seemed to be about, Colvin, that is. I'd be in the garden and I'd look up, and he'd be—staring at me." She let out an unsteady breath. "Once, when I was in the dark cellar, counting the produce jars, I finished and turned to leave, and there he was. He scared me witless. When I asked him what he wanted, he offered to help."

Rafe's muscles tensed as she spoke again.

"They worked for two weeks. Finally, they completed the job. I was relieved, I must say, for there were many other incidents. A couple of days later, Mrs. Galston asked me to put up some new drapes in her living room. Mrs. Perkins and I pressed them, and I climbed the ladder to hang them. Mrs. Galston was in one of her difficult moods and demanded we remove them several times and press the fabric over and over." She sighed. "By the time we finished, it was well after dark, and I usually walked to the orphan home at the end of the day."

Jubilee worried the sheets, and Rafe fixed his eyes on the far wall to tamp down his uneasiness.

"Mrs. Perkins told me I should have Ramsey, the butler, give me a ride in the carriage. But Mrs. Galston pitched such a fit about not finishing the dining room drapes, I slipped out the back and headed to Eighteenth Street on my own."

Here Jubilee pushed herself to a sitting position, and Rafe couldn't keep his eyes from her shadowed form, head bent, hands wringing in her lap.

"I walked along a particularly dark section of street." Her voice dropped to a whisper. A long pause stretched out. "I remember being afraid and looking all around. I think I could actually feel something wasn't right. As I passed some bushes on the left someone popped out of the dark alley and grabbed me."

Rafe threw his legs to the floor as Jubilee's hand fluttered to her mouth.

"Was it Colvin?" Rafe throat constricted and anger rose in his gut.

She nodded and her voice trembled when she spoke again. "Only I didn't realize it then. He covered my mouth with his hand and dragged me to a carriage house some distance from the main road. He wrestled me to the ground and poured a vile-tasting liquid down my throat. That was the last I knew for the next twenty-four hours."

Rafe took a deep breath but kept his eyes on Jubilee.

"When I awoke, he'd tied me up and slung me face down over a horse. There was a gag in my mouth and a blanket over my body." A sob broke from her and Rafe moved to stand beside the bed. "He…he stopped for the night, removed me from the horse, tossed me to the ground and tied my hands above my head to a tree. Then he started to drink."

She put her hands to her mouth and took a few shuddering breaths. Even in the moonlight, Rafe could make out the sparkle of tears running from her eyes.

"He told me all kinds of wild stuff, like," her voice broke, "how he'd show those rich biddies. He'd be respectable, and they'd wish they hadn't trifled with him. Then he straddled me and screamed I was his now…" She sobbed now. "I remember kicking and kicking, but nothing helped."

Rafe's clenched his jaw, and his heart wrenched as she covered her face with her hands. He sat on the bed and gently gathered her in his arms. The rest came in a broken whisper.

"The next morning he put a gun to my head and told me I *would* marry him. He'd won a farm in Indiana in a card game. He wanted to go there, somewhere new, and make folks respect him."

Rafe tamped down the burning rage mounting inside him and tightened his arms around her, praying in a low voice while her small body trembled. She burrowed her face into his neck and he stroked her back.

"Everything's all right, now. He's gone. He can't hurt you anymore," he murmured.

"I didn't have anywhere to go. I had no idea where we were." She continued to sob. "What else could I do?"

Rafe smoothed the flyaway hair that had escaped her long braid. His voice grew tight with emotion. "You had no choice. He was just plain evil."

Her sobs eased, and she pulled away from him. Rafe reached to grab a handkerchief from the nightstand and pressed it into her hand.

"Life with him wasn't always horrible." She sniffed. "Only when he drank. We settled at the farm, and he actually worked for a couple of months. There was so much to do. He left for long periods of time and came home with perfume all over him. And then he began to hit me."

Rafe massaged her shoulders and rubbed his hands down her arms. *Dear God, help me not to hate Colvin.* "No one should treat a woman like that, Jubilee. He was wrong, you know that, right?"

She nodded. Then she shrugged one shoulder, fingering the handkerchief. "I didn't know how to fix things or what to do."

Rafe sucked in a deep breath and gave a silent prayer of thankfulness. "I think God took care of the situation for you."

Her head came up. "You think so?"

"I know so. God is with us, even in painful times. And he delivers us because he loves us, Jubilee."

"I guess it's hard to believe God loves me. I have nothing."

Rafe stood, but reached over to stroke her face. "You've got me."

* * *

Next morning, at breakfast, Jubilee sensed Rafe's gaze on her. She tried to keep her attention fixed on her plate, yet her traitorous eyes kept dashing to his. Never had she told anyone such intimate information about herself. She'd had special friends at the home, like Ellen. They'd shared childish hopes and dreams with one another at night. Yet they'd been childhood friends. This was…what *was* it?

"Everything all right this morning, Rafe?" Everett grinned and glanced at Addie, his wife.

His oldest brother and his family had joined them for breakfast. Jubilee was thankful for six children who chattered continually around the table. Their prattle more than made up for her quietness.

Rafe paused and looked his sibling over. "Yes. Why?"

Everett raised his brows to Addie across from him. "No reason. Just wondering."

"Oh, leave him alone, Everett." Jennie waved as she passed the butter to her husband. "He's in love, for Pete's sake."

Jubilee's face burned, and she focused on the bacon in her plate.

"I was surely not *that* bad." Everett chuckled.

"Oh, goose and gander. You were mooning after Addie for months. I was never so glad as when you finally proposed." Jennie laughed.

"Leave the boy alone." Will laughed. "I worked him so hard yesterday he barely got to see her. He's gotta make up for lost time."

Rafe cleared his throat. "Speaking of the wheat, shouldn't we be off? The grain doesn't harvest itself."

Everyone laughed except Rafe and Jubilee. The men rose and collected their hats from the pegs by the door. Jubilee caught Rafe pulling a face at her and grinning before he disappeared outside.

* * *

Rafe groaned. *Why did I agree to run to town with Everett?* A rawness still gnawed at his belly with thoughts of the abuse Jubilee had suffered at the hands of his cousin. Now Everett was doing his best to be irritating. And succeeding.

Rafe pinched the soft leather reins between his fingers as Everett continued to talk.

"Just saying you oughta make some time to be with Jubilee, that's all. Take her on a buggy ride through town. Borrow the Johnson's little Phaeton carriage. Maybe have a picnic by the river." Everett spat over the side of the wagon. "Women like that stuff."

Rafe scratched the side of his head. "We're fine."

"Well, you two don't act like you are. You carry on like you'd like to gobble each other up. Which probably means you've been spending too much time in the fields. Addie gets all teary-eyed when I work too much." Everett stretched out his legs and set his heels on the edge of the wagon's footrest. "And why don't you get her a ring? Tanners give their women rings. And another thing, you shoulda told us about the wedding. Mom cried for two days when she got your letter. Made things downright unpleasant around here, that's for sure."

"Everett, you don't understand."

His brother snorted. "What don't I get? That yer acting addled? Yeah, I think I got a handle on that one."

"Everett...I don't want to discuss this." A warning throbbed through Rafe's voice.

"You never do. You lit outa here like a fox with his tail set fire. I told you that fancy pants Rosemary was no good. Why, she never thought of anyone but herself. Then you up and left."

Rafe gritted his teeth. "Everett. Be quiet."

"You beat all, you know. I'm the eldest and I'll have my say. Now Jubilee seems to be a good woman, and you best be taking care of her. I won't twiddle my thumbs while you make a shambles of your vows."

Rafe could stand no more. He pulled back hard on the reins and turned fiery eyes upon his brother. "My marriage isn't real!"

CHAPTER SIXTEEN

Everett's mouth snapped open and his eyes grew large. He brought his feet down onto the floorboards of the wagon and sat up straight.

Rafe sighed and turned his gaze to the road. "I married her because she had nowhere to go."

A smile stretched slowly across Everett's face. "Well, that's perfect."

Rafe reached up and wiped his jaw with both hands before turning to his brother. "Everett, I understand you're the eldest and all, and I should respect that. And for the most part, I do, but you have way too many opinions about how your family ought to live their lives. Just do me a favor and leave my private life alone."

Everett still grinned. "You don't even know, do you?"

Rafe leaped down from the wagon and started to walk back the way they'd come.

"Where are you going?" Everett called.

Rafe turned enough to yell an answer to Everett, who now stood in the wagon watching him. "*You* go get the gunny sacks we need for the wheat. I'm heading to the farm to do something productive."

His brother's laughter followed him as he strode away. Rafe gritted his teeth and refused to give in to his carnal desire of connecting his fist with Everett's face. *I'm addled? More like Everett's lost his cookies.* One minute he berated him for not spending time with Jubilee, the next gave him the business about leaving the farm. Yeesh.

Rafe growled and kicked a clod of dirt. How'd he let Everett make him blurt out the real state of his marriage? He slowed and set his hands deep into his pockets. Now he'd tell the rest of the family. Soon the whole story would leak out and be all over town.

He didn't need that grief. *And neither does Jubilee.* His tread slowed to a stop in the middle of the road. She'd been so soft and pliant in his arms last night. So broken. He ran his hand through his hair before swiping the back of his neck in frustration.

He spun. He couldn't do that to her. The wagon jangled a piece down the road now, and Rafe began to jog to catch up. Somehow he'd have to convince Everett not to let his secret out to the rest of the family.

* * *

Jubilee fell into the ladies' pattern of work each day. Monday was washing day, Tuesdays were for gardening, Wednesdays, baking, Thursdays, cleaning the house, and Fridays for sewing. The ladies fussed about a guest who insisted on doing her part, but they seemed pleased, nonetheless.

By Friday, the ladies gathered on Anna's back porch, a stone's throw from Rafe's parents. The huge wooden frame stretched out the beautiful log cabin quilt while the ladies surrounded the brown and red pattern, stitching and chatting. They spent the morning applying small stitches to the face of the covering as the children ran about the yard. They lunched under the maples and were soon back sewing.

"Sure enough." Jennie stared at her needle through the glasses perched on the end of her nose. "Rafe tied a string through a piece of corn and watched that poor hen gobble it up. Why, I think he waited near fifteen minutes for one of them hens to be stupid enough to grab it. No sooner had that red layer gulped the kernel down, when Rafe jerked it clean out of her gullet."

The ladies laughed and grimaced.

"I don't know where these boys get their ideas." Jennie laughed. "But, thankfully, he grew outa that stage. Everett used to grab the hens by both legs and spin them round like a pitcher's windup. Gracious, those hens were dizzy. Poor, pitiful chickens. All my boys earned their whippings, that's for sure."

Jubilee smiled, visualizing a mischievous blond boy with snapping green eyes. A shadow crossed her heart, realizing she'd never have an opportunity to raise a child. Her hands stilled at the thought.

"All right, I think it's time, don't you, Anna?" Phoebe stood and brushed her skirt off.

Anna gave a grin. "Most certainly."

"Jubilee?"

Coming out of her sad reverie, Jubilee looked up, surprised to see seven smug smiles on the ladies' faces around the rack. "What?"

Anna rose and motioned her to follow. "Come on. We've got a surprise for you."

185

"We'll slave away out here on this project, you girls don't worry none," Jennie joked as Anna and Phoebe pulled Jubilee into the house.

"I hope you aren't angry with us," Anna began, "but we thought you'd enjoy an evening alone with Rafe."

"Just the two of you," Phoebe chimed in as they guided her to Anna's bedroom.

Jubilee's heart fluttered. What were they talking about? "I...no, really, it's not necessary, I mean..."

Anna laughed. "Oh, Jubilee, you're so sweet. I understand exactly why my little brother fell for you. You two have been hard at work all week, and deserve some time together."

Jubilee compressed her lips. Oh, gracious. Now what?

Anna pulled a white skirt and matching shirtwaist from a peg and held the outfit up. "What do you think?"

Jubilee's eyes swept the garments. "They're lovely."

Anna smiled and Phoebe clasped her hands against her lips as her eyes danced.

"They're yours," Phoebe blurted.

A full twenty seconds ticked by as Jubilee stared at the glorious creation. Anna's face lost its smile, and she folded the skirt and blouse over her arm. "Don't you like it?"

"Oh, yes, I do. You've already given me so much." Jubilee wavered, her gaze taking in the crisp new outfit with delicate lace and layers of ruffles.

Anna looked at Phoebe. "Well, at least let us tell you our plan. And if you don't want to follow through, it's your choice."

Jubilee blinked at them and settled on the edge of the bed. "All right."

"We've planned a picnic outing for you and Rafe this evening, complete with a handsome carriage—borrowed, of course, but it's new." Anna's face began to reflect her original enthusiasm.

"Isaac and I rented it a few weekends ago. Wait until you sit in the green velvet seats," Phoebe chimed in.

"Oh, my." Jubilee brought her hands up to her cheeks. The room seemed terribly warm. She cleared her throat. "You see, it's like this. Um, well, I mean, Rafe…"

Both sisters' brows came down. *My, I'm making a mess of this.*

"If you're worried about Rafe, don't. Our mother will take care of him." Anna's voice was firm.

"The problem is this." Jubilee searched for something to say, anything to convince these ladies to cancel the picnic without casting blame upon Rafe. After gnawing her lip, she burst out in a rush, "I don't think Rafe will want to take time away from helping in the fields."

Pickle juice. That was lame.

Both ladies relaxed and tipped their heads back in relief.

Anna fanned herself and laid the dress on her bed with care. "My stars, if you're worried about Rafe missing a little work, don't. We have plenty of hands around to finish pulling and burning a few stumps in the new field. Shoo. You scared me for a minute. I thought you didn't want to go."

Jubilee gave a tremulous smile. This wasn't good. No, not good at all. The sisters began measuring her and chatting about the wonderful location of the picnic on the banks of the Ohio. Phoebe assured her she'd love a night drive in the carriage, lit by the light of the stars.

Jubilee swallowed as they fitted the dress to her body. She and Rafe. Alone. On a romantic picnic. She blinked to keep her eyes from filling with tears, extending her arms while the ladies measured. Rafe wasn't going to understand this and most likely wouldn't like the forced outing one bit.

I'm just his business partner. She'd have her first picnic as someone's business associate and not as a cherished wife. A shiver went through her as she pictured herself with Rafe under a starry sky. And, for a brief moment, she imagined endearing love burning in his eyes as he leaned toward her.

"Ow," Jubilee cried.

Phoebe's covered her mouth with her hand. "Oh Jubilee, I'm so sorry I poked you with a straight pin. Are you all right?"

"Yes," she said over the lump in her throat. *That's my payment for dreaming about something I can't have.*

* * *

"What?" Rafe pulled one last time on the chain, trying to get enough slack to unhook it.

They had a double team of draft horses connected to the stubborn tree trunk, but thus far had managed to yank only one free from the ground. Several more stumps waited to be pulled. Rafe's dad and the younger boys were some fifty feet south, burning small branches.

"You're supposed to go to the house."

Rafe glared at Everett. "It's not near on dinner time yet. I thought you wanted this field done."

"Mom wants you back up home."

Rafe looped his gloved fingers into his pocket and struck a relaxed pose to take a breather. "What for?"

Everett shrugged and attempted to look innocent, and Rafe narrowed his eyes.

"How do I know? Head home and you'll soon find out."

Rafe bent to work the huge hook loose once more. Failing, he stood. "Who else is supposed to go? Does she have a job to be done?"

Everett shouted a command at the big horses, and they backed up. He unfastened the chain and pitched the heavy links into a pile, the lead falling with loud clunks. Then his eldest brother leaned over to grab the axe from Rafe's hand. "I don't know. Just git."

Rafe grunted. If it weren't for the fact he needed Everett to keep his mouth shut about the true state of his marriage, he'd unload a bit of his frustration on his oldest and *bossiest* brother.

"Fine." His voice clipped as he spun on his heel and strode to the house.

No one questioned him as he walked away, and Rafe found that odd. By the time he reached the yard, he'd decided it was just as well. He could use a good drink of water and another axe from the barn. First though, he'd better check with his mother and find out what in the Sam Hill was going on.

His boots echoed on the wooden back porch. He pulled the door open and, without stepping in, hollered for his mother.

"Come in, Rafe."

He sighed. "I can't, Mom. I'm filthy."

"I'm in the pantry."

"Mom." He tried again with a little more volume. "I've got soot all over me."

"I know. Come in."

He glanced down at his blackened shirt. Seriously? Never in his born days had he been allowed to walk across the clean kitchen floor in such a state. With a groan, he reached down and removed his boots. *This had better be important.* His socks weren't much cleaner, so he tugged them off, too. He tiptoed barefoot through the kitchen, trying to keep his body from touching any surface.

His mother backed out of the pantry backside first. "Oh, there you are. Right on time."

Rafe stopped. "Right on time? For what?"

"Your bath."

Rafe coughed. "My what?"

"Bath? You do recall the word?" Her eyes flicked up and down him as she grinned.

Rafe shook his head. "Mom, what do you need done? I gotta get back to the fields. I'm not taking a bath now. I've got more work to do."

Jennie laughed. "No, son. You don't. I've got your clean clothes here and your new boots under the chair. Here's the soap and towel. You need to be ready to roll at six."

Rafe's mouth slid open. He scanned the large pantry, filled with the sink-to-your-neck tub, full of water. His clothes lay in an orderly pile on a ladder-back chair. "What's going on?"

"I thought I was perfectly clear."

Rafe closed his eyes and took a deep breath. "Mom, out with it."

Jennie huffed. "Fine. You're not any fun, you know that? We've got a carriage rented for you and Jubilee to take an evening picnic. Anna and Phoebe are busy getting her ready. There. Sure would've been more enjoyable if you'd have just gone along."

"What?"

"Honey, you're being a little dense. A pic–nic." She stretched out the last two words as if explaining to a small child.

"Mom, there's not going to be a picnic. Jubilee understands I need to get some work done while I'm here."

Rafe held in a groan when a flash of iron entered his mother's eyes. He was more than familiar with *that* look.

"Now you listen, Rafe Tanner." Jennie seemed to grow two inches. "You won't disappoint that endearing girl. I've never seen a person with such a sweet, gentle spirit, and she's happily jumped in and assisted in all chores around this household since she arrived. You'll not only go on this picnic, my youngest son, you'll be charming, romantic, and loving. And if Jubilee so much as mentions you failed in any of these areas, I'll personally haunt you for the rest of your stay. Am I clear?"

A smile tugged at Rafe's lips.

Jennie pointed her finger in his face and squinted her eyes, now lit with humor. "I'm serious, Rafe."

He threw back his head and laughed. "Yes, mother."

"Now, get in that tub." She started to shut the pantry door, and then whipped it open again. "And don't splash all over the floor."

CHAPTER SEVENTEEN

R afe eyed the carriage, brand spankin' new, black as night with a green velvet seat, and then turned his eyes upon the audience of his entire family.

"Go ahead, Rafe. Propose to her. Just like you did when you asked her to marry you." Jennie smiled and clenched her hands together in anticipation.

Rafe cleared his throat and fumbled with the ring in his pocket, which his mother had presented to him directly after his bath. *This has gotten out of hand.*

"Now, Mom. This is embarrassing."

"Embarrassing?" His mother's tone chided him. "Rafe, I missed everything, including the wedding. The least you can do is re-enact the proposal."

Rafe eyed his family members one by one, hating the knowing grins. He flicked his eyes to Jubilee, who stood immobile like a beautiful porcelain doll. Even Rafe's dad had an expectant grin on his face as he gestured with his head to go ahead. To repeat the actual event, if memory served correctly, he'd mutter some gibberish about a 'business arrangement,' and how marrying would save both of their reputations. *My family ought to love that.*

He turned to Jubilee with a deep breath, his Adam's apple jumping.

"Get on one knee, Rafe," Anna's voice chimed in. "Surely you did that. I think we've got him all flustered."

Rafe stretched his neck a bit with unease. Flustered was right. He bent down, and grabbed Jubilee's left hand. Her dark eyes grew huge and reflected her nervousness.

"Jubilee, will you marry me?" Rafe pulled the ring from his pants pocket and returned his gaze to hers, waiting.

A long silence ensued as she searched his face. And, for a moment, the world seemed to contain only him and her. A rush of emotion thickened his throat, and he found himself almost wishing it were real. Her cheeks flushed, haloed by ringlets of hair carefully coifed by his sisters. The darkness of her complexion contrasted against the white creation she wore, giving her an exotic look. Her mouth slightly parted in surprise and her eyes drew him in as they always did. Never had he witnessed a woman so lovely.

"Well, answer him, girl." Rafe's father chuckled.

"She's so in love she can't speak, poor child." Jennie laughed.

At that statement, Jubilee blinked and raised her head, as if realizing where she was. Glancing back to him, she answered without hesitation.

"Yes."

The family clapped around them as Rafe slid the ring onto her third finger. The fine sapphire had belonged to Jennie's aunt, reset in a band of silver. He stood as Jubilee fingered the new piece of jewelry, a look of awe on her face.

"Now, kiss her," Phoebe squealed.

Rafe put up his hands. "I think you all have seen enough."

"Come on, ya big baby," Everett said, his eyebrows dancing. "Lay one on her."

"That's a private matter, not something we do in public," Rafe replied firmly. *That's not something we do at all.*

"This is not in public, Rafe. This is family." Jennie was almost pleading.

"Come on. Kiss her."

That dadblasted Everett.

Soon everyone echoed the mantra and clapped to the beat.

"Kiss, her. Kiss her."

Before he could change his mind, he grasped Jubilee's waist and brought her against him and pressed his lips to hers. Her body stiffened and she resisted his arms, but he held her as his mouth moved over her soft lips. Just as he sensed her begin to relax, she whimpered. The memory of her past rushed upon him and he abruptly released her, grabbing her as she stumbled back.

He searched her face, and he couldn't help but direct his attention to her swollen lips. As he brought his gaze to hers, he froze. Was it fear in those beautiful brown eyes? He clenched his jaw. Why had he allowed himself to be goaded into kissing her? And what was worse, he'd enjoyed every second. *I'm nothing but swine.*

"Oh, Rafe. How romantic," Sarah murmured, starry-eyed.

Rafe tried to shake off his self-hatred. He guided Jubilee's reluctant body toward the carriage. "We're off."

* * *

Jubilee's legs turned to apple butter as Rafe settled her into the plush seat. She still trembled. He'd kissed her. Actually *kissed her.* And it hadn't been horrible, it had been...enchanting. She touched her lips as he went around the back of the carriage to climb in on the drivers' side. He climbed in and released the brake.

Rafe set the beautiful white horse in motion and Jubilee, still in a daze, waved to the departing family. Complete silence filled the space between them for the first fifteen minutes, and Jubilee took the time to slow her breathing and her speeding pulse. Surely the man could hear her heart thumping. She bit her lip and kept her face averted, pretending an interest in the passing scenery. Rafe cleared his throat.

"I seem to be constantly apologizing to you, Jubilee." He gave a deep sigh. "I had no idea this whole thing was going to turn into a spectacle. I'm really sorry."

She pushed the new ring around her finger. "No, it's I who should be sorry. Everyone has gone to a lot of trouble with this new dress, the carriage, and now this ring. I simply must give back this ring, Rafe."

He chuckled. "Are you kidding? You deserve a reward for putting on such a show."

Jubilee's heart sank and moisture filled her eyes.

"Besides, my mother would want an explanation, and that's what I'm trying to avoid. You're not angry, are you?"

The emotion clogging her throat wasn't anger. Thankful she didn't have to lie, she replied. "No, I'm not angry."

198

"Listen, Jubilee. That won't happen again. I promise."

She shrugged one shoulder. *Not even if I want it to?*

The road opened and the river appeared to the left. "Well, we can do one thing."

"What's that?"

"We've got a basket full of food in this handsome carriage, so I propose," he cleared his throat, "I mean, suggest, we just enjoy the evening and the meal. You in?"

She nodded. What choice did she have? How silly to actually think he might've enjoyed the kiss as much as she. "Yes. I've never been on a picnic. It'll be a treat."

Silence returned. Rafe slowed the carriage and turned the horse around in a wide spot in the road. "Well, in that case, we'll do this trip up right. Let's head to town and I'll give you the deluxe tour. We have some unbelievably gorgeous houses in New Albany and several impressive businesses on the river front."

A tour was just what Jubilee received. They went down each street, and he described the houses and the families that lived in each. She breathed in awe as he took her past the architecturally splendid houses owned by wealthy families. She imagined Rafe driving home in the regal neighborhood with their beautiful carriage and fancy dress clothes. Her mouth parted in a smile. She'd be wearing some crazy fashionable hat.

Her eyes took in every detail, her face bathed in wonder and enjoyment.

"And now, milady, I shall direct our interests toward engaging our appetites, overlooking the stately Ohio River. We're approaching the Johnson property, the self-same Johnsons who own this splendid carriage we currently drive. This area sports the loveliest location to view the impressive expanse of water." Rafe grinned at his pitiful attempt at a British accent.

Jubilee couldn't help but giggle as he pulled the buggy to the side of the road. When she turned her gaze on the landscape, she gasped. He certainly hadn't exaggerated. They were on a high, grassy bluff that offered an incredible view of the beautiful, shining river to the west as the sun set, changing the water into ripples of liquid mirrors. Jubilee swept her head to the east, taking in the multitude of steamers dotting the water's surface from the distant crowded beachfront of New Albany and Louisville on the Kentucky side.

"It's breathtaking," she whispered.

Rafe smiled at her as he gathered the basket and the quilt from the back.

"My accent might be lame, but the view isn't. Come on." He motioned toward the river with his head. "Let's go to the edge of the knoll. Here, grab my arm. The grass is a bit uneven."

Jubilee slipped her hand into the crook of his elbow and they walked about fifty feet until the bluff leveled out.

"Here's a good spot." He placed the basket on the ground and began to unfold the quilt.

Jubilee swallowed as she helped spread the beautiful double wedding-ring quilt from the church picnic. He held out his hand to assist her as she seated herself, his touch like embers on her skin. She directed her attention to the basket to cover her nervousness.

"Good thing they packed this." He raised the lantern. "I think we'll need it."

She glanced up to where the stars began to blink. "Not yet. Let's watch the sun set first."

"Good idea."

The fried chicken tasted delicious and the pound cake was sugary sweet. They hardly spoke as the sky grew dimmer. The steamboats below gave off tiny pinpoints of light on the darkened waters. A small strand of contentment rushed through her. Despite its uncomfortable beginning, the night had blossomed into quite a special rendezvous. Rafe's crooked smile and exaggerated tales of the local folks had her smiling and laughing. She couldn't imagine enjoying a real picnic any more. Only…she stopped her thoughts. *Be happy with what you have.*

Rafe stretched his legs out on the blanket with the soft curve of the hill. "Well, you heard way more of my family than you ought to, and I know so little about you."

Jubilee breathed in the air, scented with a distant honeysuckle bush. "I've already told you, there isn't much to tell."

"So you've no clue about your family?"

She shook head, glad for the bright moonlight breaking through the clouds. The knoll took on an ethereal quality. A gentle breeze from the water cooled her brow. "No, nothing."

They both fixed their gaze on the river shimmering in the moonlight.

"They ought to have a file on you at the orphan's home."

Jubilee sat up a bit and turned to him. "You think so?"

He nodded, leaned back on his hands, and crossed his legs at the ankles. "Sure. I bet you could send a letter and request any records they might have on you and your family. You're of age now."

She turned her attention to the stars overhead, pinpoints in a moonlit sky. "I'm not sure, Rafe. I didn't finish my term with Mrs. Galston. They may demand I return." A shiver ran through her. Would he want her to go back?

"Here, you must be cold." He handed her his jacket and helped her slip it on her shoulders. "The rain we had last night has left a chill in the air."

She clutched the lapels to her neck.

He leaned toward her on one arm. "It hardly seems your fault you were kidnapped. They surely wouldn't hold that against you. I'll write the letter if you think it'll help."

"Really?" she breathed. "That might be better."

"Good. I'll write an explanation as soon as we return to my parent's house. Do you know the address?"

Despite the serious topic, she gave a small giggle. "I lived there for practically sixteen years. I'd hope I could figure it out."

Rafe chuckled as he stood. "I guess we'd better head back. It's late.

Jubilee sighed. "I suppose so."

He helped her rise and then folded the blanket. "I had a good time, Jubilee."

She took the quilt from him and slid her hand into the crook of his arm. "Me, too."

"And now, milady, might I assist you to the handsome carriage and our patient steed?" He lapsed into his horrible accent.

"Yes, dear sir, you may." Jubilee's laugh echoed over the knoll as he sent her sailing into her seat.

It was terrible hard for Jubilee not to dream of a life where Rafe was more than a business partner as the stars twinkled over their moving carriage. Terrible hard.

* * *

Sunday came and went with church activities. The following week, Jubilee barely saw Rafe, as he spent most of his time with the men, threshing and bagging the wheat and clearing the new field. The work was hard, but made easier with the help of so many. She was sure Rafe would wish he had such aid when he returned to the chores on his own farm.

Yet working without his family ribbing his newly married state might make up for the lack of help. She grinned. They did love to tease. But her favorite time was late in the evening, when she and Rafe talked about anything and everything. He on the chaise, and she in the bed. Then they'd grow drowsy and wish one another goodnight.

On Friday, she and Sarah visited the creek with several of the older nieces and nephews. Staying away from the cooling water proved too difficult. The refreshing liquid felt wonderful, but when they all began to fling mud, Jubilee ended up in the middle, laughing harder than the rest.

Arriving back at the house, still very damp from the dip, she ran up the stairs to her room and found Rafe pulling clothes from his satchel. Her heart sped up for just a moment, remembering the last time she'd walked in on him. But he was fully dressed and gave her a tired grin as she entered.

"Been at the creek, huh?" His eyes took in the wet dress and plastered hair.

"Uh…yes." Suddenly she felt very silly.

One of his eyebrows went up as he walked toward her. He stopped and reached up.

"I think you forgot this one." He laughed as he pulled a wad of muddy moss from a lock.

CHAPTER EIGHTEEN

"Oh, no," she exclaimed and hurried to the mirror. Sure enough, a glob of spattered mud hung on top of her head. She reached for the pitcher and poured a bowl full of water. Dunking her hand over and over, she rubbed at the dirty spot, then slowed and stopped. He'd taken a seat on the chaise lounge to watch her.

"You need a hand?" he asked with a grin.

Jubilee took a deep breath. It'd help if he'd just pour the water over her head. Still, she hesitated. "Okay."

She dipped toward the bowl, and he pressed against her to tip the pitcher over her hair. His fingers rubbed the spot a bit as the water kept running. Her locks filled the bowl, and her

206

attention drifted to the warmth of his body. She had no choice but lean over and wait until he finished. At last he stopped pouring, and she felt a towel being handed to her from underneath.

After dabbing her hair dry, she bent over, wrapped the towel turban-style around her head, and stood up. He sat on the chaise again. Patting the towel with nervousness, she sat on the bed.

"Did you realize we leave tomorrow at eight?"

Her mouth opened. Was it really time to go home already?

"Oh, I'd...forgotten." She glanced toward the window. Memories of his arms wrapped about her rushed in.

"Time's gone by fast."

Their gazes locked and held. Had the clock stopped? She tried desperately to read his expression. Finally, he rose.

"I better get downstairs. Dinner will be ready soon." He put his hands in his pockets as if reluctant to leave. "I...guess I'll take this bowl of dirty water and ditch it."

Jubilee perched on the edge of the bed, her body stiff as he collected the basin and went to the door.

"I'll see ya at dinner." He opened the door and paused, his eyes flicking over her.

"All right. Thank you for your help," she replied, her voice quiet.

He nodded before the door clicked shut. They'd be going home. She took a deep breath and tried to be happy about the journey. But a sadness washed over her. She'd miss sharing a room with him. She, Jubilee, who'd been scared stiff of that man, would miss lying in bed next to him...well, across this small area. She gave an audible sigh. How she'd miss the closeness. Ugh. She'd miss him.

* * *

Jubilee cried when she hugged Rafe's family for the last time on the loading platform at the dock. It'd been wonderful to experience a real loving family, up close and personal. Sarah, the last to hug her, smiled through her tears, and pressed a small frame into her hand.

"It's not very good. The verse isn't one I'd normally use, but your name appeared in it and I couldn't resist."

Jubilee glanced down and read through a blur of moisture.

'It shall be a Jubilee unto you:
And ye shall return every man unto his possession,
And ye shall return every man unto his family.
Leviticus 25:10b.'

The letters were stitched in blue with a surrounding border of pink and red flowers, and Jubilee felt a swell of love for

Rafe's younger sister. She hugged her neck a little too long, thanking her in a choked voice.

The family departed while she and Rafe moved to the loading platform. They were early, so he left her on a sunny bench while he went to purchase their tickets. She took one more look at Sarah's sampler before sliding the frame into her satchel for safekeeping. Closing her misty eyes, she leaned into the seat and smiled. Happiness bloomed in her chest.

A shadow fell across her, and she opened her eyes before putting up a hand to block the sun. She expected it to be Rafe, but it wasn't.

"Oh, my, Mrs. Tanner," a scathing voice noted.

Rosemary. Jubilee stood up. She had no desire to meet this woman sitting down.

"Hello, Rosemary," she greeted, her tone flat.

"Actually, you may call me Mrs. Harper." Her voice all but froze over. "We hardly know one another."

Jubilees nodded in acquiescence. Fine, the woman wanted to be a rat, let her.

"I hope you're aware Rafe only married you because I'd become unavailable. Perhaps that will explain if he happens to call out my name in his sleep. He is, obviously, still pining for me."

Now, what exactly did one say to that? Especially when Jubilee knew the real situation of their marriage and Rosemary did not.

"You're a very beautiful woman, Rosemary," Jubilee kept her voice soft.

She gave Jubilee a second perusal and then narrowed her eyes.

"Exactly what is your game, little miss?" she all but hissed.

Jubilee shook her head, wishing Rafe would return. "There's no game." Exhaustion washed over her, and Jubilee's shoulders sagged. She just wanted this obtrusive woman to leave.

Rosemary's chin lifted suddenly and, as she looked over Jubilee's shoulder, her face transformed into a charming smile. The change in her countenance appeared almost comical. Jubilee turned and saw Rafe approaching. Ah, that explained the metamorphosis.

"Oh, Rafe, darling, I so wish you and your lovely wife could stay a bit longer. We barely had time to talk." She gave a mock pout, and Jubilee resisted a strong desire to roll her eyes.

Rafe stepped to Jubilee's side and brought his arm around her shoulders. Jubilee stiffened. What was he doing?

"Well, I've got to get the little wife home." He paused and looked down into Jubilee's face. "Right, darling? We have chores to do and things to take care of."

He brought up his other hand and brushed Jubilee's cheek in a caress as he gazed at her. Jubilee's eyes widened, and then she saw his wink. Still, knowing 'twas a masquerade did nothing to stop her heart from racing.

Rafe looked at Rosemary now, and Jubilee struggled to throw herself into yet another role. The other woman's face stiffened into a stern mask, her mouth pressed together in a disapproving line.

"You understand, Rosemary. You and Dale are building a house. It takes a lot of time and planning. Jubilee and I are creating a farm and we've got to tend it." He gave her a wide smile. "Nice seeing you again, though."

He picked up both satchels in his big hand and, with his arm still around Jubilee, he turned her toward the downward slope to the boarding gangplank. Jubilee stiffened her resolve not to turn and shoot her a smile of victory.

Once they had safely boarded, Rafe led her to the railing facing the shore. The overcrowded conditions of the steamer caught Jubilee in a crunch of tall passengers pushing her from the rail. She struggled to stay behind him while being jostled by the exuberant group. Glancing up, she had a full view of Rafe's expression and gasped.

There was pain there. No, not pain—*agony.* Her chest ached in realization. The whole visit had been a terrible masquerade. The nightly talks, the picnic, the ring. What was the old saying? You can't make a silk purse from a pig's ear. He only wanted...Rosemary.

Jubilee stumbled through the throng until she reached the Salon wall and leaned against it. Behind her the people laughed, cried, and waved. Tears rushed to her eyes. *What a fool I've been.* So this was how life would be. A return to their sense of normal. He in the barn, and she in the cabin. Who would possibly want a pig's ear? It was business. *Pure business.*

She barely had time to collect herself when he returned, questions flying. Blinking and sputtering excuses, she begged him to escort her to her cabin. No need to fake a sickness. She *was* ill.

Inside the small room, she dropped her satchel at the door and flung the small bunk down. She sat on the edge of the bed, clutched her rolling stomach, and began to sob. As the tears fell, she tried to understand why this realization hurt so much. He'd never indicated their status had changed, so why did this upset her so? She pulled her legs up and tumbled into a fetal position on the hard mattress.

Because really, her reaction made no sense. She sniffed, breathing in spasmodic gasps. Perhaps she was tired. Or maybe she missed the family atmosphere. Wiping her face, she pictured Rafe across the room on a chaise lounge and fresh tears washed down her cheeks.

This must be her fault, she realized, sucking in a shuddering breath. Rafe hadn't changed. She had. Not sure what to do with that thought, she pulled the sheet to her chin.

How would she make this journey home? She was too raw to join Rafe. As much as she enjoyed being on deck with the sun and wind caressing her skin, she needed to remain right here. Practicality reigned. After all, she was sick. The girl who'd never missed a day due to illness would lie in partial pretense to avoid seeing him. Perhaps by the time they reached Evansville she'd have recovered her wits.

Tomorrow they'd arrive and ride that stagecoach all day long to reach Princeton. Jubilee squeezed her eyes closed at the thought of it. Then load up in the wagon and drive to the farm. Back to life as usual. Or, perhaps, back to life as unusual. She spun the sapphire ring on her finger and more tears seeped from her eyes.

* * *

Rafe stared at Jubilee the following morning. Dark circles rimmed her beautiful brown eyes, and she refused to meet his gaze. Even her face seemed pale. His brows drew together. Had he missed something? Perhaps she was still sick.

The woman said not a word the entire way back in the overcrowded coach. The rest of the crammed occupants were quite chatty, however, which helped the trip pass. Nevertheless, her silence weighed on Rafe's mind.

It nearly crossed his lips a dozen times to broach the subject on the way home, but she kept dozing on his shoulder as he steered the horse. Once they arrived, she scrambled into the cabin, her arms loaded with her belongings, before he could even maneuver around the wagon. There was nothing left to do but take the horse to the barn and get settled for the night.

It grew quite late by the time he had the horse bedded down and everything unloaded and put away. Still, he couldn't sleep. He avoided the cot and paced a bit before striding to the door.

Rafe stood in front of the barn, hands in his pockets, looking at the cabin. Through the night's deep darkness, he could barely make out the structure in the distance. He hung his head and reached a toe out to scrape the dirt for no particular reason. He wanted to go to the door and knock and…just talk.

They hadn't had a conversation the entire trip. He...missed their talks. He lifted his head. He missed her.

Grunting, he turned away and went back into the barn to his cot. Back to business as usual. He had to get used to his role on their farm. Why in the world was his head filled with Jubilee? Sleep eluded him as he lay thinking of her shy smile and her long, shining hair. He sighed.

Would she wear that white thing she'd worn at his parents' house? Would she raise the window tonight to let the air in? Would her thick curls be unbound and gathered about her delicate shoulders? He groaned and flung his arm over his eyes. First Rosemary and now Jubilee. What was he thinking? Some folks might say he was fickle. But the truth was, Rosemary paled in comparison to Jubilee, just like the feelings he'd once had for his former fiancée.

Firmly, he pushed thoughts of Jubilee away. It was just because he'd spent some intimate time with her, that's all. Now life would be different. Everything would go back to normal.

* * *

But it didn't. He worked the farm, ate dinner at the house. He prayed over the weather and the crops, hoping for a good harvest.

They went to church. Jubilee ogled that baby, making Rafe cringe. Elsa stopped by the cabin, and Jubilee spent the day on the front porch with Britta. He struggled to keep his eyes on the barn as he painted, and Ivan's thick Swedish accent faded to unintelligible syllables.

It made him realize the emotion he'd felt for Rosemary had been very shallow next to the all-encompassing nature of what he now felt for Jubilee. And what did he feel for Jubilee?

He pondered this as he wandered along the edge of the corn patch the next day. It rose chest high and as green as grass. The wind stirred the stalks and shuffled them, filling the field with whispers. He kept walking until he came to the verge of the woods and parked his body beneath a young pin oak tree, its branches dipping low and enclosing him in his own thought cave.

Pressing his back against the smooth bark, he found himself mouthing a prayer. *God, what's wrong with me?* His thoughts were consumed with Jubilee's smile, her flushed face, that gorgeous hair, and her uncertain, dark eyes. How fragile she seemed, yet how strong. A huge swell of protectiveness rose. He was so drawn to her. A longing tugged at him to pull her into his arms. He…his eyes opened wide. Holy hornets. He loved her. He was in love with Jubilee!

He sat a long while, blinking, mouth agape. At last he stood in shock. When had this happened? How had this happened? He picked up a small rock and flung it. What an idiot. He was in love with his business partner.

Yes, yes, she was his business partner. *Business.* All business. He'd promised her they'd work together to make a home for themselves—a cooperative effort. She'd clean, blither and blather, and he'd plow, harvest, etc., and so on, and *this…* This had not been part of the arrangement. A dawning fell across him. Everett had known. Rafe recalled his laughter that day in the wagon. *I've been so blind.*

Now what? She'd been such a sport during the visit home, battling with Rosemary, saving his face. And he'd…*great.* He'd made sure she knew the whole charade was nothing more than a ruse. He brought to mind the day he'd dropped to his knee to propose. Hadn't he then wished the whole scene was real?

Wait a minute. Why was he standing here ruminating as if there were nothing he could do about all of this? *She's my wife.* That sort of gave him an edge. Yeah. Where could she go?

An idea formed in his head. Only, if this failed, what a difficult situation they'd both be in. He raised his gaze to the robin's egg sky and let his soul cry out. *God's plan.* Hadn't his father assured him things happen for a reason? *Is this your intent, God? I love her. But I can't go off on my own again. I made such a mess before. Should I pursue my wife? My…wife.*

Warmth spread through his chest and sureness settled in his gut—an Almighty assurance. He grinned.

Business was about to be mixed with pleasure because, as of this moment, he was gonna court his business partner.

CHAPTER NINETEEN

Jubilee's eyes widened. Rafe's broad smile caught her off guard and took the breath from her body. She dropped her gaze to her plate, then cut her eyes back to the wild daisies that sprang from the pewter coffee cup in the middle of the table. She had no vase, so when Rafe had appeared for supper, clutching those flowers, she'd scrambled around to find something, anything, to put them in.

"Do you think you can?" he asked as she stared at the white and yellow posies.

She swallowed, her glance colliding with his. "What?"

Somewhere amongst the disarming smile and the playful daisies, he'd shot her a question, but she hadn't the foggiest notion what he'd asked. Her face suffused with heat.

"The swing?" He prompted and shook his head with a chuckle. "I'd like to hang the thing on the porch. I wondered if you could help hold the sides."

Ah, the swing. "Uh...yes."

That crooked smile swept across his face, mesmerizing her.

"Good." His brows rose and the dimple deepened.

She quickly dropped her eyes to the plates on the table. Her nervous hands itched to be busy, so she stood to gather them.

"Let's leave the dishes for now and get to hanging while there's plenty of sunlight. I'll be more than glad to give you a hand with those afterward."

She hesitated before setting down the stack she'd collected and rubbed her hands down the front of her dress.

He rose, took a step to the door to open it, and indicated with his muscled arm that she should precede him. She allowed a small smile to flit across her features in a response to his bold grin.

'Twas one thing to interact with him under the cover of darkness as they had at his parents' house, but this was daylight, when his masculine presence seemed to fill the corners of the room. And without his family's expectations, well, this situation became a different thing indeed. His warm smiles and flirting eyes confused and hypnotized. Feeling like a dolt, she slipped through the door ahead of him.

He jogged to the barn, her attention on his easy movements. A few moments later he reappeared with the large swing, easily slung over one bunched shoulder. She stepped back as he arrived at the cabin and flipped it down on the left side of the porch.

The muscles of his shoulders rippled and snugged the shirt tight. Jubilee dropped her gaze as a rush of attraction tugged at her, causing heat to rise up her neck. With a deep breath, she coached herself. *Nothing has changed. Everything's the same.*

Liar.

He adjusted the swing on the floor in the exact location of where it would hang, then tightened the rope and picked up one armrest. He held the side easily in one hand.

"Can you hold this while I reach and tie it off?" he asked, as he grabbed a stool from beside the front door.

"O...kay."

He handed the arm to her with an encouraging grin, and stepped up on the stool. Her shoulder brushed his leg, and she strained to lean back. She kept her head down to hide her hot face. *I'm being ridiculous. I've sat by the man in a buggy seat, slept across the room from him, but I can't lean against him without embarrassment?* Yet she couldn't stop her body's reaction to his nearness.

He brushed her again as he secured the rope to the porch beam before stepping down. With his knife, he split the fibers through the two holes in the arm rest.

Bent over, his focus intent on the knot he made, their faces drew together. Jubilee blinked and caught her breath. He straightened and winked. More heat pulsated up her neck.

"All right. One more." He stepped to the other side. "Here, why don't you stand right about there?"

He pulled her to the exact spot, his hands upon her waist. Jubilee licked her lips when he didn't release immediately, and her heart tripped a fast beat.

The other side was accomplished in the same order, with the space even more limited because of the wall of the house. Jubilee concentrated on keeping as far away as she could and ignoring the pounding of her heart. She gave a thankful sigh when she could step back. He tugged on the ropes to ensure the sturdiness of his project, and she turned toward the door, intent on making her escape.

"Whoa, there," Rafe said. "Don't you want to try this contraption out?"

She spun and shrugged one shoulder.

He sat, none too gently. "See, sturdy as an oak." He patted the seat next to him and grinned. "Come on. We deserve a few minutes of rest in the breeze. Those dishes can wait."

Reluctantly, she perched on the edge.

"Sit on back and let's set it in motion."

As soon as she complied, he pushed gently against the floorboards to set the seat swinging. She gripped the armrest, feeling the muscle of his leg push against hers. Wasn't this swing smaller than normal? How silly to notice such a thing. They rode in the buggy seat all the time, which was a tighter fit than this. They'd sat together on the steamer, with her head on his shoulder, not to mention the crammed ride in the stagecoach. She'd practically been in his lap.

Still, this was an activity of choice, not necessity. After a few minutes, her body began to relax despite her over-awareness of his presence. The gentle sway soothed like a rocking chair, with a tiny breeze cooling her skin.

"Nice."

"Yep." He crossed his arms over his chest.

They swung back and forth for several minutes.

"Fields are looking good."

"Oh, uh-huh." She sensed his perusal. One hand lit to her skirt to swirl a knot in nervous circles.

"Why do you do that?" Stopping the swing, he leaned toward her.

She caught her breath, sat stick straight, and flung her hands in her lap.

"I'm sorry," she whispered.

He gave a low chuckle. "You're sure strung up tight. Ain't nothing to apologize about. I didn't mean anything. Just noticed you worry your dress a lot."

His eyes were like searing coals on her face. She shrugged one shoulder. "I suppose I'm a bit tense."

"Why?"

She blinked and took a slow breath. "I'm not sure."

They rocked some more, and Jubilee clenched her hands firmly in her lap. He spoke again. "I miss us talking, ya know?"

Boy, do I. She nodded. Only the birds' songs echoed around them for a few moments.

"Been thinking of going over to the Larsson's on Friday. He wants me to help clear another field for next year. You want to go?"

"Oh, yes. Elsa and I can visit and make some raspberry jam."

Jubilee thought of the jars in the barn she needed to gather and wash. Rafe uncrossed his arms and laid his hands on his legs. She wiggled in her seat, glancing at his big hand edging closer. Why had this talking thing seemed easier in the dark?

"I think I'm going to get those jam jars in the barn before I start the dishes." She stood, setting the swing in a series of jerks at her sudden departure.

He rose too, with a bit more leisure. "I'll be glad to get 'em for you."

She told him where they were stored and retreated to the sanctuary of the house. Taking a deep breath, she seized upon the abandoned dishes, pausing on her way to the washtub to watch Rafe stroll with easy strides to the barn. Gracious, the man took her breath away. She was as agitated as a kitten in a water bucket. *Why can't I relax when he's near?*

The swing had been a great idea, and she'd enjoy cooling herself on the shaded porch in between daily tasks. But to sit beside him and carry on a conversation proved unnerving. They'd talked of all kinds of things at his parents' house. She shook her head and decided to get to the task at hand instead of analyzing the whole situation.

She dumped the hot water from the stovetop into the tub and stepped outside to fetch another pailful. As she swung the door open, in came Rafe, and they collided. It was like hitting a brick wall.

Jubilee lost her footing until a large hand wrapped around her waist to keep her from tumbling to the floor. In a fluster, she tried to collect herself as she pulled from him, trembling from surprise and the close encounter of their bodies meeting.

"I…I'm sorry." Her voice sounded a bit too high and loud.

A wooden box rested on one of his shoulders, a grin plastered on his face.

"I almost flattened you out." He chuckled. "You all right?"

She brushed a stray strand of hair behind her ear and gave a stiff nod.

"Here. He swung the large box down and moved to deposit it on the table. "Let me get the water."

Before she knew what he was doing, he pulled the pail from her unresponsive hand and strode out the door, leaving her in a pool of confusion. Swallowing away the start she'd received, she rubbed the base of her neck and headed back to the washtub.

The water was too hot to start on the dishes, so she wet the dishrag to swipe over the table. He was back in two shakes and poured the cool liquid into the tub, testing the temperature several times. Then, to her astonishment, he plunged his hands in.

"What are you doing?" Her voice low, she walked with hesitation toward the washtub.

"Well, at the current time, I'm searching the water for a dishrag."

She held the cloth up to him.

"Ah. That's the thing." He pulled it from her hands and turned back to the tub.

"No, really, Rafe, what are you doing?"

He froze, his brow knitted. "Am I doing something wrong?"

A small smile stole across her face. "No."

His eyebrows lifted and a dimple lit the side of his mouth. "Are you laughing at me?"

Jubilee's grin widened, and she gave her one-shouldered shrug. "I've never seen a man do dishes."

He panned an incredulous face. "You're kidding?"

She shook her head, but the smile wouldn't leave her face.

"Well, I'll have you know my mother raised me right. We boys had dish duty along with my sisters. And my sisters frequently did outdoor chores."

Jubilee tilted her head and picked up a towel to dry. "Really?"

"Yes." He grinned with a nod of his head. "Our parents always said, 'work is work, don't put no gender on it.' Yeah, I hated to hear that when time rolled around to my dish night."

Jubilee gave a little giggle.

He stopped washing a moment but didn't remove his hands from the water. He stared at her. "I like to hear you laugh. You should do it more often."

She picked up another dish and refused to look at him. "I haven't always had much to laugh at."

He started to wash again while elevating one eyebrow. "I guess we'll have to change that then."

Jubilee found herself smiling as quivers shimmied down her arms.

* * *

"That the sampler Sarah made?" Rafe stood in front of the fireplace the following night, peering up at the frame while Jubilee finished mashing the potatoes.

"Uh-huh."

"Sorta've a strange verse. But I like your name in it."

Her gaze flicked to the frame. "Me, too. I'm not sure what it means, but I enjoy the words, nonetheless."

She placed the potato bowl on the table next to the fried steak and corn bread.

Rafe turned and approached the table. "It's about God's people, the Israelites, getting back all their possessions and family homes during the year of Jubilee."

They sat and Rafe put out his hands to clasp hers for prayer. His huge fingers closed about hers, and she tried to concentrate on the rumble of his voice instead of the rasp of his work-roughened skin.

"Did the people sell their things or lose them?" Jubilee asked as she passed him the potatoes.

He chewed his bread, letting his eyes roam the far wall in thought. "Well, the way I understand, folks would come on hard times, and they'd sell things to make ends meet. Sometimes they would even sell themselves. But at the end of fifty years, everything was restored."

"Huh. Since it's 1850, I suppose this would be a year of Jubilee, then."

He smiled. "I reckon."

Her eyes grew serious. "If you could restore something, what would it be?"

His fork paused in mid-air and he searched her eyes. "I'd restore you."

She caught her breath and dropped her gaze. "That's very kind."

He put down the utensil and reached into his pocket, then pushed a white envelope across the table. "Maybe this will help a bit."

Sitting up straight, she glanced from him to the letter. The Orphan Society's address was clear on the left corner. Her eyes returned to his and her mouth dropped in surprise.

"Go ahead. Open it."

A trembling took a hold of her as she wiped her hands on the napkin. "Oh, I can't. You read it."

"Are you sure?"

She nodded, the fluttering in her stomach all but making her sick. With a grin, he tore the back flap of the envelope and slid out a single sheet of paper. His eyes flicked over the contents then settled on hers. An ominous sensation tumbled in her stomach.

"Is it bad news?"

He cleared his throat. "Perhaps I should read the letter aloud.

Dear Mrs. Tanner,

'Tis with regret that we decline to send the file for Miss Jubilee Charlotte Dupree. Miss Dupree, bound out to Mrs. Gertrude Galston for the purpose of household chores and sundry duties, failed to complete the set time of service. Therefore, the Board of the Orphan Society of Philadelphia decrees that Miss Dupree, and/or Mrs. Rafe Tanner, return and fulfill her indentureship, or forward financial restitution for release from this contract. Please reply in regard to Miss Dupree/Mrs. Tanner's reimbursement of said obligation.

Cordially,

The Board of the Orphan Society,

Philadelphia, Pennsylvania."

Rafe raised his eyes to Jubilee. Her face had lost all color and her mouth hung open. He shot to his feet, sure she'd tumble from her bench, and strode to the other side of the table. Settling next to her, he realized she hadn't moved one whit. When she spoke, he barely recognized the hoarse whisper.

"I have to go back."

CHAPTER TWENTY

"You're not going to Philadelphia," Rafe said in a firm voice.

Jubilee turned her face to his. "I need some air."

She jumped up and scurried to the back door, Rafe following her.

"Listen to me. I'll work the situation out. There's no reason for you to return to be someone's servant. Jubilee?"

But she kept on walking faster past the outhouse. *Great, my courtship plan was right on track.* He rubbed his face with his hand and hiked up his britches. Déjà vu swept over him as she hurried through the field to the tree line.

He parked his fists in his pockets and watched until she disappeared into the woods and fingered the other letter he'd received. All the anxiousness to share his mother's news with Jubilee had evaporated.

In his head, he'd visualized the whole after-dinner scene, with them both smiling and laughing over his mother's stories of the family's exploits. They would've retired to the swing and, there in the moonlight, he'd have moved closer, and wrapped his arm around her shoulders. He'd have leaned in and...*nuts.* He brought his thoughts to a stop.

He stomped to the barn, frustration in each step. As much as he hated Everett's intrusions in his life, he would've given anything to be able to walk to his house, plop in his chair, and seek his advice on this love thing. It'd been hard to watch the shore of his hometown drift away that day on the departing steamer, knowing his family would be out of reach for a very long time. And right now, he needed them.

Once he reached his cot in the barn, he pulled out the letter and tossed it on the nearby crate where he kept a lantern and matches. He stared at the crumpled envelope for a few minutes. There had to be something he could do.

His head came up. Hadn't his mother mentioned Loyal and his wife taking a trip? Grabbing the letter, he scanned down to the phrase. How had he forgotten that Elizabeth's family lived in Philadelphia?

He grinned and pulled up a chair. There was more than one way to skin a cat. Rummaging through his few possessions, he quickly located a piece of plain white paper. He dipped his quill in the inkwell and began, 'Dear Loyal.'

* * *

Rafe turned the bedframe upright to maneuver it through the barn door. Sticking his head out, his gaze glided to the northern tree line. It was nearing dusk, and Jubilee hadn't yet returned. He sighed, then whispered a prayer for her before turning and hauling the frame to the door of the cabin.

It was quite a task wrestling the awkward piece of furniture through the small cabin door, but he managed to squeeze it in. He hoped Jubilee liked it.

Once he settled it into the corner, he tightened the ropes with the rope key and lost no time arranging the straw tick on top. He grabbed the quilt then froze. It was the double wedding-ring quilt they'd received from his home church.

His eyes went to the back door. Surely she'd return anytime. He arranged the pillow and made the bed before striding to the door to exit.

The trees were nothing but a dark shadow. He was done waiting. With a grunt, he stepped out the back door to head for the barn. Halfway to his destination, a big cat's scream echoed across the fields from the north. Alarm raced up his spine. *Cougar.* He jogged the rest of the way. Setting his jaw, he saddled Horse in record time and tossed his shotgun in the scabbard, his mind in constant prayer.

While Horse galloped over the field, Rafe pushed away the thought of the snake and chipmunk holes littering the ground. He looked behind him at the shadows of young corn plants flying off Horse's hooves. All irrelevant. He *had* to get to Jubilee.

At the tree line, Rafe leaned back, slowing their pace. Horse flung his head and snorted as they approached the woods. Rafe narrowed his eyes, his gaze taking in Horse's twitching ears. *Oh, glory. Lord, let her be safe.*

Rafe edged the shotgun from the scabbard and laid the weapon across his lap before urging the horse forward. Horse stamped and had to be nudged once more to encourage him to move. Rafe scanned the area, trying to get a lock on any movement, his pupils utilizing the last few remaining shafts of light.

"Jubilee?" He called. "Jubilee?"

Horse stopped and stutter-stepped backwards. He pulled the gun up and leveled it to his left. Rafe drew a lungful of air to test for the musky smell of the cougar's territorial scent. The hairs on his neck stood up.

A gasp caught him off guard, and Rafe lowered the gun barrel instantly. There stood a shadowed form.

"Rafe?" a voice squeaked.

He groaned and dropped his head. "Woman. You near scared me outa ten years of my life. I nearly shot you."

Rafe threw his boot over the back of his horse and dismounted. "What were you thinking, Jubilee? There's a cougar out here somewhere and you're traipsing around creation scaring the jeebers outa me."

He strode to her and, none to gently, pitched her into the saddle and remounted behind her. The horse jumped at Rafe's heels before shuddering to a stop. The few trees that stood between them and the field were backlit by the orange of the final rays of sunset. In a tree some fifteen feet away, a huge cat-like figure glided to a stop on a thick branch and settled on its haunches, claws kneading the bark. The animal's urine smell hit him in the face.

"Oh, dear God, help us," Jubilee whispered.

Rafe didn't dare breathe but leaned toward her ear. "Shhh…"

With Jubilee sitting in front of him, he had no option but to shoot one-handed. Horse quivered beneath them as Rafe slid the gun from its resting place and, with all the stealth he could muster, brought the muzzle up and fired.

Jubilee screamed, and the cat howled, bounding away into the woods. Rafe dug his heels into Horse's flanks and they galloped out of the woods and across the field to the barn. When Horse drew to a stop, Rafe slid off the animal in one backward bound. He led them to safety in the darkness of the barn. Only then did he realize how fast his heart was pounding.

Since he knew his way through the dark, he felt for the lantern and the matches on the post at the entrance. Once the lamp lit, he hung it back on the peg. He flicked his gaze over Jubilee, still astride Horse. She was visibly shaking, her hands clenched in the animal's mane. He walked over and reached up to assist her. She flinched.

"Look, I'm sorry, Jubilee." He stepped away and scrubbed the hair at his nape "I didn't mean to yell at you."

She threw a leg over the horse's neck and attempted to slide from the animal. Rafe stepped up, caught her, and brought her to the ground with gentle hands.

"Jubilee, look at me."

She refused to bring her head up. He tipped up her chin with his fingers. Her face was covered in tears, and he groaned, locking his gaze with hers. "I'm sorry. I was scared stiff. When I heard that cat, I thought the worst."

She closed her eyes. "I'm nothing but trouble."

Rafe tucked a stray dark lock behind her ear before wiping away the wetness on her cheeks with his thumbs. "Trouble, huh? Yeah, you're lots of trouble."

Her eyes opened, and he took his leisure searching her face before moving his gaze down to her moist lips. His voice dropped to a velvet undertone. "Very interesting trouble."

"Rafe?"

"Shhh…"

Refusing to hesitate, he brought his mouth to hers and leaned into her softness. His arms came around and drew her against him, her hands spayed on his chest. With a low moan, he deepened the kiss, and she rose to meet his demand. He pulled his head away and buried his face in her neck, filling his senses with her scent, his lips caressing her neck, as he moved his hand to cradle her head. His other hand searched her back and settled on her tiny waist as desire flamed through his gut.

Like a splash of cold water, she shoved him and, in confusion, he let his arms go slack. She fought out of his embrace and scurried to the door of the barn, breathing heavy, her eyes wild.

"What's wrong?"

Her eyes darted around the barn as she leaned on the door. "I…can't."

"Don't leave, Jubilee. We need to talk."

She shook her head. "This is not talking."

He took a step closer. "Don't go. I'm not going to hurt you."

Her eyes flashed, and she lunged against the door and fled.

* * *

Jubilee stared at the rafters from her new bed, her eyes continuing to leak tears. He'd made a bed for her. He'd rescued her. He'd married her. And now he'd kissed her. Not a forced, supposed recreation of his imaginary proposal, but an ardent kiss that commanded more. *Demanded* more. She groaned.

How had everything become so misaligned? Her thoughts darted around. First the whole Philadelphia muddle, and now Rafe's kiss. He seemed determined to keep her from returning to Mrs. Galstons. *And that kiss....* Her face burned as she relived the passionate incident over and over. His body pressed against hers, his lips on her skin.

Her eyes flicked to the jar of daisies still on the table, highlighted by the moonlight through the window. Never had she experienced such delicious emotions tumbling over her as she'd just experienced with Rafe. To be there, breathing his breath, touching his lips, feeling the rasp of his face against her neck. The mutual ardor shook her with fevered intensity. But, along with that sweet desire had been a strange sense of distress.

She threw the quilt from her body, impatient with herself, and swung her legs to the floor. After padding across the floor in her stockinged feet, she squinted at the marks she'd scratched into the wood. That seemed so long ago. Her eyes fixed on the sapphire ring that shot blue fire with a beam from the moon. She ambled through the room and stopped in front of the cold fireplace to peer up at Sarah's sampler.

"I'm so confused, Lord. I don't know what to do." Her voice was a hoarse whisper. "Please don't make me to return to Philadelphia. I want to stay here. I love Rafe and..."

Her gasp resembled a gunshot in the still night. *I love Rafe?* Realization hit her like a plunge into an icy river. She *did* love Rafe. It was so obvious. How had she not realized this before? It must've happened weeks ago, she mused, remembering her misery on the ship at Rafe's reaction to leaving Rosemary.

Rosemary.

She pressed her hands to her chest, knowing without fail she'd loved him even then. How miserable she'd been on the return trip, almost physically ill. Her stomach rocked. She was in love with a man who loved another married woman. In a daze, she wandered to the window that faced the barn and sought her own eyes in her reflection. Could he ever forget Rosemary? More moisture wet her chapped cheeks. *What do I do now? Oh, God. What am I going to do?*

* * *

Jubilee strained to keep her face emotionless. Before this point, the meal had passed with agonizing tension.

"We need to talk." He put the fork down by his now empty plate before folding his arms over his thick chest. "Things are going to change here, Jubilee. First of all, you're not returning to Philadelphia. You *will* stay here. There's no reason for you to traipse across the continent when we can resolve this from Indiana. I forbid it."

Jubilee narrowed her eyes and ire rose. *Forbid?*

"Secondly, you'll not venture to the woods alone," he continued, his startling hazel eyes boring into hers. "It is too dangerous for a vulnerable woman like you. This cougar has marked the territory and is stalking prey within those boundaries. Therefore, you'll remain close to the cabin at all times. And thirdly…"

"Thirdly?" Her voice barely restrained her anger.

"Yes, thirdly—"

"No, Rafe," she interrupted, stood, and began to collect the dirty dishes. "There is no thirdly."

Her nervousness at meeting him this morning evaporated in the heat of her fury. How dare he?

He rose as well, and Jubilee winced. "Don't do that, Jubilee. I'm not going to hurt you, and you know it. This is all for your own good."

She shook, her tone shrill. "I…I…can't even think what to say to you."

He stepped toward her. "I'm trying to protect you. Now, thirdly…"

"No." Her voice hardened. "*Get out.*"

Never had she been so abrupt. Hurt reflected in his green eyes, but he froze, and then backed away. His eyes became slits, his face stiff planes. He spun and tramped to the door, slung it open, and disappeared. Jubilee sucked in a gulp of air and leaned against the dry sink. A jumble of emotions threatened to unseat her breakfast.

Was he now reduced to commanding her about? Did he resent her because she wasn't Rosemary? In a daze she prepared the dishwater and slung slivers of soap on the floor. She'd been a fool to think he'd let go of Rosemary and embrace someone as plain as her.

She gripped the tub and squeezed her eyes shut. Her chest throbbed as she fought to hold in unshed tears. She tossed the soap and knife down on the table and marched to the door.

Once on the porch, she tarried, the smell of fresh wood melded with her vexation. Now what?

Esther. The name whisked through her thoughts. Just the thing. She trotted toward the path to the parsonage. By the time she had reached the edge of town, her wrath had died considerably. Perhaps she should've told Rafe where she was going. She hunched her shoulders. It was too late now.

After rounding the church house, Jubilee picked up her pace as she entered the Barnett's yard. Her thoughts turned to the flowers Esther had plucked from this very spot the day of her wedding. Thrusting the memory away, she raised her hand to knock on the door.

Inside she could hear movement, and Pastor Barnett soon appeared through the darkened door.

"Howdy," he said, pushing the door open. "Mighty fine to see you today. Where's Rafe?"

She cleared her throat while her gaze went beyond him.

"He's not with me." She rubbed her chin. "I was wondering if I could speak with Miss Esther?"

"Oh, sure, sure. She's round back hanging clothes, I believe. You want me to holler for her?"

Jubilee shook her head. "No. I'll run around. Thank you, Pastor."

She shot off the porch like an arrow and soon caught sight of Miss Esther, bent over, wet linens flapping on the line. As she drew near, the older woman stood and applied a hand to her lower back.

"Well, gracious. I didn't know we had company."

Jubilee furrowed her brow. "I'm not really here as company."

"Oh?" Esther approached, her keen eye searching her face. Jubilee stared at the grass.

"Where's that man of yours?"

"Home."

Esther motioned for Jubilee to follow and, settling on a bench against the shed, the older woman sighed. She patted the spot beside her.

"Why don't ya take a load off?"

Jubilee eased herself down onto the edge of the seat and sensed the woman peruse her.

"Sure is powerful hot today."

Jubilee chewed her lip and caught her hand in its habit of worrying her skirt fabric. "Uh-huh."

"So, if we're not visiting as proper company, what are we doing?"

Jubilee let out a long breath. "I don't know."

"Got yourself into a lover's spat?" The woman chuckled and patted Jubilee's knee.

"Huh? Oh, no." Jubilee stilled. "Well, maybe."

Esther nodded and looked out across the lawn at her white sheets dancing in the breeze.

"It's just…"

The woman grinned and returned her gaze to Jubilee. "What's he gone and done now?"

CHAPTER TWENTY-ONE

S uddenly Jubilee didn't know what to say. How did she spill her guts about the whole multifaceted mess? Could she ever make Miss Esther understand her situation when it was so bizarre Jubilee couldn't comprehend it herself?

"I'm unsure if Rafe loves me." She sat back on the bench and leaned against the shed's warm wood. Tears pricked.

Esther chuckled. "Thorns and thistles, child. There's certainly love in his eyes."

Jubilee straightened and peered at her. "What?"

"Lots of folks try to define love. However, Jesus Christ was our true example. Think what he did. He gave his life for us. As much as husbands are a chore at times," she laughed, "and just as difficult to understand, their job is to show the love Christ had for the church toward their wives."

Confusion washed across Jubilee's face.

Esther smiled. "Love ain't feelings and fuzzy stuff, hon. That's just some nice extras. It's something you do. Does he do things for you? Take care of you? These are what you oughta think on."

Jubilee sighed. "I wish it were so simple."

"Perhaps it is."

Jubilee blinked. "What can I do to show love to him?"

"Same thing. A little hand holding and such don't hurt none either."

Jubilee shook her hands in frustration. "You don't understand, Miss Esther."

The older woman sat back and swept her gaze across the blue sky. "I understand you married a near stranger and getting to know each other will take time."

Jubilee gasped. She was clever.

Esther turned her weathered blue eyes on her with boldness. "Do you love him?" A chuckle stopped Jubilee's reply. "You don't have to say the words. I see the answer on your face. Take some advice from an old lady who's been married near on forever. The Bible says to make friends you have to be friendly. I expect the same works for love."

"You have to be friendly to get love?" Bewildered, she jerked her head, her eyes wide.

Soft laughter flowed from Esther, and a lock of her white hair tossed in the breeze. "Oh, child. You're a delight. I reckon being friendly won't hurt. But showing love may lead to love."

She swallowed. "Doing what they want is love, isn't it?"

"Yes, Jubilee."

Jubilee shot up. "I need to go."

Esther rose and embraced Jubilee. "Now you walk up to your man, that fine man, and show him all the love in your heart."

Jubilee gave a slow grin. "Yes, ma'am."

The trip home went much slower. Jubilee noticed each part of the landscape while contemplating Esther's words. She caressed the cerulean bachelors' buttons growing along the path and swept her chin high to take in the expanse of blue sky emulating the awesome glory of God. *Eternal, infinite, indescribable.*

Why had she gotten so angry with Rafe? Such a complete foreign emotion to Jubilee. She'd learned very young that life went much smoother with simple acceptance. Humble obedience. Even with Colvin, she'd never experienced anger. Fear, yes, but never anger.

She strolled toward a pink wild-rose bush and paused to pluck a petal. As she marveled at the exquisite softness in a seemingly insignificant piece of creation, she also pondered something Rafe had said in New Albany. Perhaps the Lord *had* protected her from the very beginning.

The red maple branches beckoned to her from above and she reached to pick one, fingering the delicate leathery leaf. Life hadn't been easy. Without a family, working hard each day to satisfy the Society's demands had been her lot. Another had been church attendance. She'd awakened to the call of God at the young age of eleven.

She stopped. The memory rushed upon her. Pastor Reeker had left the church a few months earlier. She, in all her childishness, had assumed pastors were comparable to the rigid reverend, old, bald and fat, screaming about God's punishments and judgments.

Then like a dream, Pastor Sheffield had arrived, fresh, eager, kind and, to young Jubilee's mind, extremely handsome. The drudgery of church attendance had flown. He'd talked of God's love, forgiveness, and renewal. With a glad heart, she'd gone forward to express a desire to be part of such a powerful legacy.

Though what stuck in her mind was not God's great mercy, but Pastor Sheffield's sparkling eyes, earnest upon her confession. She and her best friend, Ellen, had whispered dreamily about the encounter for months afterward. In time Jubilee had outgrown her childhood crush and, in the process, she'd absorbed the reality of what God had done for her.

There'd been many times Jubilee wished she could have questioned the good pastor. He'd talked so much about serving God and living the abundant life, yet she wondered how to accomplish that. Then Colvin happened and everything went awry.

Or had it? She caught her breath. Surely she'd certainly not wish to experience those days again. She'd never once thought those trying times would make her stronger, yet she knew they had. Through her survival, she'd gained an extra dimension to her character, an extra appreciation of Christ's suffering. And with Rafe's kindness, a healing confidence grew within her.

I ordered him out of the cabin. A cringe rippled through her. It'd been his tone, his commands. Yet everything he said made sense. She didn't want to return to Philadelphia, although how she could avoid this was beyond her. The sighting of the cougar had scared the wits out of her, so avoiding the woods seemed wise. And thirdly…oh, my, she hadn't waited to hear him out. She let out a frustrated breath, threw the leaf down, and plopped on the soft grass.

The tall weeds around her put her in seclusion from the world, and only the sky peeped in. What did she really want? *Truly?* It was time to be a mature person and make a goal of some kind. She'd been swept along by circumstance forever, and now she needed to make a decision.

She leaned back until the grass pillowed her head. She tapped her lip, contemplating the sky. If she could have anything—anything at all—what would it be?

Rafe.

The tapping stopped. Yes, definitely Rafe. But…another thought collided. Did Rafe even want her? As an orphaned widow, she had little to offer. Yet Esther had claimed he harbored love for her. Was this possible?

Wait. She brushed away an insect. Wasn't this about doing what God wanted? Jubilee covered her eyes with her hands and sat up. God, I can't solve this. Esther says I should look to you to know what to do. I need help, Lord. I don't know which way to turn.

The heat became oppressive in her little weed burrow, so she stood to catch a breeze and meandered toward the shade of the maple. The fact remained, she loved Rafe. She *loved* him. Simple as that. And she was his wife.

She took a deep breath. Time for her to apologize. She shouldn't have ordered him out of his cabin, and she should've honored his requests, well…commands. So she'd take Esther's advice and be…*friendly*.

The cabin was quiet when she returned. Rafe must be in the fields. She sighed. As much as she wanted this settled right now, she had work to do. There were plump green beans waiting in the garden to be picked, snapped and canned. Four buckets of blackberries and raspberries rested on the table, needing to be washed and separated for making jelly with Elsa tomorrow. The bread needed to be baked, and this morning's milk needed to be churned into butter. Resolution would have to wait until this evening.

* * *

Rafe chucked the hoe harder than necessary to uproot the weed from the corn row. It was backbreaking work, but his mind was a spin. Had he actually come at Jubilee like some wild, lowing bull demanding this and that? He grunted. Yes, he most certainly had. Again, not a great tactic to entice the woman's affections.

He had no business commanding her in such a way. The woman was free to return to Philadelphia if she so desired, as much as the idea raised his hackles to admit it. Of course, the cougar spawned a whole other problem. He hoped, at least, she'd heed him on that point, cutting a glance at the shotgun resting in the row behind him.

He paused and jerked his head to the left to work out a kink in his neck. *Okay.* Back to plan one. He hadn't buried himself—yet. He'd apologize. Then hope the woman would listen to his third request.

* * *

Later in the evening, Rafe and Jubilee finished supper as always. Neither spoke. The atmosphere in the cabin was oppressive. As if they sat within a huge animal trap waiting for the tripwire to snap, the metal claws shut at any moment. This apologizing thing was more difficult than she could've imagined.

He cleared his throat. "Let's sit in the swing."

Finally—words. Jubilee's tension eased a bit. "Okay."

She took a deep breath as they both rose, and Rafe held the door for her. Sweeping the crumbs from her dress, she tried to amble past him with a false calm.

Settling into the seat, she mused how much more comfortable it was to talk as they worked side by side, or when the lights had been off at his parents' house. Conversing seemed plain awkward just sitting. Her body tensed as he lowered himself next to her.

"The garden looks good," he commented, crossing his arms across his chest.

"Thanks," she replied, fearing the small talk made it glaringly obvious they sat together like a real married couple.

"The corn's sprouting several ears on each plant."

"Well, that's good." She cleared her throat and tried to relax. *Apologize to the man.*

"I'm working on a pair of rockers for the porch," he said, bringing his hands down.

"Oh? A few chairs would be nice," she replied, breathless as his fingers brushed her leg.

"Figured on going in to town next week. The barn needs a little more paint and the house must be re-chinked in some areas."

"I see."

"You wanta ride along? Maybe we could stop and eat at Millie's," he said, rubbing his hands back and forth on his legs.

"Yeah, sure."

Suddenly his right arm came up and over her and rested on the swing behind her, his fingers leaving a flaming spot on her shoulder. *Friendly, friendly, friendly.* The words beat into her brain, and her apology went sailing.

"Listen, Jubilee. I got carried away this morning." He paused and Jubilee stared straight ahead, ever conscious of his arm, hot as flames, across her shoulders. "I think I made a fool of myself, demanding things from you. I had no right to do that."

"Uh huh." Witty comeback.

"I want you to know I've sent a letter to Loyal, my brother, who lives in Ohio. He's taking a trip to Philadelphia soon to visit his in-laws. I've asked him to check into the problem."

His hand caressed her upper arm.

"Oh." Her voice squeaked.

"I probably should've gotten your permission, but I'm hoping we can solve this matter without you having to return to Philadelphia. I mean, if that's what you want."

His other hand grasped hers and she caught her breath. Turning her head, her eyes collided with his green ones. "Is that all right with you, Jubilee?"

"I…" Where had her ability to speak gone? Her heart hammered. No thought of apology crossed her mind. Warm rushes of sweet emotion washed over her as he leaned forward. Her breath slowed. His eyes grew hooded.

"Jubilee?"

His voice hit her like a gust of icy wind. She jerked to a standing position.

"I've got," she couldn't look at him, "dishes…uh…to do."
Her pulse pounded. *That took forever to say.*

He stood, ramming his hands into his pockets.

"All right," he said, his voice flat, "I'll help."

"No!" Who'd screamed? Oh my, it was her. She backed to the door. "You, uh….can work on the rockers."

She glanced at him and the disappointment on his face was obvious.

He nodded his head.

"Sure, whatever," he said shortly and took both stairs in one step and strode for the barn.

She crept into the cabin and peeked at him from the window. Oh, good gracious. What was wrong with her? She leaned back against the door while tears rushed to her eyes, and she pressed her hand to her throat. Why? Couldn't she sit there and chat with the man? Why hadn't she apologized? Every word seemed glued in her throat.

An overwhelming sense of attraction for Rafe filled her senses, yet she battled even allowing his arm to rest along her back, or him to steal a small kiss. She trembled and covered her face with her hands. Her heart squeezed in agony. Were they still just business partners? She didn't want to be. It certainly didn't feel that way in her heart.

How did this whole relationship thing work? She swallowed. Why couldn't she sit and face what followed? Colvin, that's why. A wave of nausea swept through her. If what Colvin had done to her was the way of a man with a woman, she wanted no part of such a liaison.

Tears splashed to her cheeks. Developing a relationship with Rafe proved too chancy. What if the attempt didn't work? Would she be just a stand-in for Rosemary? Ugh. That would be the limit.

Perhaps Rafe's idea of a real marriage wasn't much removed from Colvin's? Yes, Rafe was good and kind and he'd stuck by his promise. Yet…this physical matter was very frightening.

She couldn't visualize talking to Miss Esther about such things. Her mind flicked to Elsa. She certainly seemed to be very much in love with Ivan. They'd no doubt consummated their marriage. If this joining were so terrible, could Elsa look to her husband with such deep devotion and respect? Her face grew hotter as she contemplated her thoughts. However, she *had* to know. With a deep breath, she resolved somehow to talk with Elsa about it. *Somehow.*

CHAPTER TWENTY-TWO

Rafe beat himself up all the way to the barn. *I'm an idiot. A royal idiot.* Why had he pushed intimacy so quickly? Because he was an idiot. He gave an audible growl. Of course the woman was jumpy. She'd been married to his cruel cousin.

He entered the shadowed barn and began to pace, trying to figure a reason to be knocking at the cabin door. After swiping an impatient hand across his neck, he grabbed up the rocker and set it on the low bench before reaching for the planer. He was going to be an expert furniture maker if this kept up.

He ran the tool down the side of the armrest. Wooing Rosemary hadn't been a problem for him, but he'd been much younger and he'd viewed it more as a game. A challenge. She'd been a prize of sorts. A prickly prize. He smiled as his mind likened Rosemary to a cactus.

He stared at his hands, covered in wood shavings. How much finer it'd be to have Jubilee's thick hair in his palms, to caress the softness, to run his hands across her smooth skin. To inhale her scent and finger the soft shift she wore to bed. He groaned. This wasn't helping. It would take time. He had to remember courting her would take *a lot* of time. And prayer.

He tossed the planer to the soft dirt floor in frustration and walked to the open door. Parking his fists on his hips and shifting his weight to his right foot, he scrunched his face in thought. What kind of terrors lived in Jubilee's mind? She'd appeared almost fearful. He hung his head and prayed for his wife. Prayed for her healing.

Tomorrow they'd take a trip to Ivan and Elsa's. He hoped this meeting wouldn't be as tension-filled as dinner had been. He'd been so set to tell her the third aspect of his plan—his plan to re-evaluate the 'business,' part of their marriage. He lifted his arm and leaned against the door.

Too bad his sisters weren't about. They could milk out her reason for her reluctance for his touch. Did the woman despise him? He shook his head. No, he'd seen interest flash across her face. He smiled when he thought of her walking in on him bare-chested. She'd been so positively shocked, she hadn't been able to wipe the surprised fascination from her eyes.

No, there was definitely heat between them. If only she'd let him explore that avenue a bit. The kiss at his parents' house, false as it was, had awoken a desire in him that was hard to tamp down. Then the encounter in the barn. And from the look on Jubilee's face, she'd felt something too.

So, furniture maker he'd be. He turned from the door and tried to push her beautiful face from his mind as he picked up the discarded tool. Pastor Barnett's sermon from a few weeks past entered his mind. He was learning a whole new dimension for, '*charity suffereth long.*'

* * *

Early the next morning, Jubilee brought out the buckets of fresh blackberries and raspberries she'd cleaned the day before, along with the jars, and Rafe stowed them in the wagon. But Jubilee's mind wasn't on the berries. It was on how she could possibly discuss her questions with Elsa.

The ride over was made in complete silence. As soon as the men had the berries and equipment unloaded on the rough outside table Ivan had built for such chores, both men strode to the barn, deep in conversation.

Jubilee was grateful the work would be done outside under the tree. With the August heat, it'd be much cooler. Elsa already had a fire going and several pots were strewn on the tabletop.

"Hello, Elsa." Jubilee greeted.

Her friend smiled. "I so glad you come. We cook berries and chat all day. Come." Laughing, Elsa wrapped her arm around Jubilee and the women walked to the cabin. "Da men are 'bout business today, yes?"

Jubilee relaxed, chuckling at Elsa's broken description. Rafe had insisted they needed to get right to work. Jubilee giggled. "I suppose so."

"No worry. We make breakfast, then we work jelly. First, tea." Just as the woman opened the door, a wail echoed from the back of the house. "Ah, Britta awake."

Elsa flashed a smile as she disappeared into the bedroom. Jubilee kept busy, filling cups with tea and pouring in the hot water from the teapot.

"Ah, here we be," Elsa singsonged as she came through with her sleepy bundle.

"Jubie, Jubie." Baby Britta chattered and grabbed Jubilee's sleeve.

Jubilee gratefully gathered the little tike into her arms and closed her eyes, taking in her baby smell before dropping a kiss on the child's forehead. Holding Britta was like a warm hug, and Jubilee reveled in it this morning. How pleasant to cradle her, a balm to her spirit. She doubted she'd love her very own any more than this precious girl. She could hardly stop her mind from visualizing herself holding Rafe's child.

"She still sleepy, I think." Elsa laughed when Britta popped her thumb into her mouth and sank into Jubilee's body.

"I have good news."

Jubilee blinked to scatter the moisture in her eyes, then looked up. "Oh?"

Elsa tilted her head, smiled, and patted her belly. "Britta soon be a sister."

Jubilee's mouth popped open. "Oh, my. That *is* wonderful news. Congratulations, Elsa."

Elsa's fair face turned a touch rosy and she bustled about, bringing over the tea and sugar to the table.

"Yes, Ivan and I so pleased. I try tell Britta. She no understand, yet." She sliced several pieces of bread and lathered them with butter and honey before she returned to the table.

Jubilee touched her finger on the tike's nose and was rewarded with a smile from around the thumb. Her heart swelled and tears returned to the back of her eyes.

"Bed, bed." Britta roused and reached toward her mother.

"Is she tired again?" Jubilee brought her head up and drew her brows together.

Elsa laughed, a cheerful sound. "No, she like bread with butter. Her favorite. Here, sweet."

Britta slid from Jubilee's grasp. Her lap felt bereft without the comfort of the child's soft body snuggled against hers. But she smiled at the toddler's joy as she grabbed the bread and made a beeline back to Jubilee.

"You are so blessed, Elsa." Jubilee dropped her head to hide the longing in her eyes.

Elsa passed her a plate with a slice of bread. "Yes, da Lord is good."

Britta finished her bread in a flurry of crumbs and slid off Jubilee's lap. The child tottered across the room, cooing and swinging the wooden spoon her mother had given her. The women finished their tea and started a simple breakfast of muffins and bacon. An hour later, the ladies delivered the breakfast basket to the barn.

Outside, they set about pouring the berries into different pots, and gathering spoons and crates to sort the finished products. About mid-morning, Elsa excused herself and took the yawning child to the cabin for a nap. Jubilee busied herself with the dishes, and Elsa returned a few minutes later.

"Let us boil berries now while little one rests." Her voice was low.

"All right."

The ladies soon had part of the berries in a large kettle hanging from a spit over the fire. Jubilee stirred the liquid while Elsa set out the jars. While contemplating her purple hands, she searched for a way broach the delicate subject that plagued her mind. Elsa unwrapped the brown paper from the wax squares and placed them in a smaller pot.

"Are you happy, Elsa?"

Elsa's head came up for a moment and a confused expression crossed her fair face.

"Happy?" She glanced down as she adjusted the wax chunks with a long spoon. "Why you ask?"

Jubilee bit her lip as she stirred the hot liquid, already regretting her question. She shrugged one shoulder.

"I don't know," she murmured. "Forget it."

Elsa finished her task, brought the wax pot to the fire, and set it amongst the glowing coals at the edge of the fire. Jubilee could feel her eyes on her.

"No, I wish to answer for you. I very happy."

Jubilee glanced up, and her friend searched her eyes.

"You not happy?" Elsa brows puckered.

"I…uh, well, yes," Jubilee stammered.

Elsa flicked her eyes to the pot of wax, but glanced at Jubilee from time to time, a concerned pucker on her face.

Finally, her friend pulled the spoon out to set it on a large rock, wiped her hands on her apron and stood.

She laid her hand on Jubilee's upper arm. "You tell me the wrong you have."

"There's no wrong, I mean, there's nothing wrong." Jubilee sighed. She was so flustered she sounded like a Swedish immigrant. "What I mean is, are you happy being married?"

"Yah, Ivan good man," she said.

Jubilee shifted her weight, wishing Elsa would go back to stirring the wax instead of pinning her with a pitying stare.

"Uh-huh. I mean, would you wish to not be married? I mean, if you were able?" That was about as delicate as Jubilee could think to phrase it.

"Oh, no, no, I love Ivan. He good man. Rafe no good?"

"Uh." She closed her eyes for a second, and shook her head. How to be clear? "Of course he is, I…didn't mean that, I…oh."

Jubilee looked down and realized she'd forgotten to stir and the blackened raspberry juice had bubbled over the side of the pan, causing the campfire to hiss and sizzle. Quickly she grabbed a towel, spread it out to grab both handles, and pulled the pan from the hook suspended over the fire. Only the cloth failed to completely cover one handle. She literally threw the pot with her bare hands onto the table and sloshed the burnt mixture across the rough wood as she cried out.

"Oh, my." One look at the white weals across her palm had Elsa dashing to the cabin to bring butter.

After hurrying back, Elsa smoothed the yellow lard over the burns on the underside of Jubilee's left hand as tears brimmed her eyes, her face scrunched in pain.

"Oh, Jubilee. Hold still. I help."

Jubilee dragged in a few calming breaths and forced herself to immobilize her hand long enough to allow her friend to smear the cooling butter across the red skin and the raised white stripes. Elsa dipped a thin towel in cool water and wrapped it around Jubilee's hand.

"Now, you rest. I finish," Elsa murmured.

Jubilee watched with tears on her cheeks as Elsa cleaned off the table and dumped the ruined batch of juice. Jubilee's palm throbbed. Finally, Elsa sat across from Jubilee and, from the look in Elsa's sincere blue eyes, Jubilee knew what subject was about to come back up.

"Please, Jubilee, I must know. Rafe, he good?"

Jubliee nodded. "Yes, truly," she whispered.

Elsa nodded but still looked confused. Jubilee swallowed. She had to tell her something.

"My first husband," Jubilee took a calming breath, astonished she was about to share this information, "he was not…good."

Elsa's mouth parted, her eyes wide with understanding. "He die?"

Jubilee nodded.

"You love Rafe?"

Jubilee caught her breath. To tell another human, to dare whisper the truth. Jubilee's throat clogged. "Yes."

Elsa gave a small smile. "Then what is wrong? No baby?"

Jubilee's eyes shot open.

Elsa continued. "You must wait. Sometimes take long time. God send baby when day is right. You see. I pray for you."

"But, I…"

As Jubilee opened her mouth, she heard Britta's faint cry as she awoke from her nap inside the cabin. Elsa quickly patted her arm and jumped up to scurry after her little one, leaving Jubilee in a confused heap. Oh, her hand hurt. But her heart ached worse.

She pressed her cheek to the table and felt tears push through her lids while a sob rose in her throat. How in the world had this conversation swung around to having children? But, as Jubilee lay there against the wooden table, she realized she did want children. And she wanted them with the man she loved.

Rafe was achingly sympathetic when he saw the angry red marks across the tender underside of Jubilee's fingers. Her misery increased as she watched Elsa following Rafe around with a bit of suspicion in her eyes, constantly trying to figure out the situation. It was a tremendous relief to bid them goodbye and to kiss Britta's sweet blonde head before they climbed into the wagon.

"You okay?" he asked.

She shrugged.

"Hurts, huh?"

"Yeah." She wished they were home so she could soak the towel around her hand in fresh, cool water.

"You and Elsa have a good visit?"

Jubilee shrugged again. If only he knew.

He glanced at her twice and the second time, he dipped his head to capture her glance. "Something go wrong?"

Jubilee wanted to cry. His compassion made her grief intensify. Hoping he wouldn't ask any more questions, she answered, "No, I just hurt."

She tensed when his arm crept around her shoulders and pulled her to him. "Relax. Rest your head on my shoulder."

Her eyes pulsated with tears, but she tried to do what he asked. She sniffed to try to keep them at bay and only succeeded in letting a sob escape. Rafe stopped the buggy and put the brake on, and gathered her into his arms as another snuffle broke from Jubilee.

"Shhh..." he whispered into her ear. "It's all right. We're almost home."

Home? Her whole situation rose up and mocked her. What kind of home was he talking about? A home where a person just married the next stranger that happened to buy a plot a land? Where two strangers just lived together, coexisting on the same farm, but never really becoming a family? Two business partners working only to make each of their single lives slightly better? Her heart tore. A home where she was hopelessly in love with a man who wanted nothing more than a dinner in the evening and clean clothes in the morning?

Yes, her fingers hurt, but her heart writhed in agony. While keeping her head down, she pulled away from him. After a couple of moments, he took the reins back in hand. He clucked to the horses and they continued down the road. When they arrived, she scrambled from the wagon without waiting for Rafe to help her and hurried into the house. Her last glance revealed Rafe, mouth open, looking from the basket of raspberry jelly, still in the back of the wagon, to the cabin door

CHAPTER TWENTY-THREE

"Enough of this business arrangement. I think we should have a real marriage," Rafe said, shoving his hands into his pockets. "I want to move into the cabin tonight."

Rafe stood in the middle of the creek, soaking wet, talking to air. He'd finally taken a break from harvesting the corn and, feeling filthy dirty, he'd dunked himself. The wheat was finished, and the straw cut and stored in the huge barn loft. But his mind wasn't on work at that current moment. His thoughts dwelled on a certain delicate brunette who kept him at arm's length.

Ever since the visit with the Larsson's last week, Jubilee had closed up like a corn plant in a drought. He'd suggested taking a walk, sitting in the swing, going for a wagon ride, but nothing seemed to penetrate the fortress she'd built. She shooed him out of the cabin or made some excuse to hurry to the garden to finish the harvesting and the canning. And if he dared to suggest his assistance, she turned all red and puffed up like an old hen.

"I just don't get it," Rafe muttered to himself.

"Yah, Rafe. You talk to birds now?"

He swung around and there sat a smirking Ivan, up on his big bay. "They give answerings to yourself too, my friend?"

Rafe shook his head, a half-smile crossing his face as he waded to the edge of the creek and scaled the bank. "Little good those blackbirds do. They never have helpful advice."

Ivan chuckled before his eyes grew serious. "You have problem?"

Rafe snorted. "Yes and no."

"Ah." Ivan tilted his head back in understanding. "Dat sound like vimen trouble, no?"

Rafe ran a hand through his damp hair. The man may have a limited grasp of the English language, but he certainly understood the universal confusion over a woman's behavior.

"Sorry—fix things. You say 'sorry.'" Ivan encouraged him with a gentle smile.

"I wish it were that simple." Rafe walked over, untied his horse from the yellow poplar sapling, and led him back to the travois he'd made to carry his tools.

"I help?" Ivan swung down from his horse, and the two of them collected the scattered implements. "I mean, with wife."

Rafe let one side of his mouth curl up in an attempt to smile. "Naw. I gotta settle this on my own. You could pray, though."

"Oh, yah. I and Elsa pray. Talk good to God in Svedish."

Once the tools were loaded, Rafe turned to his friend. "What brings you this way?"

"Franz Schlater got trouble. It rain like dogs. Roof cry. Franz climb roof to fix. He fall. He break arm. Need help. You help?"

Rafe tipped his head back and shifted his weight to his right foot. "Is that old coot your neighbor on the east side of you?"

Ivan nodded his blond head. "Yah, yah. He old...what you say? Coot. He need da Lord. We help him and he see. Okay?"

"Sure, why not?" Rafe wouldn't miss anything at the cabin with Jubilee avoiding him like a cholera epidemic. He gave a chuckle as he pulled himself aboard Horse. "It's the least I can do. Can't have Old Coot Franz with a crying roof."

* * *

Jubilee paced, twiddling the sapphire ring around her finger on her left hand as she waited for the beef stew to boil. She paused to gaze up at Sarah's sampler. Being restored to a family seemed farther away than ever. She reached up to remove the offending verse but hesitated. With her eyes closed, she summoned the memory of Sarah's happy face, her eyes moist with tears as she presented the handmade craft to her. Jubilee brought her hands to her sides and formed them into fists. Elsa once told her God never broke his promises. Could she be right?

The sound of the bubbling stew startled her thoughts to the present. She hurried back to the stove and snatched up the spoon. Burning dinner certainly wouldn't benefit anyone. Rafe could arrive at any minute. Right now she had to concentrate on getting through a meal with him.

* * *

Jubilee could barely swallow the last bite of stew. Rafe's eyes hardly left her face during the entire dinner. She was as jumpy as a grasshopper on school grounds full of insect-loving children. The apology she'd intended to give him long ago hung in the air and became a huge cloud that filled the room.

She pressed her hand to her stomach and closed her eyes for a moment. But the weight of her unspoken apology was nothing compared to her longing for a child, for a real family.

"I…ah, agreed to help Ivan work on old man Franz Schlater's house tonight." Rafe said.

Jubilee nodded and kept her gaze focused on her empty bowl.

"He fell off the roof and broke his arm. Ivan's got several men lined up to hammer down some shingles and to help him get the rest of his harvest in over the next week or two. That is—unless you need something."

Jubilee chewed her lip, glad he'd be away in the evenings. No, not glad—relieved. She sighed. If his absence were so liberating, why did she feel so gloomy at the thought of his absence?

"Uh…no. That's fine." Did he notice she hadn't mentioned going back to Philadelphia to fulfill her obligation? Had he realized she hadn't stepped into the woods since the day he'd commanded her not to? Maybe no apology was needed.

Rafe rose and Jubilee flinched. He strolled to the dry sink, already filled with sudsy water, and washed his plate. When he'd finished, he turned to her. "There's something else. I wanted to wait and give this to you after we ate. One matter or another has come up to interrupt our meals. Hope you don't mind I waited."

He approached and pulled a white envelope from his pocket and extended it to her.

Puzzled, she put her hand out as if accepting a poisonous viper. After shifting her gaze from his unreadable one to the address on the envelope, she gave a gasp. It was from the Orphan's Society.

"How?" was all she could mutter.

He shrugged, his eyes warming. "My brother. Go ahead, open it."

She swallowed a lump of emotion and held the letter in midair and stared at it. Suddenly it seemed hard to breathe. "I can't. Would you?"

He blinked at her a few moments before reaching for the envelope. Wasting no time, he pulled his pocketknife out and made a quick slicing motion across the top. He removed two white pages and flicked his gaze to her before settling on the first page. His eyes moved back and forth a moment then looked at her. He cleared his throat. "It says,

Dear Mrs. Jubilee Tanner,

With much gratitude to your brother-in-law, Loyal Tanner, the matter concerning your indenture to Mrs. Galston has been resolved. We apologize for any inconvenience this might have

caused you. We also thank you for the large donation in your and your husband's name.

Unfortunately, we possess few details about your family, but the standard form filled out by a friend of your birth mother reveals basic family information. We, of course, would encourage and appreciate any further monetary gifts to assist in our mission as we strive to undertake the duty of providing for the orphans of Philadelphia. May this find you in good health.

Cordially,

The Orphan Society of Philadelphia. "

Rafe pulled a separate sheet of paper from behind the letter. He scanned the document before handing it to her. "You need to see this."

She puckered her brow, while her mind raced. "Rafe, how much do I owe your brother?"

"Later." He motioned for her to take the paper.

"I must know. I'm going to pay him." Though by what means was beyond her.

"Jubilee, Loyal took care of the problem as our wedding gift. Now would you please look at this form?"

Pursing her lips in disapproval, she fixed her gaze on the document. A quiver shot through her. There, in front of her, were her father's and mother's names. And a sibling.

She shot up, her voice in awe. "My mother's name was Margaret."

Jubilee began to pace from front door to back, her eyes eagerly devouring the information. "Margaret Charlotte Dupree."

Stopping short, she looked up at Rafe. "That's my middle name. I was named for my mother."

She glanced down again and resumed pacing. "My father's name was Latham Lee Dupree, and I had a brother who died at delivery. My mother..." her throat closed and tears wet her cheeks, "...died giving birth. My father died several months before, of tuberculosis."

Rafe shoved his hands into his pockets. "I'm sorry, Jubilee."

She gave him a weak smile and whispered, "I'm not. I knew they were gone. But this proves my parents were real live people. I really had a family. And now I know their names."

Without a word he moved towards her and she flung her arms around him. Rafe held her close and stroked her hair. Joy soared in her breast. "Thank you so much."

His warmth spread through her like an aloe salve on a burn, weakening her resolve not let him get near. A knock sounded on the door and she sprang from him. His gaze clung to hers, and she took a slow breath to ease the trembling in her body. She couldn't pull her eyes from the intenseness of his green ones. The knock came again.

"You should answer it." She kept her voice even as her emotions heaved.

Rafe turned with a quiet growl and strode to the door.

Ivan stood at the door, a huge grin on his face that faded a bit as he glanced from Jubilee to Rafe. "You no come?"

Rafe cleared his throat and looked at her. "I'm not sure."

She wanted to beg him to stay, to share this discovery with him and lean on his strength. But Jubilee pulled her gaze from his and shook her head with haste. "No. You go right ahead with your plans. I'm fine, really."

Her eyes lifted and witnessed what seemed like reluctance cross Rafe's face.

He nodded, but kept his eyes on Jubilee. "All right."

Jubilee turned toward the back door and walked into the shadows of the house. The silence stretched.

"Rafe?" Ivan's voice was quiet with a touch of concern.

"Yeah…let me get my tools from the barn."

Jubilee stood with her back to the door until she heard the latch click. New tears spilled from her eyes. She didn't have Rafe. Or a child. But she held a document that proved she had been part of a loving family. And at this point, that was all she had.

* * *

Rafe pounded the nail into the shake just a bit too hard and split it right down the middle. His frustration at having to leave Jubilee in such a vulnerable state ate at him. Franz Schlater jumped from his rickety chair beneath the scraggy cherry tree and stalked his bent-over form to the edge of the roof.

"Ya done ruined another one. Don't you boys know nothin?" The old man swore. "I'd do better than that with this one broken arm."

Rafe settled back on his haunches on the slant of the gable and gritted his teeth while the four other men continued to pound the new shakes in, one by one. Ivan, perched at the top of the ladder, turned a toothy smile on him as he launched a heavy load of shingles from his shoulder to the roof.

"This was a great idea, Ivan. Old man Franz is eating up our help."

"Eating up? No, no. No eating. He go church next Sunday. He promise."

Rafe grunted. He'd better, or Rafe would prod him there with the pointed end of a broken shingle. He set his fists on his thighs and turned his eyes toward home. What was Jubilee doing? Had he finally shattered her wall of silence? Was she lonely? Could she still be crying over her records from the Society?

"You come to work, Tanner? Or daydream?" Odie McFarlen ribbed with a streak of humor as he tossed a bent nail at him.

The men sniggered and Rafe took a deep breath, swiping his brow before he grabbed another shake. "Well, if we all worked as hard as you, McFarlen, we'd be here till spring."

More laughter danced across the rooftop. Everyone knew Odie was right fond of keeping the water bucket company. Ivan reared back and started a tune, his English improving greatly as he followed a familiar church hymn. Several of them joined in, but Rafe settled into his sour mood that increased the speed of his hammer.

'Twas nigh on ten o'clock by the time Rafe urged Horse into the clearing in front his homestead. The cabin was dark, which put him in an even blacker mood. The porch swing hung neglected and silent in the moonlight. He supposed Jubilee sat in it from time to time to snap beans or cut apples for applesauce, but there sure wasn't any romancing going on in that seat.

In front of the barn, he swung down from the saddle, groaning at the ache in his knees. The crickets chirruped through the soft, dark night and a gentle breeze caressed his skin, but the glory of the evening was lost to him, for all he could think of was a delicate, dark-haired beauty.

He closed his eyes and remembered the sweet lilac scent of her neck, the vibrancy of her small body that fit so well against his. The ache in his heart far surpassed the pain in his knees. Rafe lifted his head and ran his gaze across the spattering of stars. In a whisper, he sent a prayer heavenward.

* * *

She dried the last of the onions and garlic from the beams of the cabin and plucked the remaining apples and peaches from the trees. With Rafe helping Ivan over at the Schlater place, she'd begun leaving food for him in his room in the barn.

He'd be in late again tonight, so Jubilee prepared some jerky, leftover fried chicken, a couple of apples, and some bread and cheese. As she swung through the door that separated Rafe's private room from the rest of the huge barn, toting her food basket covered with cheesecloth, she noticed his Bible on his bed. He often left it there, yet today a folded paper with an envelope lay across the cover of his Bible.

Rafe hadn't mentioned receiving any mail but, then again, they really hadn't been talking. As if she were drawn by a string, she moved toward the bed and picked up the page. Her heart nearly died when she saw the author of the letter. *Rosemary.*

CHAPTER TWENTY-FOUR

With a strangled cry, Jubilee plunked on the bed, her eyes scanning the words. The letter was dated a few weeks back. Rafe's basket of food thumped to the floor.

My Dearest Rafe,

It was so refreshing to see you this summer, and I won't deny my life has become a bit gray without your presence. The thought has brought me, many times, to a place of solitude to ponder a number of things. Although I'm aware this letter is so very improper, I can't bear the thought of not penning a few lines to you.

I won't chatter incessantly about the small affairs, such as the weather and the neighbors' comings and goings, or discuss your family, as I'm sure they're in constant communication. I will, instead, get right to the point which, I must add, is quite unlike me.

My marriage to Dale is not at all what I dreamed it would be. Oh, it's not that he's unkind or boorish, but rather stuffy and a tad dull. I might add he has a bit of greediness about him, too, which, without a doubt, you are already familiar with, you both having spent a great deal of time together.

Things have gotten much more difficult since we began this building project. Even Father, who has the patience of Job, has mentioned Dale had fallen short of his expectations.

Perhaps, you are wondering why I'd alert you to such goings on. Well, I blush to tell you, as this letter is already quite scandalous, so I beseech you to keep this an utmost secret. I noticed you married rather below your station in life. Oh, please don't despise me for the words I've just written. I beg of you to instead finish reading what I have to say. Rafe, I made a huge miscalculation in breaking off our relationship, and I know by your marriage that you, indeed, seemed to regret the way our lives have turned.

But perhaps this can all be mended. I urge you to write to me as soon as you're able. I need to know, my treasure, your thoughts on this matter. Please send your response by means of the name and the box I've left you below as you realize this must only be kept between my heart and yours. The days will stretch into cold eons until I can turn my eyes upon your letter. Please don't delay, my dear.

Always yours,

Rosemary Marie

Jubilee wasn't sure how long she sat on Rafe's bed, thoughts swirling in wicked patterns of anguish and pain. She only knew that, when she looked up, the window was dark. Rafe would soon be home from Old Man Franz's. Like a sleep-walker she rose, refolded the letter, and walked stiffly from the room, through the barn, and out into the darkness. For the next twenty-four hours she barricaded herself inside the cabin.

The first snap of cold weather showed itself on Sunday morning after a good, hard rain. Jubilee wrapped herself in her heavy black cape as Rafe guided the horse and wagon amid the mud to church. The peach dress hung loose, the result of some weight loss since the discovery of the horrid letter. There was little conversation between them, which had become the standard for the last several weeks. Jubilee supposed silence made everything easier. She could barely speak with the ever-present lump in her throat, and the rock permanently residing in her stomach.

Year of Jubilee

She was relieved when they arrived at church and she could converse with Elsa and coo over Britta. Jubilee kept the child on her lap during the service, her little hands eager for every new prize Jubilee pulled from her hankie. She brought several trinkets each week. Holding Britta gave her the chance to separate herself from the anguish gnawing on her heart. Yet Elsa's sympathetic glances were difficult to endure.

It pained her that she and Elsa hadn't talked privately since the last confusing conversation at the Larsson's home. Jubilee desired to ask her friend to pray for the awful situation, but they were seldom alone. Even with the complication of Rosemary's letter, Jubilee still yearned for a baby of her own.

Her thoughts turned to Elsa's promise of prayer. Was this the answer she needed? A child would be a blessing, but without Rafe, a child would be an added burden. She'd never want a child of hers to experience the hunger she'd suffered last spring. Tears sprang to her eyes as a great sadness washed over her, even as little Britta beamed at her. *God, I'm so confused as to how to pray. I don't know what's best. I love Rafe, yet his heart yearns for another. God, tell me what to do.*

To hand Britta over to Elsa at the end of the service seemed pure torture. Britta pitched a fit when her mother pried her from Jubilee's arms. Elsa laughed and shushed the child.

"Jubie, Jubie," Britta called in a pitiful voice.

It was all Jubilee could do not to burst into tears. Instead, she put her head down and marched for the doors. Her arms seemed weighted and empty as they rolled home in the wagon. The constant silence between her and Rafe only accentuated her loneliness.

Rafe withdrew, his eyes heavy with so much work and not enough sleep. Obviously, he was eaten up with remorse at having married her now that Rosemary had declared her desire to take him back. She yearned to reach up and caress his handsome face and tell him how much she loved him. To bury her hand in his darkening blond hair, revel in the feel of those locks, and lose herself in his burning green eyes. She averted her head and squeezed her hands together to resist the urge as the wagon seat lurched.

Esther was wrong. She could *never* initiate such a display of her deep love. If Rafe rejected her feeble offer, she'd be devastated. Besides, men like Rafe wanted women like Rosemary, not some small, skinny, orphan girl with eyes too big for her face. Rosemary, despite her arrogance, was gorgeous and bore the carriage of a true lady who understood how to move in social circles. But she was a wicked woman, nonetheless.

Once home, Jubilee threaded the needle to work on the blue baby quilt she'd started. She'd long since finished Elsa's yellow creation for their anticipated new arrival. This one was for the next newborn of the church, whoever that might be. She caressed its softness and visualized her own child resting in its folds. Her tears dripped onto the fabric.

Any day now, Rafe would reveal his plans to go back home to be with Rosemary, the one he loved. Then he'd sell the farm, send her packing, and be done with her. She groaned and swept her hand across the intricate pattern of the blanket. She'd be *divorced* and alone without a child to comfort her. Then she'd have nothing.

She wiped the tears from her eyes. He was taking his time, distancing himself. Her stomach clenched. Why? Why had he married her only to reject her for another?

She threw the quilt on her bed and stood to pace. There had to be something to do to stop him from pining for this *woman*. She bit her lip as she stomped back and forth across the wooden floor. What would detain Rafe from returning to Rosemary? She froze in the middle of the room. Did she want to keep him as her husband if he hungered only to be with *her?*

She gave a quivering sigh and crossed her arms. More than anything, she wanted Rafe to love and desire her as a real wife. She closed her eyes in anguish while fresh, hot tears spilled down her chapped face. She wandered toward the window and pressed her forehead on the cold pane. This would never happen. Not with Rosemary so blatantly offering herself back to him.

So if her marriage—or rather business association—was over, perhaps the matter of having a child was not completely out of the question. Even as the thought whipped through her mind, she flung her hands to her mouth. She couldn't express her desire to conceive with him. Suddenly there was a tug-of-war in her mind. They hadn't been *unable* to have a child. They'd never *tried* to have a child.

She spun from the window. No, she could never actually voice her need for a baby, could she? No. No, *no.* Nothing more than business. Furthermore, would she be willing to commit *that physical act* to become a mother?

She jumped as a knock sounded. Wiping her eyes and waving cool air across her hot cheeks, she took a deep breath. She stepped to the door to whip it open. There stood Rafe with an empty supper basket.

"I'm caught up with the harvest and we've finished over at Franz's. You won't need to leave a meal for me anymore." He handed her the basket. "Thought I'd start coming back here for dinner, if that's okay?"

She stared at him with her mouth open as cold air swirled about her skirts. Heat raced up her neck.

"Uh…sure." She started to close the door, but he put his hand up. She glanced at his eyes and found them searching her face. His brows drew together.

"You want to take a break and sit on the swing?"

That swing. Tilting her chin up, she shook her head before shifting her gaze to the crisp leaves rustling on the pin oak near the driveway. "No."

He nodded a couple of times before looking down. "Probably too cold, anyway."

Shoving his hands in his pockets, he turned and shuffled off the porch. Despite being angry with him earlier, her heart ached as he walked away. She quickly shut the door, reminding herself of that awful letter. Her pity evaporated with the knowledge he'd soon leave her completely alone and abandoned.

* * *

Rafe bellied up to the woodpile. He was mad as a hornet at himself and had to work a bit of his frustration off. He grabbed the axe out of the tree trunk he used to split timber on and snatched a huge log, placing it on the stump. He'd worked like anybody's business to wrap up the harvest, helped at that ungrateful Old Man Franz's place, and now it was too late. He'd done ruined his chance to get close to Jubilee.

The woman seemed to be hiding from him. Every time he'd have a few minutes to stroll to the cabin, she worked in the garden or hauled jars to the cooking pot in the yard. If she wasn't working, she was barricading herself inside the house. What was going on in that woman's head? *Vimen.* Ivan's dialect bled into his brain.

He swung the axe, bringing it down with a satisfying chunk, which split the large log clean in two with one swipe. His mistake cost him plenty. *Putting my arm around her on the swing.* Why, he was nothing but a plain dunce. Then she burnt her fingers and didn't talk to him for weeks. He wasn't sure what that was about.

However, the coldness he'd experienced from her the last week or two would freeze a lake in a hurry. What in the world he'd done of late to keep her so isolated had him befuddled. He thought the letter from Philadelphia would've softened her attitude toward him. And it had, for a few minutes. If only Ivan hadn't chosen that moment to pound on the door.

He that is slow to anger is better than the mighty; and he that ruleth his spirit than he that taketh a city. Proverbs 16:32 had become his mantra since Pastor Barnett had preached on it a couple weeks back. He mumbled it to himself as he brought the axe up in a mighty swing.

Church. The word sent another thought ricocheting thought his brain. Yesterday Elsa had leaned toward Jubilee to whisper something about praying for her. Maybe Elsa knew the root of Jubilee's stony silence. All he knew was Jubilee's face had flamed a charming shade of pink, but she'd clammed up even tighter.

He whipped the axe over his head and two pieces jumped away from his blade. And then this mess with Rosemary. What was the woman thinking? He hadn't dared to write her back for fear it'd be misinterpreted. He'd quickly sent off a brief note to Dale about her letter, which outright stated she wasn't happy.

He hoped Dale took his advice kindly. Not sure why he even bothered. Dale hadn't afforded him the same courtesy when he'd stolen Rosemary away. Rafe grunted as the axe rose again. He ought to thank Dale. His friend had saved him from certain heartache, which was why he'd been so eager to tip him off. He paused. *Or, rather, God had saved him.* Rosemary had certainly proved to be a changeable and difficult woman. He was glad he didn't have to deal with her anymore. *Thank you, Lord, for your perfect plan.*

His mind flipped back to Jubilee, with her haunting brown eyes and thick hair. Sometimes he dreamed of the night at his parent's house, with his arms wrapped around her slight, trembling body and her tresses brushing his skin. His motions came to a stop, and he propped his hand on the worn wooden handle. His gaze wandered to the horizon as he continued the dream sequence.

He always stared into her fathomless dark eyes, the moonlight filtering through the sheer white curtain, his hands in her thick curls. And she'd whisper his name. He'd groan and bend over to touch his lips to hers, feeling her arch against him, her breath hot on his cheek, and then she'd vanish. He'd wake up in a sweat of desire.

Blast. With a growl he grabbed the axe and arced another swing. He scowled at the stack building on either side of the stump. What a romantic fool he was turning into.

Elsa. He could talk to Elsa and see what had gotten into Jubilee. He paused a moment in his task and wiped the perspiration collecting in tiny beads on his forehead. Yeah. That's what he'd do. He'd ride over in the early morning after breakfast and put it on the line with Elsa. Surely she'd know *something.*

CHAPTER TWENTY-FIVE

Rafe stood with his mouth open. *Jubilee wanted a baby?*

Elsa, a bit pink at the subject matter, shrugged once more, glancing at Ivan next to her in the doorway.

"That what she say. She ask first if I happy. If I marry Ivan again. I say yes. But she not happy, but she say yes when I ask her. Then, I say not happy because no baby. She say yes."

Rafe closed his mouth and swallowed. "Did she say anything else?"

Elsa tilted her head, her lips twisted in a thoughtful pose. "Yes, she say first husband bad."

Rafe nodded, his mind occupied by the previous topic.

She huffed. "Maybe I no say these things. Maybe Jubilee be angry."

Rafe rubbed his hand down his bristled cheeks he'd declined to shave this morning in his haste to visit the Larssons.

"No," he said, "I appreciate your help. She does seem very cross with me lately. I thought you might understand why."

Bouncing Britta on her hip, Elsa brought up her other hand to point at Rafe. "You talk to her then you know."

Rafe sighed. *Easier said than done.* Surely Elsa, with her broken English, had misunderstood. He thanked them, turned to mount his horse, and made his way back to the farm. The weather was sure putting on a cold shoulder early this year, but his mind barely registered this fact. He pulled the coat tighter about him. His thoughts were wrapped around Elsa's claims. Rafe let the horse meander to give his brain a chance to absorb this startling information.

He chopped more wood when he arrived home, knowing the weather seemed determined to start off with a good cold snap. He glanced toward the cabin and where Jubilee worked in the garden, cutting the pumpkins, the last of the squash, and the rest of the fall produce.

He wasn't exactly sure how he was going to approach her about this whole 'baby' subject. And if this proved to be untrue, *man*, he'll have stuck both feet in his mouth and a couple of neighbors' feet to boot. He twitched his head in aggravation and set off for the barn to put some finishing touches on the jelly cabinet he'd started.

* * *

Jubilee placed the produce in the bushel basket, thankful for the thick cloak that draped her shoulders. Despite exerting herself in the cold weather, she still felt chilled. Perhaps it was a sign of a bad winter ahead. Or plain anxiety. She glanced toward the barn and watched Rafe swing the heavy axe over his head with ease. Her hand went to her throat and gathered the wool material tighter about her neck. Would he wait until spring to dump the bad news on her, or leave her right before the holidays?

She sucked the frosty air into her lungs to clear her mind. *Don't dwell on it.* Elsa said she was praying—albeit a bit left of center, but praying, nonetheless.

Yet had she taken the time to pray for herself? Surely the Lord, in all His splendor, knew her true situation and what was best for her. Her eyes moistened, and she determinedly turned back to her chore. It was just too cold to cry.

As Jubilee prepared supper, she dreaded Rafe's presence, always on edge that he'd tell her their marriage was over. It made it difficult to enjoy the meal. Tonight there was a beef roast, potatoes, carrots and celery in the Dutch oven that had been cooking most of the day on the banked fire in the fireplace. While she busied herself with the gravy on the stove, Rafe's three knocks sounded before the door swung open. His huge figure swept into the room, and he removed his hat before he approached.

"Jubilee." He nodded his head at her.

"Hello." Tension tightened her belly.

He paused a moment, turning the brim of his hat around in his big hands. She ignored him and stirred, noting how difficult it was to keep her roving eyes from him. Surely he wouldn't break the news while she blended gravy. A blue flash caught her eye and her gaze fell on the sapphire ring on her hand.

From the corner of her eye, she saw him turn and hang his hat on a peg before stepping to the fireplace on the other side of the room. Her gaze flicked to him as he held his hands out to the fire. Jubilee gathered the plates and placed them on the table. With his back to her, she took the opportunity to scan him.

His hair had darkened a bit with the changing of the seasons. The simple work shirt and pants set off his broad shoulders, hardened with labor, which tapered to his slim hips. He rubbed his big calloused hands together, hands that had effortlessly lifted her time and time again onto the wagon seat.

Her stomach jumped in response, for his strength and form both lured and fascinated her.

He turned slightly, as if sensing her gaze, and she spun to gather the rest of the utensils to set the table. She grabbed her potholders to remove the huge Dutch oven from the fireplace but found him next to her, taking it from her hands

She took a quiet breath to steady her nerves before stepping back to the stove for the gravy. Did other women feel so useless and breathy when the man they loved came near? She'd never experienced this with Colvin. *Never.*

"I'll get the pan, too." He approached with the potholders.

She removed her apron as he carried the skillet, and then stepped back to an appropriate distance from him so her equilibrium could return to normal. At least as normal as it could be with him in the same room. Exhaling between pursed lips, she seated herself across from him. As had been their custom, Rafe grasped her hands before bowing to ask God's blessing on the food. And although Jubilee wanted to gaze on him as he prayed, she dropped her head and closed her eyes.

* * *

He looked at her when he finished and gave a weak smile.

"You have a good day?" He grabbed a biscuit from the basket on the table.

"Uh-huh."

Rafe stabbed a piece of meat. This was not starting so well. "Get all the garden crops in?"

"Uh-huh."

That again. Frustration clawed at his gut. Perhaps he'd need a more direct route. He filled his mouth and chewed, keeping his eyes on her.

When he'd swallowed he said, "Talked to Elsa this morning."

That brought Jubilee's head up. Her forehead puckered. "Oh?"

He cleared his throat. This wasn't going to be easy. Jubilee put her fork down and eyed her plate.

"You see, I've been concerned about you."

Her eyes came up and searched his face.

"You've been so quiet." He shrugged and stabbed his fork into a potato but didn't lift it. "I was wondering if there was something bothering you."

* * *

She eyed him as he raised a bite of potato to his mouth and chewed, his eyes narrowing and watchful as if he were trying to read her mind. Oh, dear. He'd talked to Elsa. Praying Elsa, who'd mistakenly thought Jubilee craved a baby. She took a quivering breath. The problem was, Elsa wasn't too far off the mark. She did want a baby, but she wanted Rafe's love as well.

"No, there's nothing." She grabbed for her glass, and it tottered before tumbling over. Water splashed everywhere and both of them jumped up from the table, rubbing water drops from their clothes. The water spread across the table and dripped to the floor. An apology leaped to Jubilee's lips, but so did an immediate anger. She threw her arms down to her side in a huff, her hands clenched in fists.

"Why? Why are you going behind my back, asking Elsa about me?"

He looked up in confusion and a scowl crossed his handsome features.

"What am I supposed to do, Jubilee? You've practically stopped talking to me. How else can I figure out what's going on?"

Her anger climbed to a higher plane. "You don't have to know anything about me. We're just business partners, remember?"

Rafe opened his eyes wide and slung his head as he spoke. "Well, according to *Elsa*, you want a baby, and that's more than business in my mind."

Jubilee gave a gasp and brought her hands to her face. She closed her eyes and shook her head. *Elsa. Oh, why had she told him that?* Suddenly, the uncharacteristic anger that had exploded from her dissipated and nothing but a horrible sadness rose up. She clenched her fists to her cheeks, vaguely aware that water dripped from the hem of her dress. He grabbed a napkin to wipe the front of his shirt.

"No," she said quietly, "she misunderstood."

Rafe's movements froze.

"So you didn't tell her...that?"

She hung her head. How could she lie to him? No, she hadn't told her exactly that, but she did indeed yearn for a child of her own. She took a quivering breath. "Let's...just drop this."

She rubbed her right hand wearily across her forehead. He came around the table, picked up her unused napkin and wiped the moisture from her face. A fervor burned in his eyes. From anger? Jubilee wasn't sure. Then he moved to dab her throat, pausing a split second before moving lower. He continued until he'd wiped her dress down the front, ending at her dripping hem. Then he stood, tossed the napkin to the table, and reached forward to put his hands upon her elbows, pulling her closer.

"Jubilee." His voice thickened and her head came up. "We can do whatever you want."

His hands slid up to her upper arms, moving up and down in a gentle caress. Jubilee swallowed a lump, warmth cascading from his touch, mesmerized by the bright flecks of yellow around the pupil of his startling jade eyes. His words grew deep and hushed. "If a child will make you happy, I'm willing to do my part."

Jubilee barely heard the words he'd crooned as his face came closer. Softly, so softly, he touched his lips to hers, and Jubilee drew nearer to him until their bodies met. All the love she possessed for him seemed to blossom as she sighed against him, bringing her arms up to encircle his neck. Rafe's embrace tightened at her response and the kiss deepened, awakening a shadowed fear in Jubilee. Suddenly, with all her might, she pushed him away and stumbled backwards several steps. They were both breathing heavily, eyeing each other with yearning and wonder.

"Jubilee?"

She took a shaky breath.

"I...just need a couple of minutes." Her voice warbled with emotion. When he didn't move, she whispered, "Please, could you go to the barn for a few moments?"

Confusion clouded Rafe's eyes but failed to mask the light of desire. He shook his head before backing toward the door. "Okay."

After the door shut she closed her eyes and raised her face to the ceiling. *What in the world was she thinking?* She needed a couple of minutes for what? She couldn't do this. She couldn't...*oh, I love that man.* The power of the emotion snatched her breath away. She moved to sit on the edge of her bed, putting her hand to her breast. She ached with love for him. Absolutely ached.

She had no thought of Rosemary's letter at this point. Her only thoughts were of him and how wonderful it was to have his arms around her. And his kiss had been sweeter than the finest honey. Holy gracious, what was she going to do when he returned?

Oh God, I love this man. What am I to do? Like a whisper through her brain came Esther's wise words, 'show him all the love in your heart.'

Suddenly her chin lifted. She knew exactly what to do when he came back, come drought or high water. She was going to fight for her husband with all her being. Taking deep breaths, she rose and began removing her dress.

At last she stood trembling in her thin cotton shift, a puddle of clothing encircling her ankles. *Why is it so hard to breathe?* Quickly she pulled the band from her hair and unbraided it with shaking fingers. She shook it free and it tumbled about her waist with thickness and shine.

Oh, Lord. Of all the times to pray, but she couldn't stop herself. *I love Rafe so much. So very, very, much. Oh, Lord, how I so desire to have a normal, loving family with him. Please let the love he had for Rosemary be completely wiped from his memory and let him learn to love me, oh, Lord, please!*

Tears dropped to her cheeks and she quickly kicked the dress from around her feet and underneath the bed. She wobbled as she drew back the blankets on her mattress. Perhaps, if nothing more, she'd have his child to hold when he left. A baby to ease her broken heart.

She walked across the cold floor and blew out the lantern on the table, throwing the room into shadows. With a tremulous smile, she noticed dinner still on the table.

Thankful for late fall's early darkness, she went to the door to wait for his signature knock, trying to keep her courage up. Surely if she survived life with Colvin and his abuse, she'd survive this night with the man she loved with all her heart.

When the knocks came, she opened the door with quaking fingers. Rafe stood there, his eyes widening as he scanned her figure down to her bare ankles. When his gaze returned to her face, the light of desire burned brighter and he groaned her name. He stepped in, wrapping his arms around her trembling form. After exhaling a husky sigh, Rafe picked up her slight body, swung the door shut, and carried her to the bed to gently lay her down.

"Are you sure about this, Jubilee?" he murmured in her thick hair, laying a sweet kiss against her neck.

His warm breath on her neck sent tingles of desire through her and she arched to meet his body. "Yes."

With a moan he joined her on the bed and the two strangers, who'd been impartial business partners, became a true married couple indeed.

CHAPTER TWENTY-SIX

J ubilee blinked in the morning light. Her face seemed very cold but her body was snug under the double wedding-ring quilt. As she took a deep wakening breath, she wondered why she hadn't banked the fire. Now she loathed getting out of bed.

She closed her eyes and relaxed into the soft warmth of her little cocoon of blankets. A large hand crept over her belly, pulling her backwards against an equally bare chest. Then a bristled masculine face and sleepy sigh nuzzled her ear. Jubilee's eyelids flew open.

She caught her breath as the memory of the previous night swept over her. Allowing a slight smile to tug at the corners of her mouth, she remembered the sweet, gentle caresses of the man she loved. Rafe, who still slept behind her, snuggled against her warm body.

His tenderness gave her yet another reason to give her whole heart to him. She basked in the heat radiating from his form. Nothing about their mating had frightened her. She pondered how such passion burned between them, with his affections set on his previous fiancée. Perhaps he wouldn't ever love her, but maybe he could learn to be happy with her. Perhaps…no, she wouldn't allow that woman's name to come into her mind this morning.

As she lay there, enjoying the closeness of her husband, she became increasingly aware of how late the hour was. Jubilee forced her eyes open and flicked her gaze to the strong sunshine washing through the window. Her brow puckered when she heard the cow lowing insistently from the barn. Then the unmistakable squeaks of a wagon pulling up the drive.

With haste, wondering who rolled up to the cabin, she flung the blankets off and hopped around, grabbing at her shift to cover her chilled body. Her hand went to the wall below the peg next her bed, but her fingers moved through empty air. A flush covered her face as she recalled her dress had been discarded and kicked beneath the mattress.

Rafe stretched and rose up on one elbow, the blankets falling away to expose his muscular chest, sprinkled with dark blond hair trickling to his navel. Her gaze made it to that point before she sensed his eyes on her. He gave a sleepy, wolfish grin. Her face heated even more.

"Good morning." That grin still in place, he raised an eyebrow at her thin shift. He patted the mattress. "The bed was much warmer when you were in here."

"Someone's outside." She ignored the longing to do just what he suggested. "And I think it's late, because the animals are fussing."

His smile faded and his eyes went to the door, listening for the things she'd mentioned. Sure enough, the cow let out a painful bellow.

She bent to grab the dress from beneath the bed and wiggled into the garment before someone knocked on the door. Rafe stood behind her, pulling on his wool pants before reaching for his shirt. A second knock sounded. She plaited her hair into a braid as Rafe strode across the floor to answer the door, buttoning his shirt. He swung his head back to check if Jubilee was decent before swinging it open. There stood Ivan and Elsa with baby Britta balanced on her hip. Oh, my, what a time for a visit.

"Your cow seem hungry maybe," Ivan remarked. "You have trouble?"

Rafe cleared his throat. "Uh, no, I haven't fed them yet."

Jubilee cringed at the odd look that crossed Ivan and Elsa's faces.

"You sick?" Ivan pressed.

"Uh, no."

Ivan's bushy brows came down in confusion. "You remember we kill hogs today?"

* * *

Rafe wanted to kick himself. How could he have forgotten he'd made arrangements to slaughter hogs with Ivan? But then, last night had been an *unusual* evening.

"Yeah, yeah, come on in. Let me put my boots on. As soon as I take care of the milking and the feeding we can get started."

Both of them came in with hesitation, and Elsa's eyes went straight to the bed where the covers lay in a mess. Ivan turned immediately to Rafe, sat next to him at the table, and began a conversation about curing the ham and bacon portions of the hogs.

Rafe ducked his head and concentrated on pulling the stubborn boots on while Ivan talked in butchered phrases. He couldn't feel less like cutting up those hogs. Ivan paused and

Rafe realized his friend had just asked a question. Rafe shrugged, hoping his gesture gave an adequate answer. Ivan began blabbering again, but Rafe found his thoughts wandering back to Jubilee's soft skin. *Oh, and her hair.* Rafe suppressed a groan.

By all that was good and holy, it was going to be hard to walk outta this cabin and pretend something life-changing hadn't occurred between the two of them last night. He stood, then grabbed his hat and gloves. *Doggone it.* He shot a glance at Jubilee wandering toward the stove, Britta toddling close behind. Elsa's narrowed eyes fastened to him.

Ivan babbled some gibberish about the new smokehouse he'd built, and how he'd be glad to smoke the meat with the hickory and maple wood he'd acquired. Rafe was just short of busting him in the jaw to shut him up. He hesitated at the door, willing Jubilee to notice, begging to get a glimpse of her dark eyes.

Their gazes locked as Ivan swung the door open. He tried to read the expression there, but she glanced at Britta who yanked at her skirt. Finally, not about to stall anymore, he pulled a smile and lifted his hand when her gaze returned to his. He hoped, for now, the gesture was enough.

* * *

The door closed behind the men. Jubilee's cheeks burned like a hot coal as she met Elsa's knowing face. She wiped her sweaty hands down her dress and approached her friend who clutched a bag filled with her knitting.

"Let me make some coffee," Jubilee offered, with a voice slightly higher than normal, and turned away from her guest.

"You mind I add wood to fire?"

"Oh. No, go right ahead," Jubilee stuttered, having difficulty getting the stove to cooperate.

A flame finally licked greedily around the round log, and Jubilee sensed Elsa returning to the table. By the time Jubilee turned, grabbed a bowl, and dumped in the ingredients for flapjacks, Elsa had sat on the bench. Jubilee raised her eyes a bit and caught her smile.

"I'm so sorry, Elsa. I didn't know you were coming today. I guess Rafe forgot to tell me."

"I not sorry." Elsa's fair face dimpled and her hazel eyes danced. "You seem very happy this day."

Jubilee smiled but fixed her eyes on the batter.

"I suppose you be angry with me?" Elsa questioned.

Jubilee eyed her and shook her head. "No, I'm not."

Elsa looked down at her daughter toddling around the room. She'd made her way over to the bed and pulled the blankets off.

"When Rafe come, he sad, like lost boy." Elsa giggled a bit. "He so big to be little boy, no? I only want you be happy, Jubilee. I know how happy little Britta make for me. And Ivan. I want for you, too."

Jubilee set the bowl down, plopped opposite of Elsa, and laid her hand on her arm. "Don't feel badly, Elsa. You did the right thing. I'm lucky to have a friend like you."

Elsa beamed then jumped as she remembered something. "Oh, I have mail for you. Miss Rosy at post office ask I bring."

Elsa pulled two envelopes from her dress pocket and handed them to Jubilee. Jubilee gave a little cry of pleasure, having received a pair of letters when they seldom even got one. The first was from Rafe's parents but, as she eyed the other one with no return address, her breath whooshed from her body. She'd recognize that fancy writing anywhere.

She swayed. Her vision fuzzed. Had Elsa said something? Jubilee stood. She heard a strange voice ask to be excused to visit the necessary, and she realized it was her own. Somehow she stumbled out the back entrance, across the yard, and into the privy without falling over. She collapsed on the floor and pushed the envelope from Rafe's parents into her pocket. As she leaned against the rough door, her hands ripped open the letter with the fancy calligraphy. Another letter from

Rosemary. Her eyes strained to read the missive in the poor light.

My dearest Rafe,

Oh, please forgive me for writing again so soon and without having received a reply from you, but things have worsened here. I long to join you, therefore I've purchased a steamer ticket that will take me to your side, where I belong. Please meet me at the Evansville Wharf on Dec. 5th. If you are unable to, I'll find my way north unchaperoned. I'll endure the hardship through the Thanksgiving holiday, but I can wait no longer. I must see you.

All my love, my darling,

Rosemary

The little shrew. How dare she confess her passion for another woman's husband? Her stomach rocked, and she staggered to gag into the open hole. Sweat broke out on her face and the rolling in her middle continued. That awful woman planned to arrive with the full intent of taking her husband. She sat for a very long time, trying to settle her insides and her nerves.

Two weeks. Two weeks before that horrid Rosemary appeared. What to do? *What to do?* Jubilee wanted to run for the woods, but thoughts of the cougar flashed into her brain.

Besides, Elsa and Britta waited for her in the cabin. Ivan was engaged in an all-day task with Rafe. Her stomach rocked again and her teeth chattered. She hadn't even bothered to grab her shoes or her cape. Tears burned her eyes.

She heard the cabin door shut. *Elsa.* She steeled herself. Her friend would be full of questions. A tentative knock sounded on the outhouse.

"Jubilee? You okay?"

Tears coursed down Jubilee's face and her stomach clenched again.

"No." Her answer was no lie. "I…think I'm sick."

"Oh."

This is my way out.

"Maybe you should take Britta home. I'm not sure if it's catching." A sob rose in Jubilee's throat and she sealed her mouth with her hand. A broken heart was most assuredly *not* contagious.

"Oh, yes," Elsa exclaimed. "I get Ivan."

Jubilee hung her head and wiped her cold face as Elsa's hurried footsteps grew fainter.

"Jubie, Jubie," Britta called.

Not even Britta's sweet voice could bring Jubilee from her misery. She stood and leaned against the door. Heavy footsteps came quickly across the yard.

313

"Jubilee? Are you all right?" *Rafe.* Fresh tears cascaded down her face. "Do you need help? Elsa offered to stay."

"No," she burst out.

"Are you sure? Can I come in?"

"*No.*" The word tore from her lips.

Silence stretched for a moment before Rafe spoke again. "I'm going to see the Larsson's off. I'll be right back."

Not if I can help it. She listened for his footsteps to fade then eased the door open. Her mind numb with anguish, she sprinted barefoot across the field, now stubbly and pale with cut stems. She ignored the pain and cold in her feet and slipped into the dimness of the trees.

What was she doing here? A sob broke from her body. There was nowhere to go. She had no money, no clothes, no destination. Choking on tears and hating herself for her stupidity, she only knew she needed to escape.

A shadowed form shifted through the dead vegetation and Jubilee froze with a gasp. She peered into the undergrowth, then glanced around. When had the weather become so gray and formidable? She shivered, hugged herself, and looked down at the small white crystals falling on her sleeve.

A moving object caught her attention and she jerked her head up, her breath coming in foggy puffs. Her gaze shifted from tree to tree to get her bearings, but her comforting woods seemed very forbidding. *Dangerous*. Fear bloomed in her chest.

Quickly making her way to a young, sturdy oak, she shimmied up the trunk. Almost all the brown, curled-up leaves held fast to the branches. Her fingers and nose were practically frozen by the time she stopped climbing. The exertion had warmed her but, as she sat clutching the tree, the icy wind chilled her to the bone.

She licked her dry, cold lips while the frosty air bit her cheeks. Why hadn't she grabbed her cloak? *Or her shoes?* The small crystals gradually turned into fat, wet snowflakes, shrouding her view. The tree creaked and swayed, making her dizzy. She opened her eyes. Was Britta tugging on her skirt? Her brain felt fuzzy and her eyes flickered open and closed. Now open.

A ghostly voice echoed amidst the trees. No, only the cold permeating her thinking processes. She blinked. Her body slipped a bit. She had to hold on. It was a long drop to the ground. *Why am I here again?* Time slipped by.

A shadow moved below. Jubilee closed her eyes for a lengthy moment before opening them. She leaned over, trying to distinguish shapes. The wind whipped through the leaves, stealing her breath, casting snow in her face.

Was it morning? Why did it seem so dark? Swiveling her head from one side to the other, she pondered whether her mouth was open. Something brushed her arm. Blinking, she fixed her gaze and found white powder. Where had this come from? *I should brush it off.* She turned her head to stare at her hand, perplexed that it wouldn't release from the trunk.

Puzzling. A draft blew in. Was the door open? No, *no.* She was hiding. While pressing her head against the jagged tree trunk, she attempted to remember her reason for hiding. Had she broken a dish? Was Mrs. Ulster about to switch her? *Think.*

The tree tilted again. No, Colvin had come back. Well, he'd never find her here. She was safe. Besides, he'd be gone in a moment. Her head lolled from side to side, the bark scraping her cheek. She grew drowsy as the white blanket enveloped her. Inhale…exhale. Everything turned gray.

Her left hand flew out into space in an arc, colliding against a rough branch. Her whole body leaned. *Where am I?* Tired, so tired. Woozy, dizzy, faint. She huffed a short breath and groaned. Her entire being began to relax as she lost the battle with hypothermia. A distant growl eased into her semi-conscious brain.

CHAPTER TWENTY-SEVEN

Rafe returned to the outhouse, only to discover it empty. Deciding she must have made her way back into the house, he sprinted to the back of the cabin and yanked the door open. But inside was shadowed and vacant. In confusion he exited and scanned the surrounding area. *Where is she?*

He slammed the door closed and tore around the yard calling her name. Then he strode to the barn to do the same, with no luck. Had she gone with the Larrsons? No, he'd watched them lumber off down the road. He walked slowly away from the barn, searching the surrounding area.

Suddenly a terrible dread dawned on him as he looked to the left at the wooded tree line. His steps faltered to a stop. That had been where she'd gone after he'd arrived, and again later when the Society's letter had appeared. Surely she wouldn't, not in this cold weather. He looked up. The first snowflakes of the season filtered down in tiny flakes. Fear ran up his spine.

Quickly he returned to the barn and saddled up his horse with great haste. He pulled the gun from where it hung over his bed in the barn, then collected the quilt from the floor of the cabin. Wasting no time, he swung up in the saddle and kicked the horse to a full gallop toward the trees.

He first rode through the woods, calling her name. How many places might a person hide in such a desolate place? He meandered amongst the frozen undergrowth and soon reached the creek, swollen from the rains last week. He drew Horse to a stop and turned around in the saddle, searching the dreary winter landscape. Already, snow clung to every surface.

The river's current was strong, and the water cold and muddy, overflowing its banks. A large tree branch and other debris moved at a good clip with the murky flow. Yet, even with the great volume of liquid that chugged by, not a sound could be heard. The birds, as well, had vanished with their songs, and the calm seemed—*deadly*. He shuddered and searched the shores.

"Oh, Lord," he muttered aloud, "keep her safe and let me find her."

With one last glance, he wheeled his horse back to the tree line. She *had* to be in the woods. As they moved, slowly but steadily, his eyes combed the snowy landscape. How long had she been gone? He looked up into the spikes of the falling snow, the wind whipping the collar of his thick duster. The storm approached white-out. He recalled her cape, hanging on the peg near the door of the cabin. Pushing the disturbing thought away, he stopped at each fallen trunk or snowy glob of thick bushes and thickets. Puffs of frozen air huffed from his lungs.

God. Help me.

With a heavy sigh, he headed due east and happened to glance up where the weak light of the sun through the dreary morning clouds lightened the tops of the trees. His throat constricted and his heart seemed to stop dead in his chest. Thirty feet from the ground she hung by one hand, the only thing that kept her from catapulting to the ground.

Her whole body swayed away from the trunk in the stiff breeze, her left arm drooping lifelessly. And although she was still seated, her legs dangled, motionless. He kicked the horse violently, urging immediate response. He had to get to her before she let go.

At that moment, a movement from the right sent Horse screaming and lunging away. A sleek, golden cougar sprang from a tree branch and swiped a razor-sharp claw at the horse's neck. The animal's awful odor filled the air as the cat bounded up the pin oak where Jubilee hung.

Horse skittered to the side while Rafe tightened his legs around the frightened animal and eased the gun from the scabbard. Blood pulsated through Rafe's body. Hunched on a low, thick branch, the cougar pulled back the whiskers of his lips and screeched, displaying a mouth full of incisors big as knives.

"Whoa," he muttered, trying to calm the horse but keeping his eyes fastened on the huge feline.

The cougar bunched his muscles, kneading the bark, preparing to leap. The eyes were like yellow, ethereal pools shimmering in the grey light. Rafe cocked his gun, and the cougar spat and spun before grabbing the trunk with its front paws to ascend. After leveling his gun, he fired. A miss sent the cat skittering higher up the tree.

Taking big gulps of air, Rafe fumbled with the bullet as he set it in the chamber. Huge snowflakes blurred his line of vision. The cat let out a scream as it settled on a high branch, pawing at the fabric of Jubilee's skirt. Rafe's heart went to his throat. How could he aim at it now?

Like a horrible nightmare, Jubilee's right arm relaxed and her body fell backward. The cougar flinched and shot out its paws, batting in a rage at the billowing skirt. Jubilee's legs flipped up and gave up the seat in the tree. She began free-falling like a rag doll, and each branch she struck bent and spun her body.

The sickening sounds of twigs snapping and crashing sent Rafe's heels into Horse's flanks. They swooped under the tree and she landed across his lap with a terrible thump. She groaned on impact, and Rafe clutched her with all his strength. But he couldn't lose sight of the cat bounding down the tree branches after her. The golden terror gained the lowest branch and, gathering the power in its sinewy haunches, gave a tremendous leap towards them.

Eyes white, Horse shrieked and lurched sideways, quivering and dancing. Rafe tugged on the rein to spin him, bringing up the rifle that exploded in a horrifying roar, felling the cougar and redirecting its body in a backward motion. The cat fell against the foot of the tree, twitching and writhing. After thrusting in another cartridge, Rafe fired at him again, and the cougar grew still.

He quickly reined in the horse, pulled the blanket from his pack, and spread it over Jubilee's freezing body. *Dear God, she is so cold.* He brought up her head and wrapped the quilt around her back, wondering at her injuries as he moved her. After checking the cat for life one last time, Rafe gathered her against him, then urged Horse toward the cabin, going as fast as she could bear, and prayed over her lifeless body like nobody's business.

Gaining the back yard in mere minutes, he threw his right foot over his mount's head before Horse even stopped and dismounted with her in his arms. He sprinted to the cabin, cradling his precious load. He kicked the door open and laid her on the mattress. He stacked blanket after blanket on her, then pulled a warming brick from the fireplace with a poker and wrapped it in wool, placing it next to her body under the blankets.

He looked around. What to do now? He had to get a doctor fast, but he didn't want to leave her. *Ivan.* He'd ride like the wind to Ivan and have him fetch the man. He went to her bedside, but she was still unconscious. He laid his hand on her forehead. Her skin was pale and chilled.

Decisively he turned to the door. He must get help. There was no other way. He hurried out the back door, making sure the door was secured, and prayed earnestly as he boarded his restless horse once more. He tugged the reins and directed the animal around the cabin and kicked him into a run down the driveway.

He'd just turned right as he breasted the row of trees toward town when he distinguished a whistle. Relief washed over him. Ivan, aboard his mount, approached from the north. He whispered a grateful prayer to the Lord and pulled his horse around to gallop to Ivan.

He called to him through the heavy curtain of snow as he came to a sliding stop. "Ivan. Thank God. Jubilee needs a doctor." He jerked on the reins to guide his horse back towards the cabin. "And hurry," he yelled as he was off again.

He glanced behind him long enough to see Ivan shoot toward town before the trees blocked his view. Quickly he shut the horse into the barn to give it some shelter in the freezing weather. Rafe ran through the snowflakes that had picked up again with a vengeance and Rafe sent up a quick prayer for Ivan and the doctor.

He went in and tended to the fireplace to warm up the room as much as possible and checked on Jubilee. Terror sliced through him when he discovered several lumps on her head as he probed for injuries but, other than a few scrapes and bruises, there wasn't a great deal of blood. At least the cougar hadn't injured her. He made himself settle on the chair next to her bed instead of pace. All he could do now was pray.

It seemed an eternity until Ivan brought the doctor. He offered to take care of the horse in the barn while Rafe waited for the doctor to check her. Doc was an older man, slightly balding, with spectacles. His face looked grim as he returned to Rafe, who stood beside the table. He removed his glasses and stuck them in his pocket.

"Well, hypothermia won't be what does her in," he began.

"Huh?" Rafe demanded, alarmed.

The doctor held up his arthritic hands. "Now, don't go jumping to conclusions. I meant she seems to have survived the cold fairly well. It's the head injuries and the internal injuries I can't be sure of."

Doc took a deep breath. "She has four separate knots to her head, bruising along her right ribs, and a long bruise forming across her back." He clicked his tongue. "I'd say she's probably got herself a concussion, some broken ribs, and a possible spinal injury. But that's just an educated guess, son. I can't know the extent of those injuries until she wakes up, *if* she wakes up." He mumbled the last words, but Rafe heard them.

"What can be done?" he asked hoarsely.

Doc shook his head. "Not much, and that's for sure. I'll wrap her ribs the best I can without jostling her. There's no way of knowing the extent of damage she has to her back, so there's no sense in moving her a lot. I'll give you some headache powder 'cause if she wakes, she's sure to have one humdinger of a headache."

Rafe's blood ran cold. He pushed a shaky hand through his hair.

"Best stay by her so you'll know when she rouses. She needs to drink as much liquid as she can, and start her on some broth or such once she's able." After laying out the bandages he intended to use and setting out the headache powder, he snapped his black bag shut. "That's about all that can be done."

Rafe sat heavily on the bench at the table and watched as the doctor wrapped her ribs. A numbness spread through him as Doc checked her eyes once more. The older man returned to the table to grab his bag before he pulled his coat down from the peg by the door and shrugged it on.

"I'll be by in the morning," he assured Rafe before seeing himself out.

Rafe stood and took up vigil by her bedside. Ivan came in an hour later to see if there was anything else he could do, and all Rafe could do was shake his head. Ivan assured him that he and Elsa would be praying, and that he'd stop by the following day.

After he left, the cabin became so still and hot. He reached up and smoothed the hair from her forehead. *Dear Lord, why was the woman in that tree?* He parked his elbows on his knees and leaned his face into his hands. And he prayed. He prayed with all his might, well into the night. And somewhere toward dawn, he laid his head against the mattress and fell asleep.

Rafe gave a startled jerk and woke himself. He was bent over with his head pillowed on the bed. *What awakened me?* Something stirred his hair. He jerked his head upright and met Jubilee's dark gaze, dull with pain, her hand resting near where his head had been. Moisture filled his eyes, and he broke into a slight grin.

"Good morning," he said softly.

She blinked slowly and licked her lips.

"Here, let me get you a drink."

He scrambled around the room, searching out a glass and the water bucket. She sipped the water as he supported her head.

"How are you feeling?" He set the cup down on the small table near the bed.

She swallowed and shut her eyes for a moment, and Rafe feared she'd gone back to sleep. But then her eyelids fluttered open.

"I...hurt..." Her voice rasped.

"Where?" He clutched her hand.

A flash of pain shot across her face. "Everywhere."

Rafe nodded. "Doc said you had several bruises and bumps to the head. I can give you some of Doc's headache medicine."

She closed her eyes once more and answered without opening them. "No...just...too...tired."

Her expression relaxed, and he thought she'd drifted off to sleep, until she mumbled in nearly unintelligible words. "The snow was...pretty."

A sad smile quirked across Rafe's mouth. He longed to draw her up and hold her until the hurt went away, but he knew he'd best leave her to rest. He leaned back in the chair, thanking God she'd awakened. He closed his eyes and tried to get comfortable, a warm rush of relief seeping through his body. He'd need his rest so he'd be alert when she revived again.

But it was Ivan who woke him next. His friend took care of the morning chores in the barn. At the door of the cabin, Rafe realized in the clear, cold of the early dawn that six inches of snow covered the landscape. Doc Adams showed up thirty minutes later in a sleigh and, to Rafe's relief, Jubilee's eyes opened for the second time. He hovered close by as Doc leaned to examine her and to ask several questions. Finally, Doc stood and fixed his gaze on his patient.

CHAPTER TWENTY-EIGHT

"Well, little lady, you've got a concussion and a couple of broken ribs, not to mention bumps and bruises here and there, that are bound to be sore for several weeks. You need to stay in bed for at least the next week or two. Get up and stretch a bit when you can. Bending over will probably be painful, so my advice is, if it hurts, don't do it. No lifting anything heavier than a cup of milk." He turned to Rafe. "I'll leave you something for the pain, and I'll be back to check on her tomorrow."

Doc walked to the table and Rafe stared at Jubilee, who drifted off to sleep. The sound of the door opening brought him out of his thoughts. He turned and darted out the door, closing it with a soft click.

"Wait. What about her back, Doc?" Fear sliced through him as ominous possibilities haunted his mind. Doc set his black bag down on the sleigh's seat before he answered.

"She feels her toes and can move her extremities. All good signs everything's fine. Since she's conscious this morning, I figured her injuries weren't as serious as what I initially thought. You baby her for several weeks, because she's in for some pain while she heals."

Rafe nodded, his tightened muscles relaxing a bit, and he waved to Doc as he pulled away from the house. Rafe murmured in the cold, "Thanks for the miracle, Lord."

The next week and a half, Rafe spent most of his time waiting on a groggy Jubilee, cooking, cleaning, and sleeping on a pallet of quilts by the front door. Thanksgiving came and was a quiet affair. Elsa brought turkey and fixings, yet Jubilee, propped in bed, ate only a few bites. Slowly but surely, she started moving around the cabin. She was silent for the most part, and Rafe blamed the discomfort of healing.

He set a bowl of his poor excuse for oatmeal in front of Jubilee before attempting a conversation. "Christmas will be here in a couple of weeks."

Her head shot up. "What?"

He chuckled softly. "Christmas."

Her mouth fell open and she fixed her eyes on the wall in front of her. When she spoke, her words were a whisper. "What's today?

Rafe's brows drew together. "It's the seventh. December seventh."

He stared at her as her face turned sheet-white. Jubilee's throat worked convulsively a couple of times before she stood up, knocking the bench to the floor with a crack.

"Jubilee?" He rushed to her side. "What wrong? Are you sick?"

* * *

Jubilee closed her eyes for a long moment. How she longed to bolt from the room, but she could barely stand and toddle across the floor without pain radiating from her back and chest. Instead, she forced herself to move out from behind the table. In moments Rafe appeared, his hand on her arm, pulling the bench out of the way. She froze.

"Stop, Rafe. I'm not a child. I can walk to the bed." Her voice was pure ice.

He let go and swiped his hand on the nape of his neck. She ambled to the other side of the room and struggled into bed, trying to keep the expressions of agony from flitting over her face.

"I'm going for a walk." His heels pounded a beat to the door. He grabbed his coat from the peg and yanked the door open.

Jubilee panted in the bed, covered with a thin sheen of the sweat of struggle, thankful he'd left, yet moisture sprang to her eyes. Rosemary would be here anytime. Perhaps even today. Tears that had begun in her pain now flowed from a heart of misery.

Her thoughts shamed her. What must he think of her, running to the woods and hiding in a tree like some child? She could barely lift her eyes to look at him, at his face so set and stern. However, he'd waited on her hand and foot during the last two and a half weeks. How he must hate her. The claw marks she'd discovered on her skirt indicated more had occurred than even she knew. She cringed, trying to remember her fall. She recalled the snow and turning cold and sleepy. After that...nothing.

Yes, this physical pain was overwhelming, and intercepting Rosemary's love letter pure agony. But the greatest torture would be when he returned to the cabin, picked up his blankets and belongings, and turned his back on her.

* * *

Rafe quietly pushed the door shut, threw his coat on, and set out. He shoved his hands in his pockets with frustration.

They still hadn't discussed the reason she'd climbed that tree in the first place. A cloudy fog preceded him as he exhaled into the freezing air. His chest tightened and he clenched his cold hands in his pockets. He'd thought the night they'd shared would solidify them into a couple at last, but that hadn't happened. In fact, she'd drifted farther away. Jubilee barely acknowledged him, refused to meet his gaze, and hardly spoke two words to him. She slept so much. There had to be some explanation. Maybe her injuries were more serious than Doc thought. Rafe missed the spring in her step, but mostly worried about the lack of hope in her eyes.

Rafe lifted his head and found himself in the very woods where he'd discovered Jubilee. With a gruff sigh, he wandered through, soon in sight of the tree from which she'd fallen. The cougar carcass at the foot of the trunk had disintegrated to just a few bones and a skull. A large amount of the snow had melted, and the landscape appeared grey and rust from the leaves littering the ground. He kicked at a mound of them, and the light breeze tossed them in a flurry of brown with chunks of snow. A larger white object grabbed his attention. *What in the world is that?* The wind whipped the slip of paper away, and he gave chase until he finally captured it.

He pressed the sheet open and searched the faded letters across the page. The flowing script was difficult to decipher.

He studied it for a long while, trying to make out the words. At last, he shook his head. There was a five, he was sure of that. He squinted at the missive, and a sudden recognition of the flowing slant of the letters sent a chill through him. This was Rosemary's writing. But this wasn't the letter he'd received. His freezing fingers held up the paper to squint at the signature in the low winter light. Satisfied the signature said 'Rosemary' at the bottom, he stuffed the offending material into his pocket.

How had this gotten out here? And why hadn't he received it? His head jerked toward the cabin as a theory percolated in his mind. *Jubilee.* Was this note the reason she'd run and hidden, or had she fled because of the cougar as he'd assumed? He deliberated through the painful events of the day after he'd spent a glorious night in Jubilee's bed. The Larssons had arrived to butcher hogs, an arrangement he'd totally forgotten, and he and Jubilee had been thrown for a loop. They'd overslept, leaving the chores undone. But none of this explained how Jubilee had received this letter. Had Elsa brought it?

He strode toward the cabin, then stopped. If he burst into the cabin, talking all kind of gibberish about this, and not one iota proved true…well, it would have disastrous results. He took a deep breath. He'd go talk to Elsa first. Back at the barn after a brisk hike, Rafe saddled the horse in no time.

* * *

Elsa looked at him coolly from the door. Rafe's face was chapped from the cold, but he wasn't planning on staying long.

"You ask much questions, Rafe. Jubilee might not like again I tell you."

"Please, Elsa. I've got to know if you delivered any letters to Jubilee that day." At Elsa's pursing of her stubborn lips, he decided to spill the beans. "Look, Elsa, I love Jubilee and I need to understand how this happened."

Her eyes studied his for a moment. "Yah, two."

Nodding his head and yelling his thanks, he bolted for the horse. His heart soared all the way back to the house. Perhaps now they'd get everything straightened out. What had he been thinking by not telling her about his ex-fiancée's silly letter? He simply hadn't told her because Rosemary meant nothing to him. Why, he'd recognized his love for Jubilee months ago. Rosemary's problems were Dale's. Not his. Now he'd calmly explain everything to Jubilee. Then he'd finally take the chance and bare his heart. He'd tell her that he loved her.

* * *

"I'm so glad you're feeling better," Esther chimed, setting the dried-peach pie on the table. "We've been praying up a storm for you, little lady, haven't we, hon?

Pastor Barnett nodded with a kind smile, settling his lanky body on the bench across from Jubilee.

"I baked you and Rafe a chicken in the big roaster pot. I know your man has been taking care of you, so I thought I'd help out a bit." She sat at the table next to Jubilee, who was wrapped in a quilt. Esther patted her hand. "I can tell you're right suffering, poor girl."

A sob rose in her throat and she wished Miss Esther wouldn't be so kind. It tore down her weak defenses plumb quick.

"I'm fine, really." But the words came out riding a bubble of hysteria.

"Oh, hon." Esther wrapped her arms about her.

Jubilee cried and rested her head on the table, yet the comfort of the woman's embrace enveloped her.

"Why don't you go check the livestock, Raymond?" Esther murmured to her husband.

Jubilee kept her head down, hearing the door open softly before closing again.

"You poor dear. You poor, poor thing," Esther crooned, stroking her hair.

Never had anyone consoled her with such compassion, and a fresh wave of tears trickled down her cheeks. Jubilee raised her head and peered at Esther through disheveled hair.

"Please let me go home with you." Oh, she'd stored those words in her heart for so long. For years she'd hoped to say them to an adoptive family as the time passed at the orphan's society, and now she hated uttering them.

Surprise shot across Esther's face, and then concern. "Hon, what are you talking about?"

Jubilee shook her head in misery. "I won't be able to bear it, I know I won't."

Esther smoothed the hair from her face and cupped her cheeks in her hands. "What, sweet girl? What are you talking about?

"Rafe. He's going to leave me."

Silence reigned. Esther searched her eyes. "He's told you he's leaving?"

Jubilee's chin quivered. "I…I just know."

Esther pulled her hands from her cheeks before putting her right one to Jubilee's forehead. She arranged the quilt around her quivering body. "Let's get you in bed."

Anguish weighted every step as she trudged across the floorboards. Esther fussed over her and straightened the covers while Jubilee settled back onto the mountain of pillows. The older woman returned to the table to fetch a book before settling in the chair next to her bed.

"Listen to me, Jubilee. I don't know a lot about you, but I know you were an orphan child. You grew up not depending on a great deal of folks, which left a scar of distrust on your heart." Esther's weathered eyes were blue pools. "But you've got to open yourself to the Lord and allow him to take the heartache away."

She patted the book in her lap and a small smile lit her wrinkled face. "Proverbs 3:5-6 says, 'Trust in the Lord with all your heart and lean not on your own understanding. In all your ways acknowledge Him and He shall direct thy paths.'"

Jubilee swallowed a rising sob and blinked the tears from her eyes as she thought of Sarah's sampler. The stitched verse constantly mocked her from its lofty spot above the fireplace and her gaze flicked to it. "Scripture doesn't always come true."

Esther snorted. "The Lord's words aren't fairy tales, hon. They're promises from an all-powerful God. And God keeps every single one. He may not answer the way we figured, or in the manner we plan, but he most certainly fulfills every vow."

Esther pressed the book into Jubilee's palms. The leather-bound volume and Esther's comforting hands clasping hers warmed her soul.

"No matter what happens," Esther whispered, "God will take care of you."

Jubilee's mouth parted and her heart swelled. Could the answer be so easy? No, of course it wouldn't be easy. But it'd be bearable. Understanding flooded her soul. Suddenly Esther's words were clear. Yes, with God's help, she could endure Rafe's departure.

At that moment, the thunder of hooves sounded from the front yard.

"You think on what I said and read the good book." Esther squeezed Jubilee's shoulder before setting off to answer the door.

CHAPTER TWENTY-NINE

"Fire. Fire at the church. Hurry, Pastor," young Patrick Riley yelled from the back of his horse.

The yell echoed into the cabin with a blast of chilly air and Jubilee rose up in bed.

At the door, Esther caught her breath before grabbing her cloak. "Oh, my glory."

"We'll be right there." Pastor Barnett's voice was louder now as he called from the porch. "Hurry, Patrick, and tell the neighbors. We're going to need lots of help.

"They've already started a bucket brigade, Pastor."

"Good. We gotta go, Esther."

"I'm sorry, dear. It's an emergency. Please forgive us." Esther swung the black wool cloak around her shoulders and picked up her empty basket from the table. She hurried to the bed and leaned down to hug Jubilee and kiss her cheek. "Please be praying...about everything."

"I will."

The door closed, and Jubilee slid to her knees beside her bed.

* * *

"They need everyone's help." Patrick was off like a shot aboard his quick Morgan pony.

Rafe urged his own mount to a gallop and covered the ground to his home in a matter of minutes. Once at the cabin, he slid from the horse and burst through the door. Jubilee knelt beside her bed and alarm jangled his nerves. "Jubilee?"

"I'm fine." She struggled to a standing position before he could assist her. "You've got to get to the church."

A million thoughts raced through his head and he searched her tear-streaked face. So much to say, but this crisis left so little time. His arms ached to gather her to him, his lips longed to press against her ear to whisper endearments. Plus, there were countless things to discuss and restore. But these matters would have to wait. Mutely, he nodded and made for the door. He caught her words as he pulled the door shut.

"I'll be praying."

* * *

The next two and a half weeks disappeared in a flurry of cleaning the charred mess that had been the church. The people of the surrounding community rallied around the tragedy and donated the necessary building materials in a matter of days. Rafe and the men of the church were determined to raise the new structure before Christmas, and celebrate the sacred holiday within its fresh walls.

Rafe, Ivan, and several other men stayed nights at the Barnetts. They rose in the dark of early morning and worked throughout the day until well past nightfall, lighting the area with lanterns. Ladies of the church took turns checking on and preparing meals for Jubilee, and Elsa and little Britta became a permanent fixture at the Tanner cabin.

By the 24th, the men had accomplished their goal. The new church graced the landscape where only burnt ruins had been. On the last day, the men joined forces to pick up the tools and scraps of wood scattered across the frozen terrain.

When they had finished, Ivan, fatigue outlining every crevice of his face, clapped a thick, chapped hand on Rafe's shoulder. "What say ve go home, yah?"

Rafe filled his lungs with icy air and grinned as he skimmed his eyes over the clean new building, bald without a coat of paint. That'd have to wait for warmer weather. "I'm all in, my friend. Let's go."

Arriving at home, he stabled Horse while Ivan collected his wife and daughter from the cabin. As Rafe hiked from the barn, his friend tied his horse to the back of the wagon. Rafe approached and shook his hand.

"Be seeing ya." Rafe grinned.

Ivan smiled and nodded his bushy head before gesturing towards the cabin. "You treat woman right, yah?"

Rafe chuckled and nodded. He had no idea.

Ivan leaped to the driver's seat and the Larrson's wagon jolted into motion. Rafe waved as they disappeared through the trees. He turned and exhaustion transformed into anticipation. *Finally.* He hadn't had Jubilee to himself since the day the church had burnt. Now he was going to lay it on the line.

He took a deep breath and strode to the door, great purpose dogging his step. Hope rose in his gut. *His wife.* She was completely his wife. And now, with God's guidance, they'd build a life together.

He swung the door open with a smile and a gleam in his eye. Sunlight lit the floorboards before him like a beam, outlining his beloved. Jubilee knelt on her hands and knees, retching into a bucket by her bedside. Disappointment stabbed him, and the smile slid from his face. Unease shot through his brain as he covered the distance with swift strides and stooped at her side.

"No." Jubilee's voice came out in a groan. "Leave me."

She dipped her head to choke into the bucket again.

Rafe rose and grabbed a towel before kneeling beside her once more. "I'm not leaving you, woman. You're sick."

Jubilee settled back against the side of the bed on the cold, wooden floor, and he reached to wipe her face. Fear curdled his stomach. Her face was pale with pain, and sweat beaded on her forehead and upper lip. She looked so weary as she rested her head against the bed, her eyes shut. *Why didn't Elsa tell me she was still ill?*

"Let's get you back into bed." He reached for her.

She lifted a limp hand to fend him off.

Rafe pulled away and stood. He studied her face as tears gathered in the corners of her closed eyes.

"Are you hurting?" he asked, wondering what damage the vomiting had done to her healing ribs.

She nodded, weeping silently. He drew the covers in one motion and leaned to gather her carefully into his arms.

"Jubilee, you need to be in the bed. I know you don't want me to move you, but I'll be as gentle as I can."

He lifted her, drawing a gasp of pain from her lips. With great care, he laid her petite form on the mattress, smoothed the white gown, and covered her with blankets. His hand sought her forehead and, thankfully, she wasn't feverish.

"I'm going to get, Doc." He grabbed the bucket to dump it at the outhouse.

"No," she said faintly as he pulled the back door open.

"Yes." His voice booked no argument.

After returning, he made her as comfortable as possible with a clean bucket, a drink of water, and a fresh towel before tucking the quilts around her.

Outside, he jogged to the barn and mounted the horse in no time, heading for town. The cold weather trips were grueling on his mount, so he left the animal at the stable for a good rubdown while he strode to Doc's office on Main Street. It wasn't long before they headed out to the cabin in Doc's buggy, with Horse, now well groomed, tethered to the back.

Rafe waited anxiously as Doc bent over Jubilee and finally could stand it no more. He exited and paced the front yard, stopping every few moments to glare at the door before running his eyes over the dormant fields, frozen in crystalized mounds.

Doc's lengthy examination sent frustration careening though him, so he headed for the barn. What was he doing in there? Did the sickness originate from her injuries or something worse, like cholera, or the flu? He'd no sooner opened the barn door when he heard the cabin door shut behind him. He spun to see Doc pulling his long overcoat about him on the porch. Rafe sprinted back.

Great puffs of fog poured from Rafe's throat in the frosty air. "What's wrong?"

"Huh…" Doc muttered then grunted. "Oh. Ain't nothing wrong with her. Her ribs are still sore, sorer now, I reckon, with all that retching. But she'll be fine."

"What do you mean?" Rafe demanded, throwing his hands out. "She's sick, Doc. I brought you here to tell me what's wrong with her."

A slow smile spread across Doc's face at Rafe's indignation.

"She ain't sick, son. She's expecting," he grunted, one bushy brow elevated.

"She's expecting? She's expecting…" Rafe's next word was going to be 'what?' when dawning overcame him.

Doc let out a caw of laughter and slapped his leg in merriment.

"I begun to wonder if you was a little slow." Doc smirked with a huge grin while Rafe blinked in surprise.

He dropped his eyes to the ground and slowly brought them back up to Doc's.

"When…when…when's it due?"

Another smile crinkled across the old doctor's face. "Son, you ain't that green. 'Bout eight months."

Doc adjusted his hold on the black bag, stepped down the stairs, and walked to his parked rig. Rafe stood rooted to the spot, barely perceiving the sounds of Doc's departing wagon, the wheels crunching over the hard frozen ground.

Another of Doc's guffaws filtered back to Rafe, shaking him loose of his state of shock. Swallowing, he climbed the stairs and quietly opened the door to the cabin. To his relief and disappointment, Jubilee was asleep. It taxed his self-control to back up to the bench alongside the table to sit and wait.

His mouth still hung open, he realized, and he shut it with a snap. She slept so peacefully now, snuggled under the blankets, her face toward him. No wonder Doc had thought he had a screw loose. He shook his head. *A baby...his child.*

He rose and walked closer to the bed. His eyes roved the face that had become so precious to him. Such a powerful love clamped his heart, it almost suffocated him. He longed to stroke back the dark strands hovering near her cheek, ached for those deep, haunting eyes to open and fill with love.

She'd captivated him from the first moment he'd seen her. She been so abused and misused, yet so innocent and lost. An intense rush of protectiveness rose in his gut. *Oh, God. Be*

347

here, in the center of our marriage. Help me tell her my heart.
He closed his eyes as his throat tightened with emotion. *God, bless our union.*

Rafe stood a long while, gazing upon her until the animals put up such a racket he realized it was evening feeding time. Reluctant to pull his gaze from her in case she somehow disappeared, he rose silently and went to his chores.

* * *

Jubilee's eyes flitted open and she took a deep breath. Thankful the nausea had passed, she stared at the ceiling for a moment. With a sigh, she nibbled her lip. When Rafe left, she'd have a baby to care for. It'd seemed like such a wonderful idea. But now, having experienced the weakness that had settled on her this morning, she knew supporting a baby on her own would be next to impossible. Tears formed in her eyes, and she began to pray, her lips forming the words as tiny indistinguishable whispers came from her. *Trust in the Lord with all your heart...*

"Jubilee?" Rafe's voice, low and questioning, seemed very close.

She gasped and turned her head to find him sitting in a chair not two feet from the bed.

"What do you need? Are you sick again?" He handed her a hanky to wipe her eyes. "Can I do anything to help?"

She struggled to sit up, her ribs causing a moan to escape. His big, gentle hands slid under her arms and pulled her up and forward against his chest. Her face nuzzled his neck, and her heart thudded as she drew in his scent. He adjusted the pillows to support her and laid her cautiously against them. His face was just inches from hers, and her cheeks heated at his close scrutiny.

"Can you talk?" His brows lowered.

Jubilee shook her head slightly to clear it. How could she speak with him so near? She wanted to throw herself at him, promise all kinds of outlandish things, if he'd only stay. Her unnatural feebleness tamped down the urge, but her throat swelled and she swallowed. "Of course I can talk."

He drew away, scanned her face, and adjusted the covers before settling back in the chair. His knee pressed against the bed, and Jubilee glanced sideways at him. The fear she'd once held for him had completely evaporated. Instead, adoration and admiration filled her soul. His size, which at one time had intimidated her, now instilled protectiveness. How she ached to feel the shelter of his muscled arms around her. Clenching her hands, she ripped her mind from these thoughts before she dissolved into tears and climbed into his lap.

"How long have you been there?" she questioned quietly.

He shrugged. "A while. Are you feeling better?"

She nodded and placed a hand to her flat belly and inhaled. A child grew within her. Rafe's child. Would this baby have golden locks and eyes of emerald? Rational thought returned as the silence lengthened and, sensing his gaze on her every movement, she snatched her hand away.

"Are you thinking about the baby?" His voice was gentle.

She gasped and turned her face fully toward him. "You know?"

He nodded. Her head throbbed, and a sob worked its way from her stomach. *Trust, trust.* After a couple of jerky breaths, she covered her mouth with her hand. He rose and massaged her shoulders.

"No," she choked. "Please."

His touch awoke a longing that would never be fulfilled, and his tenderness all but scalded her skin. Tears cascaded down her face and his weight pressed on the bed next to her. She twisted from him. *Oh, I love this man.* It rocked her soul, and encompassed her being. How many times had she dreamed of running her hands through his blond hair and pressing her lips to his, whispering the depths of her love? He shifted closer and his leg pressed against hers, and memories of their night of passion flooded her thoughts. How would she let him go?

Oh, dear God. Help me bear what he's about to say.

CHAPTER THIRTY

Rafe gathered Jubilee in his arms, crooning and stroking her hair. He stifled plans of revealing his love, and his heart thundered with impatience. He wasn't sure what was going on. Was she in pain, or upset about the baby?

"It's all right, Jubilee, you'll see. A child will be such a blessing. I understand you're weak now, but you've time to heal before the baby comes. Besides, I'll be here to help in any way, I promise." He breathed in the lilac scent of her hair and his stomach knotted.

Suddenly, with great strength, she wrung free of his embrace and turned to him with red, tear-streaked cheeks. "You can't be much help if you're not *here*."

Rafe drew back, still gripping her upper arms, his brows crinkling. "What are you talking about?"

Jubilee inhaled stuttering breaths, shoulders heaving. "She's coming."

Rafe grimaced and brought his hands up to capture her face. "Who? Rosemary?"

Attempting to pull from him, she nodded as tears washed her cheeks.

Rafe gave a small gruff laugh. "Let her come. No skin off my nose."

Jubilee's dark eyes flew open, and her sobs slowed. His hands slid down and covered hers clutching the blanket. She blinked at him.

"There was a letter, wasn't there?" His tone grew hushed, while he searched her eyes.

"Yes." Jubilee's voice wobbled.

"And she's on her way here, right?" He narrowed his eyes, and fear lit Jubilee's face. "And it doesn't mean a hill of beans to me. I'll be glad to send her packing, because I'm already holding the hands of the woman I love."

Jubilee gasped. "What?"

Rafe grinned, a gleam dancing in his eyes. "I said *you're* the woman I love. I want to live here, with you, in this cabin, and have lots of babies and grandbabies, and sit in that swing holding your hand through it all, come sunshine or rain…if the Lord lets me."

Her eyes widened, and she opened her mouth to speak, but no sound came.

"Jubilee?" He raised a brow.

She freed her hand of his and gripped his bicep. "Are you…sure?"

"Glory, woman. What more can I say?" Ardor flamed within him as he drew her closer. "Jubilee, you need to talk to me. I understand you're working through a lot of pain from your past. If you need some time, I'll be glad to court you. We'll take all the time you need, I'll move back to the barn and we'll go slow. We'll…"

"I love you, Rafe," New tears rimmed her eyes.

His speech halted and his gaze sought hers hungrily. As he studied her, his grin appeared and grew. She wiped away the moisture, and her mouth parted with wonder into a shy smile.

He chuckled. "You sure know how to scare a fella."

Sobering, he pulled her into a gentle embrace and laid a soft lingering kiss on her lips before pressing his forehead to hers. "Can I retract the part about moving to the barn?"

She gave a giggle-hiccup, and they laughed together. Quietness grew between them as he rubbed her back with his hands, feeling her relax under his touch. Her arms crept along his shoulders and she touched the hair at his neck. When she spoke, it was in hushed amazement.

"I can't believe this is happening. God drew us together in the strangest of ways, Rafe. Everywhere I went His Word promised His love and guidance. Esther helped me realize I'd stopped trusting Him, how I'd also quit believing in everyone around me...like you. I realize now He's always there, helping me endure the hardest of times, guiding me to a better place. Sarah's sampler of God's promise *is true*. He restored me to a family, to a home of my own—our own."

He nodded and caressed her cheek. "When Rosemary left, I vowed never to marry. I thought I was heartbroken. I moved here with plans to start farming. But I bumped into a petite little snag when I arrived."

Their gazes met as he pulled the leather strap from her hair and ran his fingers through her thick locks. His eyes slid closed in pleasure. He opened them and winked at her, his lips twitching. Their gaze intensified. "A few days later I found myself married to you, thinking I'd solved not only my problem but yours. It was a nice little business arrangement, or so I thought.

By the time we'd returned home from my parents' house, I realized the truth. My feelings for you had nothing to do with business. Then the whole misunderstanding about...babies.

God must have a sense of humor, watching me trying to fix everything myself." Rafe cradled her face, pushing away the stray strands of dark hair, reveling in their closeness. His eyes softened with love and his lips quirked into a smile. "We've a lot to talk about, you and I."

"Yes." Awe and adoration filled her face.

"Merry Christmas, Jubilee."

She tilted her head and smiled, while a charming pinkness colored her cheeks. "Merry Christmas, Rafe. My, what a year it's been."

His eyes grew hooded as he memorized every feature of his beautiful wife's face. "A year of Jubilee."

"Yes." Her words were a rush of air. They exhaled together, their breath intermingling as their faces drew closer. Heat shimmered between them. "We've so much to talk about…later."

Their lips met on a sigh.

* * *

Rosemary never appeared. A letter came two weeks later from Dale, asking Rafe and Jubilee's forgiveness for Rosemary's letters. Despite Jubilee's new resolve to trust God more, a great sense of relief entered her heart.

Eight months later, Lathan Rafe Tanner arrived with Doc's skillful care and was laid in his father's arms. Jubilee gave a tired grin when Doc chuckled over the amazed expression on Rafe's face. The sunlight through the window lit the golden hair upon the baby's head.

"I can't cotton to how such a greenhorn is going to take care of a son." Doc grunted as he snapped his black bag shut and wiped the sweat from his brow. He motioned to Jubilee, who could barely tear her eyes from the vision of her husband cuddling his newborn. "You'll have to guide him along, you know."

She gave the good doctor a benevolent smile, and a soft laugh. "Doc, I don't know one thing about a baby. All I know is, I was a lost, hurting orphan, and God blessed me with a family and restored my life. If God can do that, He can help Rafe do anything."

As he ran his wrinkled hand through his gray hair, Doc nodded. "Reckon I can't argue with that."

About the Author~

Peggy Trotter's a small town Hoosier native who writes ransomed-ever-after Christian fiction/Romance that is real, raw and redeeming. When she's not crafting or DIY-ing, (or combing the house for one of her twenty pairs of cheaters) she's immersed in a story scene of some sort, always pushing toward that sigh-worthy, happily-ever-after ending with juyst a dash of heat.

Winner of the prestigious ACFW Genesis Award, she flip-flops from historical to contemporary. But ultimately, it's always about incredible characters and story lines that reveal God's guiding providence and unending love.

She has two amazing grown children, two terrific children-in-laws, and four unbelievably fantabulous grandchildren, who deserve way more than the average amount of adjectives and adverbs. Her Batman of 39 years, whose cape is much worn from rescuing his wife from one scrap or another, is the delight of her life. She's a smoldering pot of determined discombobulation who, by the grace of God, occasionally pulls it together to appear in public as a normal confident woman while privately craving a few hermit hours to woo the printed word.

Find Peggy all around the web and sign up for her newsletter:

peggytrotter.com

peggytrotter.blogspot.com

diamondsinfiction.blogspot.com

Twitter: https://twitter.com/Peggy_Trotter

Facebook: https://www.facebook.com/PeggyTrotterAuthor

Goodreads:

https://www.goodreads.com/author/show/13778873.Peggy_Trotter

Amazon Author's Profile Page:
amazon.com/author/peggytrotter.com
Instagram: https://www.instagram.com/peggy_trotter_author/
Pinterest: https://www.pinterest.com/PeggyTrotterAuthor/
LinkedIn: https://www.linkedin.com/in/peggy-trotter-44a29b95/
BookBub: https://www.bookbub.com/authors/peggy-trotter
MeWe: mewe.com/i/peggytrotter
Parler: https://parler.com/profile/PeggyTrotterAuthor
Usa.life: https://usa.life/PeggyTrotterAuthor
Gab: https://gab.com/PeggyTrotterAuthor

Dear Reader:

Thank you for reading *Year of Jubilee*. Please enjoy a sample of one of my Contemporary Christian Books *Reviving Jules*. Browse through all my books @ https://www.amazon.com/stores/Peggy-Trotter/author/B00V15P2LU

Chapter One

The house completely sucked. Which made it perfect.

Jules Summers breathed in the stale air of the vacant living room, her gaze flitting from the water-stained wooden floors to the white walls riddled with nail holes. A large black spider suspended in a cloud of an intricate web drew her eye to the upper corner near the ceiling.

Yes, perfect.

The realtor beamed, flipped her bobbed hair, and pushed the ill-fitted door shut. "Well, I know you're interested in renting only, but I give everyone the same tour, just in case you change your mind."

Jules released a pent up breath and kept her face expressionless. The slender woman in the navy pantsuit continued as if Jules had gushed with interest. The realtor approached and pressed a fact sheet into her fingers before gesturing to the expanse before them.

"The open concept here of the living/dining areas is quite convenient for entertaining. The wood floor is original and would be gorgeous if one took a little time to resurface it."

Jules ignored her and walked to the left where the sunlight streamed through the double-glass doors facing the backyard. The woman continued to talk, referring to her property hot sheet. Amy? Was that her name? Jules sighed and glanced at the paper she held. Did it matter?

"Built in 1951, it's a classic jewel—solid. There're plenty of cabinets, and all a person needs is a fresh coat of paint to perk them right up. They're charming, really. Retro, even. The appliances stay." She tapped a silver monstrosity sandwiched between bottom cabinets. "I think this oven might be a collector's item. Irreplaceable. Now, if you'll step down the hall with me, you'll see the two bedrooms."

"I'll take it."

The woman froze in mid-step and shot her a glance. "I'm sorry?"

Jules shifted her weight and pushed her empty hand into her jeans' pocket. "When can I move in?"

Amy's eyebrows lifted before her lips stretched into a small smile, and she nodded toward the back of the house. "Wouldn't you like to check out the bedrooms first?"

"No."

Her hands flew up. "Oh. Well, let's see."

She strode to the Formica-flecked counter, opened her briefcase, and rifled through the interior pockets. Jules turned to study the tall tufts of uneven grass spread across the backyard.

"I can set you up in a jiffy. You won't be disappointed. This is an older home, but Mrs. Kissel took excellent care of it. Her son owns the house now and lives in Florida. He'll be thrilled to have a dependable person here. And I'm sure he'll be more than willing to sell it to you. This property has been sitting since his mother passed."

Jules cleared her throat but continued to stare at the overgrown yard. "Right now, I just want to rent."

For the first time since meeting the chatty little saleswoman, silence reigned. Jules took a deep breath and peered through her reflection in the glass to a neglected goldfish pond amongst the weeds. The hairs on her neck prickled, and she sensed the woman's perusal.

"You'll love it here. Great neighborhood." The realtor paused. "You have family nearby?"

Tears rushed to Jules' eyes. "No."

Amy gave a soft laugh. "Well, you'll soon feel at home in this tiny community. Most folks' families have lived here for years. You from a small town?"

Jules clenched her jaw to staunch the moisture threatening to spill. "No."

"Really? Ah, there it is. All right, if you could fill out this form, including references, I can get you in here by the end of the week."

Jules blinked away the wetness on her lashes and forced herself toward the counter dividing the living space from the kitchen. She picked up the pen to fill in the appropriate information, cringing at the reference section. The ball point hovered above the blanks.

Amy threaded her dark hair behind her ears and shot her a smile. She snapped the briefcase closed. "I'm going to make a quick call to the office while you're finishing. If you need anything, just holler. I'll be right outside."

The realtor's heels clicked a victory chant as she marched through the living room. Relief washed over Jules as the woman tugged the door closed behind her. She took a deep breath and stretched her tense shoulders. After laying the pen across the document, she cracked her knuckles and pressed her clasped hands to her lips. Who could she put down? Who'd be discreet and help her get this house without spilling the whole scenario?

Moisture flowed to her lids again, and she stabbed her fists into her eye sockets. Those blasted tears. Blinking, she sucked air through her nostrils and expelled a quivering breath. Somebody, anybody. No, not *anybody*.

Maybe someone from church? School? No, not anyone from the neighborhood. She chewed her lip, her ears picking up the mumble of Amy's voice on the front porch. The realtor's dark shadow paced past the picture window. She didn't have forever. *Make the decision.*

She settled on an old teacher friend who'd moved away a few years ago, and Mr. Slatton, a previous pastor from happier times. Hopefully, no one would think to contact either of them for news of her. Her pen grated against the page as she scratched the information down. She groaned when she proofread, her penmanship nearly illegible. With disgust, she slapped the form to the counter.

Tilting her chin, she blinked at the discolored ceiling tile and rubbed the wetness from her eyes. She wandered back to the smudged glass of the sliding door. How different things seemed. A weight settled on her sagging shoulders, and she crossed her arms to ease it. But it didn't. It only made the stress on the inside bind up into a cluster of knots until breathing became difficult.

Please let her hurry.

The door swung open. "Super. All is settled at the office, and I spoke with Todd Kissel, the owner, so everything's a go. Now, I just need your application to get started on the references, and you've got yourself a house."

Jules nodded and heard her swipe the paper from the countertop. While she waited, her gaze swept the outdated exterior aluminum window canopies, once burgundy and white, now faded pink. The fresh spring air gusted, sending several grey paint chips astir across the small back porch.

"Everything looks good here. Is there anything else you need to see? Bathroom, garage, shed?"

Jules spun on her heel. "No. I'm fine."

The woman's face lit into a well-practiced grin, and she came forward, hand extended. "Great. I'll get this processed and give you a call tomorrow to pick up your key. I hope you'll be very happy here."

Jules attempted a smile, hoping the twitch of her lips qualified, as she shook the woman's hand.

* * *

Jules groaned and rolled over on the air mattress. The first night in her new home. The musty smell caused her to sneeze.

364

She focused her aching eyeballs on the clock. 5:02. Tears hovered in her scratchy eyes. She flipped over and willed herself back to sleep.

The blanket slid from her face, and light flared against her closed lids. She grimaced, squinting at the glass doors. Where was she? Recognition dawned and her gaze flicked to the red digital numbers. 8:28. Tears emerged to course down her cheeks. If only she could sleep away the next year. Or two. Or three. Anguish seemed a constant companion. A sob rose, and her throat throbbed. She buried her head under the velour blanket and clutched her pillow to her face.

Jules' eyelids blinked open, and she uncovered one eye to read the clock. After ten. Again, tears threatened. Would she ever awaken without an episode of weeping?

She clenched her hands and pushed to a sitting position. Her hair wrapped about her head like seaweed. Sunshine poured through the glass doors in a cheerful greeting, and she groaned and squeezed her eyes shut. Moisture flowed down her face again, and she let her tears spill, her breath coming in spasms.

"Stop," she yelled to the empty living room. Catching sight of the lone lawn chair sitting next to the mattress caused her lips to quiver again, but she balled her fists. Enough was enough.

She needed a plan. A goal to strive towards. First, she'd *get* out of bed. Second, a shower, no questions, no excuses. Next, she'd drive the jeep to the grocery store. Fresh donuts beckoned. Well, fresh from the donut shop in Evansville, thirty minutes away.

She'd purchase the donuts, her favorite super-charged caffeinated soda, and a paper. Such a healthy breakfast. Then she'd call her daughter. End of story. This was the plan. A sob rose while a balloon of pain bloated in her chest. Now, how to rally the desire to leave the bed?

The stagnant air tickled her nose, and she scrubbed at it. She shot a glance around the living room where she'd inflated the mattress. Her attention flicked to the glass doors, her only balm. The early spring sunshine cascaded through and warmed her mattress. She sighed and thrust her fingertips into her eyes to stem the moisture. *No more crying.*

Her stomach growled and a cramp clenched her abdomen like an exclamation point of hunger. With a sniff, Jules crawled off the air mattress onto the chilly, stained floor planks and followed her plan to a tee, ignoring her drawn face in the steamy bathroom mirror. Even the fogged glass couldn't hide her pale skin and dark-circled eyes. Ugh. She looked horrid.

The caffeinated, sugary soda had kicked in by the time she drove to the rusted phone booth. Hannah should be home. Jules took a deep breath as she swung from the jeep. She hoped her daughter understood. Come to think of it, that was impossible, since she, herself, couldn't comprehend what she'd done. *Fine.* She'd settle for Hannah not lecturing her. The coins jangled as they dropped, and her fingers trembled as she pressed the digits.

"Hello?"

Oh, glory. Hannah's voice alone made Jules want to weep. She opened her mouth, but froze. How to explain?

"Hello?" Hannah spoke again. "Is anyone there?"

"Yes." The syllable came in a hiss. Tears tumbled down her face.

"Mom. Oh, thank God. Where are you? I got your message the other day, and I prayed you'd call again. Are you all right?"

"Yes." Another hiss. A huge lie.

"Tell me where you are, and I'll come and get you. It's going to be okay, Mom, really." Hannah voice sounded gentle, but commanding.

"No." A shred of strength surged through Jules. "I'm fine."

"You are *not* fine, Mom. You disappeared for two weeks. No one could figure out what had happened to you."

"I know. Please don't be angry. I can't tell you where I am for now. I'm afraid it'll get out, and someone will show up. I just can't handle that right now. I have to work through this on my own." Jules swiped her tears.

"But why? What you need are friends and family by your side. You'll survive this mess, I'm positive you will. We all want to be here for you."

Jules cleared her tight throat.

"No, honey." Calm over swept her in a shiver. "Everyone's smothering me to death. And knowing they're right there…your Dad and…*her*. It's too much." Jules paused a moment. "Did she have it?"

"Mom, let's talk about you."

"Did she?" Jules' jaw tightened.

"Yes." A whisper-soft answer coursed through the line.

"When?"

"Last week." Hannah's tone flattened. A heavy sigh followed.

"How nice." Her tumbling emotions turned icy and detached. A breeze dried her chapped face as she squeezed the flexible metal conduit cord. She was so glad she didn't have to gallivant around Nashville while people examined her beneath their reaction microscopes as the tragedy played out.

"Mom, please. I hate telling you this stuff on the phone. I need to see you. Come home." A childish whine laced her adult demand.

"No." Jules fell into her old teacher's voice. "I'm doing well here. I'll call again with any updates. I don't have a phone right now, but when I get one, I'll let you know the number."

Fat chance of that happening anytime soon. Jules gritted her molars. "Just tell everyone I miss them, and I'll eventually be in touch."

"Mother." An audible sigh. "Okay. If this is what you need for now, I'll go along with it. You can walk out on your friends, but I'm pregnant, and I want you at that hospital when the baby comes."

"I'll be there, Hannah."

"September. You have until then, and you'd better be here." The line went still. "I love you, Mom."

A hot stone settled in Jules's chest. "I love you too."

Silence dominated both ends of the connection. A space. An understanding? After an unsteady breath, Jules spoke. "I'll call next week."

"I don't recognize the number on the caller ID other than it's out of state. Is there somewhere I can reach you?"

"No, this is a pay phone."

"But what if I need to get ahold of you?" Hannah sniffed.

"I'll keep in touch. I promise."

"All right. If that's all you'll give me, I'll try to be satisfied. Know I'll be praying hard for you."

Jules closed her eyes and laid her head against the cool, rusted metal of the phone box. "Goodbye, Hannah."

"Goodbye, Mom.

Jules narrowed her eyes and plunked the receiver into the cradle. She clenched the black plastic as her breathing sped up.

Pray.

Yes, pray. A lot of good that did. Hadn't she been praying for a year? She backed away from rusted booth and stumbled over the uneven curb.

Pray.

Her bottom lip quivered as the urge to do exactly that mounted in her soul. She wouldn't. No, she *couldn't*. Tears blinded her, and she choked for a breath of oxygen. This wasn't her life. It shouldn't be happening this way. She spun and began to run.

Sign up for my newsletter so you don't miss my next new release! Sign up @https://www.peggytrotter.com/

Find all my books @
https://www.amazon.com/stores/Peggy-Trotter/author/B00V15P2LU

www.ingramcontent.com/pod-product-compliance
Lightning Source LLC
Chambersburg PA
CBHW032133190626
46814CB00005BA/1673